CRAZY Sexy LOVE

A DIRTY DICKS NOVEL

K.L. GRAYSON

Cover Designer: Kari March Designs
Editor: Jessica Royer Ocken
Proofreader: Alison Evans-Maxwell
Formatter: Champagne Book Design

Dedication

To my son, Kaden …

Try everything at least once.
Hold the door for a woman … and her hand.
Approach everything with an open heart.
Always be on time (punctuality is a virtue)
Call your mom every day.
It's okay to cry.
Think before you speak.
Fall in love.
Say please and thank you.
Stay true to yourself.
Women are complicated—but so are men.
Wish on shooting stars.
Chase your dreams, and when you catch them, dream again.

CHAPTER
One

Rhett

"Are you crazy?"

The door flies open, hitting the wall behind it with a loud thud, and every man in the locker room—myself included—looks up. My manager, Nikki Atwood, is a sight to behold: big tits, plump ass, and thighs made to squeeze a man's head. And tonight she is dressed to the nines. Any other woman in that outfit would look out of place in a room full of bull riders, but she makes it work. I know every man in here is wondering what it would be like to dirty her prissy little ass up a bit.

Except me.

Been there. Done that.

It's not something I'm proud of, but I was young and dumb, and I refuse to dwell on mistakes of the past. And in my defense, when I slept with her, she wasn't my manager. Not yet anyway, and I was nursing a broken heart. Had I known she would eventually slide into the role that had belonged to her father, I would've thought twice before getting my dick wet. But that doesn't mean my decision to fuck her would've changed—because I was hurting, and she's hot as hell, and any man would have a hard time turning her down—but maybe I would've given it more thought.

"I ride bulls for a living, darlin'," I tell her. "I'd say crazy is part of the job description."

"Don't get cute with me, Rhett. You know damn well what I'm talking about. A bonus ride? On Lucifer no less."

"I just walked out of that arena with a 92.2 score. Thought you'd be happier about that."

"Oh, I am happy about that, and so are your sponsors." She crosses her arms. "But imagine my surprise when I find out you signed up for a bonus ride. What were you thinking, and why didn't you tell me?"

"I was thinking I could use the extra cash, and if I told you, you'd try to talk me out of it."

Her brow creases, and for a split second I swear I see steam coming out of her ears.

"You're damn right I would've talked you out of it." Nikki stalks toward the middle of the room, plants her hands on her hips, and lifts an eyebrow at some of the other guys, a silent request that they get out.

Lincoln Bennett, my best friend in this business, is the first one to move. Pushing up from the floor, he shoots me a *good luck* look and taps some of the other guys on the shoulder. "Come on. Let's give Rhett some privacy." On his way out of the locker room, he tips his hat to Nikki. "Nicole."

"Thank you, Linc," she says.

She waits for the locker room to clear and then turns to me, eyebrows raised.

She's not going to intimidate me. "What?"

"Don't play dumb. You may be crazy as fuck, but no one ever called you dumb."

"I don't know what you want from me." I shrug. "They offered a fifty-grand bonus if I stay on for eight seconds. I couldn't pass that up."

"They offered you fifty grand because no one has been able to stay on that damn bull for longer than four seconds."

"Until me." I shoot her a cocky smile, and she rolls her eyes.

"Until you. Riiiiiiiight," she says. "Lucifer has been responsible for forty-seven injuries this year alone, and unless you've forgotten, you've got commitments outside of the arena, commitments that will earn you well over fifty grand."

"I'm well aware of the risk, and as far as Wrangler and Powerade are con—"

"Gatorade."

"Whatever. The point is, bull riding is my job, and it comes first."

Fifty grand is nothing to Nikki. She was born into money, and even though she works her ass off, she doesn't really need her job.

She may come from cash, but I come from a ranch in Heaven, Texas. My parents—although they're doing well now—have practically killed themselves for every dime they have, and even though I've got a decent cushion in my bank account, it's not enough. It might never be enough. Being a bull rider is a precarious job, and it doesn't always pay the best, which is why I've let her talk me in to a few modeling gigs and the occasional commercial.

Every time I get on one of those bulls, I'm putting my career and my life at risk. If something happens and I lose the ability to work, I need to know I'm going to be financially stable until I find something else to do. So, yes, whether she understands it or not, I need that fifty grand.

"Call it off."

She's smoking crack. "No way."

As Nikki well knows, I don't back down. If I say I'm going to do something, I do it, which is probably why she pinches her lips into a thin line and strides across the room. Her hand hits the door knob and she stops, but doesn't look back.

"You better stay on that fucking bull, Rhett Allen, or so help me God, your ass is mine."

"Not a problem, darlin.'"

———◦———

The smell of dirt, sweat, and testosterone-fueled beast fill the air as I weave my way through the back pens. I hear the announcer reveal the final special event as I slip on my gloves, and when I come into view, I'm bathed in a bright light. The crowd roars to life. I raise my arm, encouraging their cheers, and I'm reminded why I love this sport.

It's the thrill I get every time the gate opens, the adrenaline that rushes through me as I'm whipped through the air by a two-thousand-pound bull. It's just me, that beast, a thunderous crowd, and eight seconds of pure fucking glory.

Most people think I'm crazy, and I don't deny it. Any man who regularly mounts a one-ton bull has to have something wrong with him.

"You ready for this?" Dad asks, placing a hand on my arm.

It's tough on my dad to leave the ranch, but he insists on being with me as much as he can. And although I feel guilty pulling him away from my mom and siblings, you won't hear me complain. He's my rock, my mentor, the person who keeps me tethered to the life I left behind to chase my dream, and I count on him more than he'll ever know.

Smiling, I look up. "I was born ready."

"We're really proud of you, son. Your mom and I, your

brothers and Adley—we're real proud of you. The whole town is piled in at Dirty Dicks to watch you tonight, and Beau is streaming your ride on his phone."

I picture the pub overflowing with patrons. Everyone packed in like sardines; beer sloshing from their mugs as they cheer me on. Dirty Dicks isn't large enough to house everyone in town, but they'll sure as hell try. With a population of 12,500, Heaven, Texas is big enough that not everyone knows your name, but small enough to have a Facebook page where you can catch up on who's who. That town saw me grow up, learn to ride a bull, and break a few laws along with a few bones. Even though I don't return very often, it's still the place I call home.

"Well then, I better give them a good show, huh?" Hoisting myself up on a rung, I fling a leg over the rail and ease myself onto the bull. Lucifer looks at me over his shoulder as if he's of-fering me one last chance to hop off and save myself. *I'm ranked number one in the world, cowboy, with a buck-of percentage of 88.89. You don't stand a chance.*

I narrow my eyes. The odds are in his favor—even I'm not naïve enough to believe otherwise—but I'm too stubborn to back out now. "Bring it on," I whisper.

Lucifer huffs and thrashes from side to side, slamming us against the chute. Three sets of hands reach for me, and when the bull finally settles, they release their grip and I'm able to adjust my hand until it's secure in the rope.

And then, with the tip of my head, the chute opens. Lucifer flies through the gate with the wild fury only a bull on a mission can possess.

CHAPTER
Two

Monroe

"You need to show more skin," Cooper says, eyeing my shirt.

Looking down at the black shirt I've paired with skinny jeans and my favorite Chucks, I wonder how the hell I'm supposed to show more skin. I was proud of this outfit, considering my wardrobe consists mostly of concert T-shirts, boot-cut jeans, and my favorite pair of Ariats.

"You didn't say anything about skin," I tell him. "If I remember correctly, you said a black button-up shirt and jeans." I look to my co-worker and friend, Sean, for confirmation, and he just shrugs.

Coop nods noncommittally while eyeing my chest. "We'll have to get you fitted for a uniform top; I don't have any extras. Until then, what color is your bra?"

I reel back. "Excuse me?"

He sighs and steps toward me. Without asking permission, he unbuttons my top three buttons and pulls my blouse open, revealing the slightest hint of my red lace bra.

"Perfect," he says.

Heat creeps up my neck, infusing my cheeks, and I look down—not out of embarrassment, but because the sight of Cooper Allen with his hands on my body is almost too much. This has nothing to do with Cooper himself, but his identical twin. Rhett Allen was my first boyfriend, my first love, and the first boy to break my heart. I can't look at Coop without thinking about Rhett. No matter how hard I try.

I have to give Cooper credit, because while Sean makes a sound of appreciation at my newly exposed state, he doesn't flinch. As if I'm a painting he's studying, his eyes sweep across my chest, down my stomach, and land on my hips.

"Lower," he says.

Grabbing my jeans, I tug them down until the waistband sits indecently low. I hold my arms out to the side, waiting for his approval.

"You look hot," Sean says, earning a wink from me.

Cooper shakes his head and mumbles something that sounds an awful lot like *I can't believe I'm doing this* and *My brother is going to kill me,* but I ignore it because I don't care what anyone thinks. Least of all Rhett. I need this job.

My days are spent running my dad's non-profit, no-kill animal shelter, Animal Haven, and up until tonight I've spent my evenings bartending at Broadway Bar and Grill, a pub two towns over. They paid well, and I made fat tips, but after working a day at the shelter, followed by a thirty-minute drive, a six-hour shift at the tavern, and another thirty-minute drive home, I was exhausted.

Needless to say, when Coop offered me a bartending spot at Dirty Dicks, I couldn't turn it down. The hourly wage is less, but I'm willing to sacrifice that for a little extra sleep each night.

"We're laid back here. Have fun, keep up with the pace, and you'll do great."

"Thanks, Coop. I appreciate this."

He smiles and nudges my arm. "Don't mention it. We're glad to have you. I have a few phone calls to make, but Sean is going to show you the ropes before we get too busy."

"Follow me." Sean nods toward the door, and I follow him to the front bar.

I've been inside Dirty Dicks more times than I can count. It isn't the only bar in town, but it's the most popular, and during my rare moments of free time, this is where I find myself. Knocking back a few with friends and shooting the shit is about the only way to spend a day off in this town—unless of course you're into bull riding. In that case, you'll need to drive a couple miles south of town to find a hoard of people every Friday and Saturday night, anxious to watch a slew of young men try their hand at riding a bull.

That was the thing to do back in the day. I was a buckle bunny for sure, but those days bring back too many memories, so I focus on the here and now.

Sean makes quick work of showing me the basics. I've worked behind a bar long enough that it doesn't take much for me to fall into a groove. When the crowd picks up, another bartender joins our crew.

"Sarah," she says, holding out her hand. I take it for a quick shake.

"Monroe, but you can call me Mo."

She grabs a pad of paper and stuffs it in her back pocket. "This your first day?"

I nod. "First day here, but not my first time bartending."

"I hope you wore comfy shoes, because tonight will be crazy."

"Most weekends are."

"Tonight is different. Have you heard of Rhett Allen?"

Have I heard of Rhett Allen? I've only spent the last six years trying to forget him. But she doesn't need to know that. "Yeah, we went to school together."

Her smile is bright and mischievous. "Lucky you."

"What does Rhett have to do with tonight being crazy?" As far as I know Rhett hasn't set foot in this town in well over a year and has no plans of doing so anytime soon. At least that's what Coop tells me, and he should know.

"Rumor has it Rhett signed up for a bonus ride." She nods toward the two TVs against the wall. "The entire town is expected to pile in for the occasion."

"Lovely."

"Sarah, get out on the floor. Table two needs refills," Coop instructs, appearing from the back.

With a quick smile and even quicker step, she's off, and I turn to Coop.

"You could've told me tonight was going to be swarming with Rhett Allen fans," I say, lifting a brow.

"It's cute when you pretend not to be one," he chides, winking before shoving me toward my end of the bar.

The next few hours fly by in a flurry of activity as I do my best to keep my eyes off the TVs. First, I served a socialite and her glittery posse celebrating...hell, I don't know what they were celebrating. All I know is they were fat tippers and brought a hoard of hot guys to my end of the bar. She and her posse eventually dissipated, leaving me with a beautiful view of Heaven's sexiest cowboy bachelors. At least I think they're bachelors—they'd better be, considering they're flirting their asses off and asking to take me home. Lucky for me I'm able to stand my ground, refusing to melt under their heated gazes. They too eventually fade and are replaced by a pair of men who have made it their life's mission to make me laugh. And as much as I appreciate their effort, I'm dying for this night to end. I am beat, and if I hear one more woman fawn over how tight Rhett's ass looks in a pair of Wranglers, I'm going to scream.

"Wait, let me try again!" The slurred voice tugs me back to the land of the living.

"Oh no." Shaking my head, I laugh, fighting back a yawn. "You've had four chances."

"Come on," Bill begs. Or is it Bob? Braeden, maybe? Shit, I can't even remember. There are too many men here to keep track of, and unfortunately for me, they're all good looking.

I hold up a finger. "One more chance, but you better recruit some help because this is make-it-or-break-it time."

He turns toward his buddy as I hustle down the bar to wait on another customer.

When I return, he smacks his hands together. "We've got it!"

Cooper walks up behind and claps him on the shoulder. "The only thing you've got is a ride home. I'm calling you an Uber."

He completely ignores Cooper. "You ready?" His glossy eyes are twinkling, and I almost feel bad for him, because he really does think he has a shot with me. If this were a normal day, and I were a normal girl, maybe he would. But that's a *big* if, and I'm far from normal.

I barely have time to sleep, shower, and eat, let alone date. And my heart…forget about it. I gave that traitorous organ away years ago, and the damn thing never came back.

"Last chance," I say, tossing a towel over my shoulder. Leaning against the bar, I give him my full attention. "Better make it good."

Squaring his shoulders, he sits up straight, only he isn't straight at all. He's leaning to the left, and I hope Cooper really did call an Uber for him.

"Feel this shirt." He gives me a lopsided smile, and I raise my eyebrows, waiting for the punch line. "Know what it's made of?"

I shake my head, and his smile widens.

"Boyfriend material."

It takes everything I have not to laugh, and not because the pick-up line is funny or unique, because it's not—it's cheesy. But the look on his face… He looks like one of the dogs at my shelter, sitting at my feet, waiting for a treat. But I've mastered the ability to deal with drunk, horny men, and I'm able to stifle my giggle.

Shrugging, I frown.

"Fuuuck." Dropping his head to his hands, he groans.

"Jace, dude, what was that?" Cooper asks, giving him a perplexed look.

Jace! That's his name.

"Don't tell me you actually use that line on women."

"If you think that was lame, you should've heard the first four," I mumble.

Cooper slaps Jace on the back and laughs.

His head rolls to the side toward Cooper. "All I had to do was make her laugh and she said she'd consider going out with me."

"And you had five chances," I add.

"I did." His head nods like a damn bobblehead. "I failed five times. Can you believe it? This angel here could've been my new girlfriend." He waves his arm toward me. "I would've given her the world. I would've given you the world," he repeats, facing me.

"Maybe you can try again next time," I offer.

"Come on, let's get you out of here." Cooper grips Jace's arm to help him up, but Jace shrugs him off.

"Not yet. I can't go home before Rhett's bonus ride."

"Fine." Cooper holds out his hand. "But no more drinks, and I'm going to need your keys."

"Done." Digging in his pocket, Jace retrieves his keys and tosses them to Coop, who tosses them to me.

I drop the keys in the cash drawer and rush to fill another order. That's when I hear the announcer on the TV.

"Lucifer has what seems to be an insurmountable resume with twenty-one straight buck-offs, but tonight that could all change as three-time world champion Rhett Allen prepares for the ride of his life. That's right, Mike, and if anyone can pull this off, it's Rhett..."

I glance between the TV and my customers as the announcer goes through a series of statistics, but when Rhett comes into view, I can't help but stop and stare.

Turns out the entire bar feels the same way.

Scuffed-up cowboy boots, jeans, leather chaps, flannel shirt, and his trusty ol' Stetson make Rhett Allen one of the most ruggedly handsome men I've ever seen. Dark brown hair curls out from under his hat, and his blue eyes shine bright under the spotlight.

I'm proud of Rhett and his accomplishments, as is the entire town, but I can't deny that part of me is bitter about the success he's found. *Maybe it's because he chased his dream while mine slipped away*, I think to myself. *Or maybe it's because his dream stopped including me when I so desperately wanted it to.* Either way, it's a feeling I hate and one I don't have time to dwell on, so I quickly push the thoughts away.

Cooper climbs up on the end of the bar with his cell phone in hand. He's been known to videotape the crowd for Rhett. "Hey, everybody," he yells, gathering the bar's attention. "Say hi to Rhett." A wave of hands goes up, and a few people shout out. When the camera makes its way across the sea of people to me, I smile and flip it off. Peeking at me from behind his phone, Coop winks. He redirects the camera toward the crowd as Rhett mounts the bull.

I hold my breath the same way I do every time I watch Rhett give the nod. The gate opens, and Lucifer propels himself forward, bucking and whipping his back end from side to side as he tries his best to throw Rhett off.

A sharp turn to the right causes Rhett to lose his balance, and I gasp as he slides precariously to the side. Somehow, by the grace of God, he's able to hold on, but it doesn't last long. Another high kick and sharp turn toss Rhett's body like a rag-doll, catapulting him toward the harsh, unforgiving ground, and the entire room goes silent. Blood rushes through my ears, my heart drops to the pit of my stomach, and the only thing I can think of is getting to him. Talking to Rhett. Finding out if Rhett is okay.

Adrenaline pushes me forward, and I jump over the bar and rush toward the TV as the crowd around me starts to bustle. All I can see is Rhett's lifeless body lying on the ground as a team of people coax the bull out of the arena.

Why aren't you moving, Rhett?

"Why isn't he moving?" I ask, looking frantically around the room, as though someone here should be helping him. "He should be moving, right?" I turn back toward the TV. "Damnit, Rhett," I growl. "I need you to move. Fucking move already. He's so still. Why aren't they helping? They need to do something."

The TV cuts to a commercial, and the room erupts in chatter.

My eyes burn as the first tear falls, followed by several more. Desperate and wild, I turn toward the back of the bar. Cooper's arms hang limp at his sides. The phone in his hand slips out of his grasp, landing on the bar at his feet, and I rush toward him.

"Coop," I cry. My heart is going crazy as every worst-case scenario flashes through my mind. My hands shake uncontrollably as I wait for him to look at me. "He's going to be okay. He has to be."

Cooper's eyes finally find mine. He climbs down off the bar, pulls me into his arms, and holds me. His heart beats wildly against my cheek, and when his phone rings, I pull back.

With one arm still wrapped tight around my shoulders, he grabs his phone from the bar.

"It's my dad," he whispers, bringing the phone to his ear.

For the second time tonight I hold my breath.

"Please tell me he's alive," Coop says as he answers.

CHAPTER
Three

Rhett

I blink heavily. It takes several seconds to adjust to the light, but when my vision comes into focus, there's a pretty blond nurse messing with an IV at the side of my bed. I try to formulate some sort of pick-up line, but by the time she looks down at me, my eyelids are drifting shut.

Next time I wake up, the pretty nurse is gone, and it's my mother standing over my bed. Her eyes widen when she sees that I'm awake.

"Hi, sweetheart." She offers me a tremulous smile, and I take her hand as she sits on the bed.

"I'm okay, Mom." I choke the words out because my mouth is dry.

She pats my hand. "I know, but that doesn't make what happened any less scary." Leaning forward, she presses her lips to my forehead and lingers there for a moment. When she pulls back, her eyes are clear with relief. "Let me go find the doctor."

She rushes out of the room, and I notice my twin brother, Cooper, sitting in a chair next to the window. He sits up and offers me one of those fake smiles. You know, the one where something horrible happened, but they don't want to be the one to tell you.

"Who died?" I ask.

"There for a second I was worried you had."

I try to wave him off, but when I lift my left arm, I end up groaning in pain. "I feel like I got run over by a train."

"Close. You got run over by a bull."

I nod, wincing when my head throbs. "I remember. How long was I out?"

"Three days."

Hmmm. Not bad. "Last time it was four. I'm improving."

Cooper frowns at my poor attempt at a joke.

"Too soon?"

"Just a little." Pushing up from his chair, he walks to the side of my bed. "You gave us one hell of a scare."

"Not the first time, won't be the last. What's the verdict?" I do a quick inventory. Rhett Thomas Allen, three-time world champion bull rider. *Check.* Nice deep breath. *Check.* Wiggle my fingers and toes. *Check.* "When can I get back to work?"

Furrowing his brow, Coop shakes his head. "I'll never understand why you choose to get on those bulls night after night, knowing one of these days you could end up dead."

"It's not your job to understand."

"Doesn't matter if it's my job; you're my brother." He looks at me for a moment, stuffs his hands in his pockets, and turns toward the door. "Trevor, Adley, and Dad went down for coffee. We've had Beau on standby. I'll let them know you're awake."

The solemn look on his face doesn't sit well with me. I'm not one to worry about what anyone else thinks of my profession, but Coop isn't just anyone.

"Coop?"

"Yeah?" he replies, looking over his shoulder.

"I'm okay." I don't know what else to say. I can't promise I'll never get hurt again or that a bull might not someday claim my life, and I won't apologize for loving my profession.

He nods and walks out.

Blowing out a breath, I look around the room. Flowers and balloons are scattered over the table and windowsill, and there are a few cards propped up on my bedside table. I reach for one, but my arm is too damn sore, and I give up at the same time a man in a crisp, white coat walks into the room, followed by my parents, Coop, Trevor, and my sister, Adley. My oldest brother, Beau, is traveling around the world, but I know he'd get here if I needed him.

The doctor walks toward me and reaches out. It takes longer than I'd like, but I manage to shake his hand.

"Mr. Allen, it's a pleasure to meet you. My name is Dr. Simpson, and I've been in charge of your care since your admission the other night." With a warm smile, he glances at my family. "We've got a lot to talk about, and I need to check you over. Would you like your family to step out or—"

I shake my head. "They're good. They can stay. I'm just anxious to find out how much damage I caused."

"Surprisingly, not much. You suffered a grade 3 concussion and lost consciousness. Most patients with a grade 3 concussion don't stay out as long as you did, but you had quite a bit of swelling in your brain. I watched the video of your accident, and after you were thrown from the bull, you were kicked in the head, which is what I presume caused the swelling. It wasn't a direct hit, otherwise the injuries would've been much different. We did a scan and ran several tests, and everything came back normal, so we were confident you'd wake up once the swelling subsided."

"Will I have any permanent damage?"

He shakes his head and pulls out a pen light. "I hope not, but your chart tells me this isn't your first concussion, so we're going to watch you for a few more days." He shines the light in my left eye and then my right. "Squeeze my fingers," he says, holding out two fingers on each hand. "I need to check your grip."

I squeeze his fingers, noticing that my left hand feels weaker than the right. If he notices it too, he doesn't show it. Instead he does a series of movements with both of my arms and moves his way down my body, checking the strength of my legs. Once he's done, he folds his hands in front of his body.

"Now for the not-so-good news."

Damn. I had a feeling that was coming. "Okay. I'm listening."

"The concussion wasn't your only injury." Dr. Simpson looks at my family and back at me. "After watching the video, I was concerned about a possible shoulder injury, and it was confirmed by the MRI. You've strained the rotator cuff of your left shoulder, and there's a partial tear. It's small, but it's there."

Closing my eyes, I grimace. A rotator cuff injury can be hell on a bull rider's career. If surgery is required, it can mean months out of work, and you're still not guaranteed to come back at full capacity.

I run the fingers of my right hand along my forehead and look up at the doctor. "What does that mean? Will I need surgery? How long will I be out of work?" I try to pull up a mental calendar of the all the events I have left this season.

Dr. Simpson shakes his head. "Don't get too far ahead of yourself. It's a small tear, barely visible. My hope is that we can rehab it without surgery."

"So what does that mean? Physical therapy?"

He nods. "That's where we'll start. I'll give you some medication to help with inflammation and pain, and we'll get you going with physical therapy. You're young and healthy, and so I'm hopeful you can get through this without surgery. But I do want you to follow up with Dr. Wong. He's an orthopedic surgeon, and I'll let him make the final decision."

"Okay." That doesn't sound so bad. "I can do that. When can I go home?"

He chuckles. "Like I said, I want to keep you for a few more days so we can be sure there's nothing else wrong neurologically. Maybe we can get Dr. Wong to come in and see you before you're discharged. Until then, I want you to be thinking about where you're going to go when you leave here."

"What do you mean? I'm going home."

"Do you have a spouse or roommate? Or do you live alone?"

I shake my head. "It's just me."

"He can stay with us," my mom interjects.

Hell no. I love my mom to death, but she'll drive me up the wall. "No. It's not necessary. I'll stay at my house."

Dr. Simpson frowns. "I highly encourage you not to go home alone—at least for a few weeks. You need to rest your shoulder as much as possible, and since you're left-hand dominant, that's going to be difficult. You're going to want to do things yourself, but it won't be easy, and if you want this to heal without surgery, you cannot strain it any further."

Damn. The last thing I want to do is go back to Heaven, but asking my family to commute an hour and a half each way to come help me doesn't seem fair.

Sighing, I look at my brother, Coop. "Can I stay with you for a few weeks?"

"You don't even have to ask," he says.

Shit. My dogs. "What about Duke and Diesel?"

Coop holds up a hand. "Already taken care of. They're in good hands."

Dr. Simpson gives me a tight smile. "I also think you need to evaluate your return to bull riding." I open my mouth to protest, but he holds up a hand. "I'm not saying you can't return or that you won't, but look at your history, Rhett. You've had several concussions—this one being the worst—and those injuries eventually add up. You have a lot of life left inside of you, son, and it's my job to make sure you live long enough to enjoy it."

He pats my leg. "Just some food for thought. I've got to get going, but I'll have the nurses get you something to eat, and we'll make sure you're able to shower tonight. Just remember to take it easy. You're going to be sore."

"Thank you, Dr. Simpson."

He nods, gives my family a polite goodbye, and slips out the door.

———°———

"Seriously." I look at Coop's jacked-up Chevy and lift an eyebrow. "You couldn't have brought your car?"

"Yes, that's exactly what I was thinking when I saw you get trampled by a bull and rushed to the hospital. *Let me go home and get my car in case my gimp brother has to come home with me.*"

"Get me out of this damn wheelchair."

The nurse steadies the wheelchair while Dad helps me into Coop's truck. Mom hands Coop my discharge paperwork, and finally—almost six days after I arrived at this hospital—we're on our way home.

Well, not my home, but close enough.

"Thank God," I mumble once we're actually moving. I lay my head back on the seat rest. "I wasn't sure how much longer I could stand that place."

"At least your nurse was hot."

I look over at Coop, and he shrugs. "What? She was. You should've requested a sponge bath before you left."

I smile and close my eyes. "Next time."

"Let's hope there isn't a next time."

"Coop."

"Yeah?"

"Shut up so I can get some sleep."

With my eyes closed, I replay my ride with Lucifer in my head and try to figure out what I did wrong. Somewhere along the way I must fall asleep, because next thing I know, Coop is nudging me in the side.

"Rhett. Wake up."

Every bone in my body throbs as I prepare to climb out of the truck. I'm not as sore as I was when I first woke up in the hospital—thanks to the physical therapist—but I still ache.

"I'm getting too damn old for this."

"You're not even thirty," Coop reminds me.

With a hand under my good arm, he helps me down from his truck, and I brace myself for Duke and Diesel's attack when he opens the front door.

When it doesn't come, I follow him into the house. "Where are my boys?"

Coop drops his keys on the counter and picks up a stack of mail. "They're at Animal Haven."

"You took my dogs to an animal rescue?" I nearly shout, grabbing the keys he just dropped on the counter.

"Chill out. They're being boarded, not sold."

That doesn't make me feel better. "Since when does Animal Haven board animals?" I've known Phil Gallagher my whole life. I remember when he opened Animal Haven, and not once do I remember him boarding animals for the public.

Coop thumbs through his mail and tosses it on the counter.

"They don't. It's a special situation, and they're being nice, helping out."

Shaking my head, I turn toward the door.

"Where do you think you're going?"

"To get my damn dogs." I respect Phil—he's one hell of a guy—but my dogs are my babies, and they belong with me.

"Are you supposed to be driving?"

"Ask me if I care."

Coop beats me to the door. "We should probably talk before you leave."

"About what?"

"Mo."

I flinch at the mention of her name. "What did I tell you about saying her name?"

Coop frowns. "It's been six years."

"Is she hurt?"

He shakes his head. "No."

"Is she in jail?"

"What? No."

"Is she getting married?"

Coop opens his mouth, and I shake my head.

"Wait, I don't want to know. Now move so I can go get my dogs."

"What happened between you two?"

"Nothing. Get out of my way."

"Suit yourself. At least take the car and leave the truck for me."

We switch keys, and I climb into his Malibu.

As I pull out, I realize he's right; I probably shouldn't be driving. But the doctor said I *shouldn't* drive, not that I couldn't. And luckily, Animal Haven is only five miles from Coop's house.

As the road spools out before me, I remember all the good

things about being here. Making the decision to leave Heaven was difficult—not just because I was leaving my family behind, but because I left Mo behind.

Mo Gallagher. The girl who got away. Our relationship was a whirlwind. We fell hard and fast, but we both had big dreams, and we made a promise that when the time came, we'd support each other in the pursuit of those plans. Turned out her version of support was much different than mine.

Shaking my head, I try not to think about the past. Now I'm living my dream. Well, I'm not living it *right* now. Right now, I'm jacked up, but I'll get back there. I have to; bull riding is my life.

My tires crunch on the gravel lane that leads to Animal Haven. The main building is tucked in the backwoods of Heaven. As I approach I see a large, red barn sitting off to the left that wasn't there six years ago, and the trees I helped plant along the lane when I was a boy have grown exponentially. Animal Haven sits on about one hundred acres, and I know at one time Phil wanted to build a house out here. That doesn't seem to have happened yet.

A small lane juts off to the right, leading toward a set of stables, and beyond that is a dirt path. It's grown over now, but back in the day, Coop, Mo, and I would spend hours out there running through the woods.

Coming back here feels familiar, and familiar hurts. I put the car in park and climb out, and a movement to the left catches my eye. A woman runs across the open yard with two dogs. *My* two dogs. Duke is a German Shepherd mix, and Diesel is a husky mix. I picked them both up at an animal shelter in Houston a few years ago. My intention was to get one dog, but they were in the same cage, and it didn't feel right to leave one behind.

The woman stops, zigs to the left, and when the dogs follow her she zags to the right and takes off again. Diesel jumps up, catching the back of her leg and sending her face first toward the ground.

Shit. I move across the yard as quickly as I'm able, praying she's okay. Diesel bends down to lick her while Duke bounces around her in circles. She sits up and pushes Diesel off of her, and that's when I hear it. Her laugh. My heart seizes inside my chest. I'd recognize that laugh anywhere.

Mo.

I can still remember everything about her—the way she'd thread her fingers through my hair before kissing me, the light smell of strawberries every time she entered a room. Her touch. Her taste. Her soft moans when I made love to her. Everything about her is so fresh in my mind that it's hard to believe we've spent the last six years apart.

Monroe always loved coming out here and helping her dad, so I shouldn't really be surprised to see her. I suppose that's what Coop was trying to tell me. If my calculations are right, she should be about ready to finish up veterinary school, and I imagine she'll soon be taking over Phil's practice. Not only did her dad start Animal Haven, he also owns and runs the only veterinary office in town, Ruff Times Veterinary Clinic.

Mo must sense my eyes on her, because she turns my way, and the easy smile on her face fades. She pushes up from the ground, brushes her hands off on her jeans, and not once does she break eye contact.

Her long, dark hair is a bit of a mess, pulled up into a knot on top of her head as her green eyes move warily over me. She's wearing tight jeans, a flannel shirt with the sleeves rolled up, and cowboy boots, and she looks gorgeous. Unable to help myself, I take a tentative step forward. She seems hesitant at first, but then she looks down at the dogs and says something. I'm not sure what—we're not close enough for me to hear—but whatever it is makes Duke and Diesel two happy pooches, bouncing and jumping around her.

I can almost hear her sigh as she takes her first step toward me, and I use the distance between us to run my eyes over her body. The last six years have been kind to her. Much kinder than they've been to me, that's for damn sure. Her chest is larger than I remember, and she fills out a pair of jeans in a way most women only dream about. I'm not at all ready to analyze the strange feeling stirring in my gut.

My eyes travel north as she comes to a stop twenty or so feet in front of me, and even from this far away, I can feel the magnetic pull that's always between us. I take a step back because I don't want to feel that attraction—or anything else that will make me see this woman as someone other than the girl who left me.

CHAPTER
Four

Monroe

"Well, well, well. If it isn't Rhett Allen. I've been expecting you," I say casually, even though nothing about this feels casual.

Rhett smiles, but it doesn't reach his eyes. "Funny, I wasn't expecting you."

At the sound of his voice, Duke and Diesel's ears perk up, and when they see him, they go crazy. Their tails and butts are wiggling so fast, for a second I think they might fall over. As they charge him, Rhett steps back, using one arm to keep the dogs from jumping on him—the other is in a sling—and that's when I remember his accident.

Not that I forgot because it's the only thing I've thought about since that horrible night, but the sight of him standing before me rendered me stupid there for a few seconds.

I knew it would only be a matter of time before Rhett came for his dogs. I was prepared for that. What I'm not prepared for are all the feelings that have picked this moment to come rushing back. Some good, others not so good. Against my better judgment, I've followed Rhett's career over the years, but I've tried not to think about him outside of his bull riding. It was hard at times, especially when his face showed up in a magazine or on a commercial. But I gave his brothers and Adley strict instructions not to tell me anything about his personal life, and for the most part, they've honored my request.

Every once in a while, Coop would let something slip during conversation, but it was always something simple.

Rhett remodeled his kitchen.

Rhett came to town to visit Mom and Dad, but he was by himself.

Adley and I visited Rhett and went to one of his events.

I like to think it's Coop's way of keeping me in the loop without keeping me in the loop. There were times I wanted to beg him to tell me more, but I knew I couldn't go there. Losing Rhett was one of the hardest things I've ever had to go through—right after my dad's stroke and my mom walking out on us. For a while, in the back of my mind, I hoped we'd find our way back to each other, but I gave up on that years ago. Rhett is lost for good to the world of professional bull riding, to his fans, to his career—and it's mostly my fault.

"Duke. Diesel." I call to the dogs and take a few steps forward. "Down." They're both overly excited, but they listen to my command.

Instead of jumping up and mauling Rhett, Duke shoves his nose into his leg—no doubt looking for a special treat—while Diesel plops down at Rhett's feet and rolls over in hopes of a belly rub.

Rhett looks up, clearly annoyed. "They listened to you."

"They're good dogs. Aren't you a good dog?" I coo at Duke when he runs back to me. I give him a good scratch behind the ear and nudge him toward Rhett, who's giving Diesel all sorts of love and attention. Duke pushes his way into the fray, demanding some hand action, and I can't blame either one of them. I know what it's like to be the center of that man's world.

It's consuming.

And perfect.

And I'm losing my mind.

"Didn't know you guys were in the dog-boarding business," Rhett says, squinting up at me. He uses his right hand to shield the sun as he stands up. There are a million questions I want to ask about his injuries and recovery, but I refrain. The less I know, the better.

"We're not."

I pull the ponytail holder out of my hair and re-knot it on my head. Not because it was falling out but because Rhett's gaze is intense. Too intense. And that feeling of excitement I always got in the pit of my stomach when he was near, well, it's back.

Rhett tilts his head and smirks. It's the same damn smile he used to give me right before he'd strip me naked and fuck me up against the wall. Only this time I'm older, wiser, and his smile doesn't hit me in the same spots as it used to.

At least that's what I'll keep telling myself.

"Wipe that damn smile off your face, Allen. I didn't do it for you."

"Then who'd you do it for? Seems to me this was a sure-fire way to make sure you got to see me while I'm in town."

Lord, give me strength. With a deep breath, I put my hands on my hips and pin him with a steely gaze. "I did it for Coop."

He lifts a brow. "Is that right?"

"He was a mess after your accident, and he knew your entire family would be at the hospital. I didn't want to cause them any more worry, so when he called, I volunteered to take the dogs."

"Whatever you have to tell yourself, sweetheart." Rhett

walks past me, his shoulder brushing mine, and I freeze on contact. It takes a solid minute to regain my composure, but when
I do, I turn around and find him grabbing the dogs' leashes,
which I'd clipped to the chain-link fence.

"What do you think you're doing?"

"What does it look like? I'm taking my dogs home."

"You sure that's a good idea, what with your arm and all?" I
say, nodding toward the sling.

"Why is it that everyone seems to think they know what's
best for me? My dogs should be at home with me, not locked
up in a kennel."

I scowl. "It's not that we know what's best for you; it's that
we *want* what's best for you. Big difference, buddy. And for the
record, I would never lock your dogs up in a kennel. They've
been staying with me. You're welcome for that, by the way.
Asshole," I add under my breath.

"Were you doing what was best for me when you screwed
Charlie Dixon?"

Once again, all the breath leaves my body. "Rhett," I manage after a moment. "I—"

Lowering his head, he rubs a hand over his face. "Shit. I
didn't mean to say that." He looks up at me. "I appreciate you
taking care of the dogs, and you're right, I probably shouldn't
take them back to Coop's with me. I can barely wipe my own
ass, let alone take care of these crazies."

I can't help it. Despite every protest, I grin. "I can't help you
with the ass wiping, but I'm more than willing to keep the dogs."

"You sure I can't talk you in to the ass wiping?" he asks,
turning to hang the leashes back on the fence.

"Not a chance in hell." I laugh, and it feels good. I can't remember the last time I laughed. "I like you, but not that much."

"You like me, huh?"

And there's that smile again. If I didn't know better, I'd think all the shit that happened between us doesn't matter. Except it does, because this cowboy broke my heart, and I'm damn sure I did the same to him—the mention of Charlie Dixon proves that.

"You know what I mean." Swallowing hard, I meet Rhett's eyes. "I've always liked you; that was never the problem."

I open the door to my truck, but Duke and Diesel hesitate to jump in. When Rhett motions for them to do so, they listen, and I shut the door.

"I should get going. I've got a ton of errands to run today."

He nods, slowly backing away.

I think about Rhett sitting next to me in the truck, about being surrounded by his husky scent, and I go out on a limb. "You can come with me, if you'd like."

He shakes his head without even thinking about it. "I'm good."

"Okay." I nod. "You can swing by tomorrow about this same time if you want to spend time with the dogs."

"I have physical therapy tomorrow."

"Right."

"Friday?"

"Friday's good."

"Okay. I'll see you Friday," he says, pulling a set of keys out of his pocket.

The look in his eyes tells me there's more he wants to say. I know we need to talk, about so many things, but today isn't the day.

"Bye, Rhett."

Before he can reply, I hop in my truck and pull away.

CHAPTER
Five

Monroe

After a long-ass day, I pull down Harris Street, put my truck in park, and stare at my childhood home.

The last few years have started to wear on the three-bedroom house. I tried to keep up with the landscaping and general maintenance, but with two jobs and caring for my dad, everything else eventually fell to the wayside. The once-black shutters are now a dull gray, paint has started to chip along the base of the house, and one of the wooden front steps is cracked. One of these days I'm going to fall straight through. Maybe then I'll muster up enough energy to have it fixed.

The bushes are overgrown, covering the windows, and the swing on the front porch is leaning to the left. I've wanted to take it down for years, but the damn thing holds too many memories, so there it sits—dilapidating more each day.

Our home wasn't always like this. When my mother was around, everything was bright, colorful, and full of life. But she left when I was eight years old, and nothing has been the same since. She couldn't do it anymore—at least that's what she told my father the day she went. My dad has tried his hardest to fill her role. There were moments he succeeded and moments he failed, but he never gave up.

When I was younger, I couldn't wait to get away. Getting accepted into veterinary school was a dream come true, and those first few months in the dorms were everything I'd hoped they would be, until one day they weren't.

I was sitting in Biology 101 when they pulled me out of class. My dad had suffered a stroke. I rushed home and the next few weeks flew by as he and I faced our new normal. He had right-side paralysis, which confined him to a wheelchair, and initially his speech was affected. Over the years, with the help of several therapists, it has improved. These days he talks slowly, but his words are clear, and in the disaster our life's been recently, that is a miracle.

Against Dad's will, I dropped out of school. It was either that or put him in an extended-care facility, and I couldn't send the only parent I had left to a nursing home. He'd spent his life caring for me, and that's a favor I was willing to return. We sold Ruff Time Vet Clinic to his partner, using the money to pay off hospital bills, pay his caregivers, and socking the rest away to help keep Animal Haven—who's main source of income are donations and grants—up and running.

With Dad's Social Security, my jobs, and what we have in savings, we manage to stay afloat. Every penny I make goes back into Animal Haven and toward bills, and on the rare occasion I have some money left over, I tuck it away for something special—which usually ends up being a beer or two with one of my friends. Although that hasn't happened in a long damn time.

I close my eyes, and not for the first time, I think about what it would be like if my father lived in a facility that could manage his daily needs. I think about what it would be like to work one job rather than two and come home at night to a husband instead of being my father's caregiver. But my gut twists at the thought, and I instantly feel bad for allowing my mind to go there.

I'm in my late twenties now, and not once did I ever think I would still be living at home at this point. I should be preparing for graduation, lining up a job, and buying my first house. I should be thinking about finding a good, decent man, settling down, and building my future. Instead, all I think about is whether or not there are enough Depends or bed pads in the cabinet, and how I'm going to get Dad to and from his next appointment.

Duke pushes his nose into my shoulder, and I reach back to give him a pet. "I know, buddy, we're going."

Opening the door, I slide out, followed by the dogs, and make my way up to the front of the house, where I'm met by Sharon Daniels. Sharon is the mother I never had. I grew up with her daughter, Claire, who is now a first-grade teacher at the local elementary school. Growing up, if I wasn't at home, there was a good chance I was at Claire's. Sharon also happens to be an RN and one of my father's caregivers.

Her husband died thirteen years ago in a fire, and since then, she does whatever she can to keep herself busy. Her sister Lucy also helps out with my dad, and they're a godsend. I don't know what he and I would do without them.

"How was Dad today?" I ask, shuffling the dogs into the house. Duke and Diesel sniff at Sharon and then head straight for their food bowls, which I have set up in the kitchen.

"Today was good. The weather was nice, so we got up and went for a walk around the neighborhood."

"I bet he loved that."

She smiles and nods for me to follow her into the kitchen.

"He did. I think it wore him out. He's back in his room sleeping."

When I walk into the kitchen, I find the mouthwatering sight of a warm, home-cooked meal sitting on the table. It probably sounds stupid, but the thought of eating a home-cooked meal almost brings me to tears.

"Sharon, you didn't have to do this. I don't expect you to cook for me."

"I know I didn't, Mo, but I wanted to. I invited Claire over. She should be here any minute."

"Thank you," I say, wrapping her in a hug. "I appreciate it."

"I know you do, sweetheart. We all deserve a warm meal every now and then, not those microwave meals you eat." She gives me a pointed look.

There's a soft knock on the front door, and when it opens, Claire walks in. Duke lets out a hefty bark and almost plows her over as she walks into the kitchen.

"Hey, Dukey," she purrs, scratching the top of his head. "I heard Rhett came home today. I'm surprised he didn't come pick up the dogs."

"He tried." I pull out a chair and sit down.

Sharon is a damn good cook, and I don't waste any time plopping a big helping of shepherd's pie onto my plate. When Sharon and Claire make no move to sit down, I look up to find them both staring at me.

"What?"

"You saw him?" Sharon asks, pulling out a chair.

I nod and shovel a bite into my mouth.

"And you talked to him?" Claire asks.

I nod again.

"Without crying or throwing a punch?" Claire asks. "Because if you cried or threw a punch, no one would blame you, but I'll definitely need to break out a bottle of wine."

Claire and her mother know a little of what happened between Rhett and me, but they don't know the whole story, and it's going to stay that way. Some secrets are better left tucked away in a dark closet.

"I assure you, there were no tears or violence involved, which is a good thing because I don't have a bottle of wine. And don't look so surprised. We broke up years ago."

Claire sits down across from her mother and grabs a plate from the center of the table. "And you still have the dogs?"

"No, they went with him," I reply dryly.

Rolling her eyes, Claire sticks out her tongue and fills her plate.

"To be honest, it was nice to see him. I might have some ill feelings toward him, but he was my friend before he was my boyfriend, and I want nothing but the best for him. He looked good."

Claire wags her eyebrows. "How good?"

"That's my cue to leave," Sharon says. "You two chat while I go check on Phil." She disappears down the hall.

Once she's out of earshot, Claire scoots her chair closer to mine. "Tell me everything."

"There isn't much to tell." I shrug. "You know…he looked good."

"I want details," she demands.

"Details. Let's see. His left arm was in a sling. He was wearing a pair of jeans and a T-shirt, and he looked tired."

"Really. That's it?"

"Pretty much."

"You're horrible at this. I want to know if he's gained muscle or fifty pounds of fat. What did his hair look like? Is his ass still as tight as it used to be, because that man had one hell of an ass back in the day," she says, leaning back in the seat and fanning her face.

Sharon walks back into the kitchen. "Would you leave her alone? If she doesn't want to talk about it, don't make her."

"Oh, she wants to talk about it. She's just making me work for it."

"Fine." Dropping my fork, I prop my elbows on the table. Not the most ladylike thing to do, but I moved way past ladylike a long time ago. "He gained muscle. Lots and lots of muscle. I don't think the man has an ounce of fat on his body. His hair is longer than it used to be, and it curls around the tops of his ears. And I didn't get a good look at his ass, but based on the rest of his body, I'd bet just about anything it's still a work of art."

"Yes!" Claire hollers, slamming her hand on the table. "That's what I wanted to hear."

"Shhhh," Sharon scolds. "You're going to wake up Phil, and he needs to rest."

"But I need details," she whines.

"Then go somewhere else and talk about it."

Claire smiles and gives me a mischievous look. "Want to go to Dirty Dicks and grab a beer? My treat."

I would love to. "No, I shouldn't. Your mom has been here all day and—"

"I don't mind, sweetie," Sharon replies. "You deserve some me time too. Lord knows if I go home I'll just plop down in front of the TV, and I can do that here. Phil's out for the night. You should go."

"Are you sure?"

"I wouldn't have offered if I wasn't sure. Now, finish your food and go."

"Thank you." I look at Claire. "But can we go somewhere

other than Dirty Dicks? Now that I work there, I really don't want to go in on my day off."

"Done." She scarfs down the rest of her food. "We can go to Red's."

CHAPTER
Six

Rhett

"You could've told me Mo was going to be there today. Better yet, you could've told me she was the one who had my dogs."

Cooper points his beer toward me and smiles. "If you remember correctly, I tried to tell you, but you didn't want to hear it. In fact, I think your exact words were 'What did I tell you about saying her name?'"

I hate it when he's right.

"Asshole." I take a pull from my beer and look around the bar in time to see my baby sister, Adley, bust through the front door.

"Hey! Sorry I'm late." Adley tosses her purse on the table and drops into a chair. "Class got out late, and my car was parked on the other side of campus. I'm exhausted and crabby and hungry. Oooh! Are those wings?" She reaches across the table and grabs one. "What were you guys talking about?"

"Rhett was about to tell me how his conversation with Mo went today."

Adley's mouth drops open. She watches me for a second and then pops the wing inside. "You talked to Mo?" she asks around her food.

"Yes. And I would've been prepared to see her if this asshole would've told me she had my dogs."

"I told you they were at Animal Haven," Coop argues.

"Yes, and I assumed they were with Phil."

Adley frowns. "Well, that would be difficult considering Phil's in a—"

Coop shoots Adley a sharp look, and she snaps her mouth shut.

I glance between them. "Considering Phil's in a what?"

"Nothing." Coop shakes his head and grabs a wing.

I snag it out of his hand.

"Hey! I was going to eat that." He tries for another, but I slide the plate out of his reach.

"Tell me what Adley was going to say, and you can have the wings."

"Come on, Rhett, you know Phil had a stroke," Coop says.

My heart clenches tight in my chest. I'll never forget the day Coop called me. I was in the middle of training—something I'd been doing nonstop for weeks—when they pulled me out of the arena. My manager, Bill, told me my brother was on the phone, demanding to talk to me. I nearly lost my shit when he told me everyone had been trying to get a hold of me to let me know Phil had had a stroke. I hung up, grabbed my stuff, and raced for my truck. Mo answered on the third ring, and when I told her I was heading home, she ripped my heart out.

"I know, but what was Adley going to say?"

Adley clears her throat. "He's paralyzed on one side and has been in a wheelchair ever since."

Son of a bitch. "What?"

Coop looks annoyed. Good, so am I.

"What did you think happened to him when I told you he

had a stroke?" he asks.

"I don't know, Coop. I'm not a doctor. Grandma Allen had a stroke, and she wasn't paralyzed."

"You really didn't know?" Adley asks.

I shake my head, and she frowns.

"It was awful," she says, lowering her voice. "Mo was a mess, but everyone rallied around her to help her get through it."

"Except you," Coop replies, reading my mind.

I shoot him a glare. "Don't sit there and act like I did something wrong. You don't know shit about what happened between Mo and me."

Coop raises his hands in surrender and doesn't say another word.

"What about Ruff Time?" I ask, looking at Adley. "Who's been running it? She should be taking it over soon, right?"

Adley and Coop share a look that pisses me off even more. It's clear they know something I don't.

"You need to talk to Mo," Adley says, resting her hand on top of mine. "This is her story to tell, not ours. I'm sorry you didn't know about Phil's condition. I wish one of us would've told you sooner, but we were only trying to follow your wishes—even if we didn't understand them."

"I wish you would've told me too." I pull my hand out from under Adley's and finish off my beer.

"Speak of the devil." Adley nods toward the front of the bar. "Look who just walked in."

I feel Mo before I see her. The hairs on the back of my neck stand on end, my heart kicks up a couple of notches, and my cock twitches before I even turn around. If I thought Mo and I were over, today has shown me I was sorely mistaken. Whatever we had is still alive and strong and growing inside of me by the second.

My chair scratches against the hardwood as I turn to look. With ease and grace, she glides across the floor and props her elbow on the edge of the bar. She's talking with Claire Daniels all the while. I'm not surprised to see her with Claire; they've been best friends for as long as I can remember. I am, however, surprised to see her at Red's. This was never her hangout.

Things change; people change. I wonder what else has changed with Mo. I wonder if she still sings when she cooks or shifts on her feet when she's nervous. Does she still prefer to eat dessert first when she goes out to dinner? Does she still leave a mess wherever she goes? Most of all, I wonder if she still makes that sweet little moan right before she—

Son of a bitch, I have to stop. I can't think about that. Not right now, and certainly not after what she did.

"Did you know she would be here?" I ask, turning toward Coop.

When he talked me into a beer, we purposely chose to stay away from Dirty Dicks. He said it was because he's there all the damn time and needed a change of scenery, but I'm wondering if he had ulterior motives.

"Nope."

I grunt noncommittally, unsure whether I believe him or not.

"Is she dating anyone?"

Coop frowns.

Adley lifts a brow. "I thought we weren't supposed to talk about that sort of thing."

"Answer the damn question."

"She's single. And don't look now, but we've been spotted," Adley whispers, trying to be discreet as she glances over my shoulder.

I can't help it; I follow her gaze.

Mo's breath hitches the second we make eye contact. She doesn't look pissed, but she also doesn't look happy. She looks... unsure. My eyes drop, drinking in the sight of her. She switched out her flannel for a concert T-shirt, and the cowboy boots I love have been replaced by a pair of tattered Chucks. But she's still wearing those tight-ass jeans that showcase her mile-long legs, and I can't help but remember what it's like to have them wrapped tight around my body.

When I look up, Mo's eyes are smoldering. *Yup, I've still got that control over you, sweetheart.* My lips curve in a smile. She blushes and looks down at her feet. Claire must say something because Mo looks up and then over at me and nods. Here they come.

"Family dinner night?" Claire asks as they draw near. "You're missing a few. Where's Trevor?"

"He's on shift tonight, and I'm sure Beau is floating around the world somewhere. We don't hear from him much," Adley says.

Trevor is my younger brother. He's a full-time firefighter and helps Dad out on the ranch. Beau, my oldest brother, is a freelance photographer, and we only hear from him when he breezes through Texas on an assignment. Much like the rest of the Allen crew, Trevor and Beau are married to their jobs.

Claire's cheeks turn red, and she smiles. "He's always working."

If I were a betting man, I'd bet she has a thing for my baby brother. I look at Adley, and she must notice it too, because she grins.

"How's work going, Claire? You're still teaching at the elementary school, right?"

"I am. It's good. I like it, although I can't wait for summer break."

I frown. "It's only August. Didn't school just start?"

Mo laughs, the husky sound wrapping itself around me like a warm breeze on a southern summer night. "She'll spend the entire school year waiting for summer break."

Mo, Claire, Coop, and Adley fall into easy conversation about all the gossip that's new in our town. I signal our server for another beer, because I need something else to focus on—anything to keep from thinking about Mo and how goddamn beautiful she is. Her hair is still in a messy knot, and I want to take it down and run my fingers through it to see if it's as soft as I remember. And don't even get me started on her clothes. Mo has more curves than County Line Road, and I want to strip her out of those jeans, toss her shirt to the side, and spend hours exploring every dip and turn.

The waitress drops off my beer, and I take a long pull from the bottle. Coming back to Heaven was a huge mistake. I was never able to control myself around Mo, and I see that's still the case. Not even one day back, and I'm already trying to figure out how I can get her alone, strip her naked, and fuck her senseless.

We're explosive between the sheets. I've pulled up many a memory from back in the day to get me through lonely nights on the road. Mo was wild in bed and it kills me that I have to keep my hands to myself when they itch to reach out to her. It also kills me that I'm still this attracted to her after the shit she pulled. What I need is to talk to her, find out these secrets Coop and Adley are talking about, and then find a way to get her back in my bed. I'll be in town for a few more weeks while I rehab my shoulder, and what better way to spend them than with a warm and sated Mo Gallagher?

I'll work her out of my system, and in a few weeks, I'll move on—for good this time, leaving Mo and a lifetime of memories behind me.

Adley kicks my chair, and I blink. "Move over so Claire and Mo can pull up a chair."

"Thanks, but we're not staying." Claire tips her head back, drains the rest of her beer, and sets the bottle on the table.

"Oh, come one, one more beer," Adley begs. "I can't remember the last time I hung out with girls, and I've enjoyed catching up with you two."

Mo smiles. It's genuine and gorgeous. "If I didn't have an eight-hour workday followed by a sixteen-hour workday ahead of me, I would. I really need to get home and get some sleep, but we should plan a girls' night."

Adley squeals in delight. "That would be so much fun—"

"Sixteen hours? What kind of job do you have that requires you to work sixteen hours?" I ask, my voice holding more bite than I intended.

"Not that it's any of your business, but I'll put in eight hours at Animal Haven and then I have a shift at Dirty Dicks."

"Dirty Dicks?" I glance at Coop, who suddenly won't make eye contact with me. "I didn't know you worked at Dirty Dicks."

I don't know why that pisses me off so much, but it does. It's my own damn fault I didn't know—I realize that—but it doesn't stop the flash of jealousy I get knowing Coop gets to spend so much time with her.

"I was working over in Brighton at Broadway Bar and Grill, but the drive was wearing on me, and Coop was always on my case about taking better care of myself."

She smiles at Coop, and I see red.

"He offered me a job at Dirty Dicks, and I couldn't turn it down. I started last weekend."

I lift a brow at Coop. "What else have you kept from me?"

He rolls his eyes, but I'm jealous and pissed, and that is not a good combination.

"First you tell me about her dad—what are you going to tell me next? That you're in love with her? Are you sleeping with my girl, Coop?"

I regret the words as soon as they leave my mouth, because not only would Coop never do that to me, Mo wouldn't either, and I sure as hell don't have the right to call her my girl. I lost that privilege a long time ago.

Mo lets out a strangled noise, and I turn to see her wide, furious eyes staring back me. "Fuck you, Rhett Allen. I'm not your girl—you made sure of that—and if you think I'd sleep with any of your brothers then you never knew me at all."

Slamming her beer down on the table, she turns to Claire. "Let's go."

"If the shoe fits…" I can't stop myself.

Her lips part.

If Claire's eyes could kill, I'd be dead and buried.

"Mo, wait." I grab her wrist, but she wrenches it away. *What does she mean* I made sure of that?

"No," she shouts. "You're a dick, Rhett. It's something I learned the hard way six years ago. Sadly enough, I let myself believe maybe we had both changed, grown up a bit, and could move on from the past. But I can see you're still a selfish prick, and I refuse to waste another minute worrying about you."

I push up from my chair and step toward her. "You worry about me? Really, Mo? Were you worried about me when Char—"

She closes the distance and gives a nice solid shove to the center of my chest, knocking me off balance. "Don't you dare throw that in my face."

We're both breathing heavily. Frustrated that I lost my cool, I run my fingers through my hair.

Mo blinks and then blinks again. "Everything was fine until you came back. Whatever this is, I can't do it," she says, her voice breaking.

Her eyes grow suspiciously glossy, and I swallow past a lump in my throat because the last thing I want to do is make Mo cry.

"No more, Rhett. I'll drop the dogs off at Coop's sometime after lunch tomorrow. I don't want to see you again."

One minute she's here, and the next she's walking out the door—and out my life for the second time.

CHAPTER
Seven

Monroe

The last thing I expected to see this morning is Rhett sitting outside Animal Haven with a steaming cup of coffee. And there's a white bag next to him with a familiar donut logo on the front, guaranteeing that whatever is in there will taste as delicious as he looks.

Last night was horrible. I didn't sleep a wink. I spent the entire time tossing and turning, replaying our fight in my head. I kept coming back to the last thing I said to him.

"I don't want to see you again."

I've learned the hard way that tomorrow isn't promised, and things can change in an instant. I would hate myself forever if something happened to Rhett and those were my last words to him. I was pissed, but I didn't mean them. Rhett was once a big part of my life, and as much as I hate to admit it, I enjoyed seeing him yesterday.

"That for me?" I ask as I approach.

"That depends. You still mad at me?"

"If I tell you no can I have the coffee?"

Rhett takes a deep breath and looks at the cup in his hand.

I've seen a lot of emotions in Rhett over the years. When we were little, I saw him cry and scream, throw tantrums that were out of this world, and when we grew up I saw him laugh and goof off, and after we became intimate, I saw so much love and affection. But not once did I see this look. I've never seen regret on his face until now.

I take a step forward, and he looks up, his bright blue eyes swirling with apologies.

"You can have the coffee regardless, but I hope you'll give me a chance to apologize. I don't want you to be mad at me, Mo." He hands over the cup.

I take it, blow across the top, and take a sip. "I'm listening."

"I was an asshole last night. Despite how I feel about you and our past, I shouldn't have acted like that."

"What you said hurt me, but I said some hurtful things too."

"Don't." He shakes his head and looks down. "Don't apologize for what you said. You didn't do anything wrong. Last night is all on me."

"Apology accepted." I take another sip of my coffee, wishing I had a shot of whiskey to throw in it. "Although I still feel terrible."

My words hang in the air, floating around us while I try to decide if I should say more.

"Why do I have the feeling we're talking about more than what happened last night?" he says, finally looking up at me.

The cup freezes on the way to my mouth. "Maybe we are talking about the past, and maybe you don't know as much about it as you think you do."

Rhett blows out a breath. "Mo, there are so many things we need to talk about."

He's right, there are. The only problem—I'm not sure he's ready for what I have to say. "I know. Just not today, okay? I've got a ton of work to do, and you've got therapy."

His gaze remains steady. "I don't know how to move forward without talking about the past."

"I don't either. Maybe we don't move forward. Not yet at least. Maybe, for now, we just agree to be civil, friendly. We've always been good at that."

"We've been good at a lot more than being friendly." Rhett leans in close, and I'll be damned if my stomach doesn't start to flutter. "The connection we share is still here, Mo. I know you feel it."

"Oh, I feel it. But I'm surprised you do."

He steps back. "I'm starting to realize I might not have much of a choice."

Don't I know it. "Just because we feel it doesn't mean we need to act on it."

He nods. "Because we've got things to discuss, and until then—"

"Until then we're friendly acquaintances," I answer for him. "Who bring each other gifts." I look down at the bag between his legs. "Is that what I think it is?"

"If you think it's a peace offering in the form of donuts from the bakery, then yes, it's what you think it is."

I grab the bag, unlock the door to Animal Haven, and lead him inside. "I accept your peace offering, and I'll gladly take a donut or two before I start my day. I overslept and forgot to eat breakfast."

"I didn't sleep well either," he says, wryly.

My dog, Ruby, saunters out of the back room to greet us and Rhett's eyes grow wide. Lowering himself, Rhett holds out a hand and waits patiently for her arthritic legs to carry her across the room.

I watch Ruby approach him and my mind drifts back to the

day she became a part of our family. Dad picked her up off the side of the road. She was a gangly puppy. He nursed her back to health and instead of adopting her out, we kept her. She's not as lively as she once was. Years of running around Animal Haven with the other animals have taken a toll on her hips. Her black and brown patchy face has faded to a dull silver. Her big brown eyes are still bright, but they're also tired.

She stops in front of Rhett's hand and takes a whiff. Her tail starts wagging, and she pushes her nose into his hand.

"Hey, pretty girl." Rhett gives Ruby a nice long rub down. "You remember me, don't you? I can't believe you still have her," he says, looking up. "I didn't see her when I was here yesterday."

"She was inside. Duke and Diesel are a little too hyper for her."

He nods and looks back at Ruby. "She's got to be what, ten?"

"Twelve."

Rhett pets Ruby for as long as she'll allow. He whispers soft words into her floppy ear. Eventually she gets tired of standing and walks off.

"Let's eat." I kick out a chair for Rhett to sit in and take the one next to it. I lay some napkins on the desk and pull out a donut for each of us.

"Does Ruby still live here, or do you take her home every night?"

"She lives here. I tried to bring her home with me a few years ago, but she hated it. She would sit in front of the door and cry for hours, refusing to eat or sleep. I eventually brought her back out here."

"This is her home."

I nod and take a bite. We eat quietly side by side, and although the air is thick with tension, it's not uncomfortable. It feels distantly familiar. It feels good.

"Where are Duke and Diesel?" he asks, licking icing off of his finger.

I've only had those dogs for a few days, and they already feel like mine. It's going to suck handing those babies back over. "I left them at my house while I do morning chores. Duke was still sleeping."

Rhett laughs. "That dog is going to sleep his life away. He snores so loud too."

I smile. "He does! And he farts in his sleep." I make a face. "I made him sleep in the living room because he stunk up my bedroom."

"You had them in your bedroom?" He looks surprised.

"Of course I did. It's like having two big body pillows with built-in heaters—until one farts. Then all bets are off."

"Please tell me you didn't let them in bed with you." There's a smile in his eyes.

"Okay, I won't tell you."

He laughs. "You did! You totally let them in bed with you. Now they're going to want to sleep with me."

We look at each other, a comfortable warmth settling between us, and for a moment it feels as though our past is just a bad dream. For just a second, we're nothing but old friends having breakfast and laughing, without a care in the world.

"You mean you don't already sleep with them?"

"Hell no," he says. "They hog the damn bed, and I end up on the floor. I make them sleep in their own beds."

"Well," I say sweetly, "that's probably about to change."

Rhett shakes his head. "If I can't get them out of my bed, I'll be calling your ass to take care of it."

"Deal." I finish my donut in three bites.

"Do you want me to send Cooper over to get the dogs after lunch?"

I furrow my brows and then remember what I said last night about dropping them off. "No, I'll keep them. I was just mad."

"You sure? Because it's really not a problem. I know they're a lot of work."

"They're really not. I've enjoyed having them around. I'll miss them when they're gone."

Rhett watches me, but he doesn't say anything as he finishes his donut.

"Do you want the last one?" I ask, offering him the bag.

He shakes his head. "You eat it."

I roll the top of the bag down and put it in the center of my desk. "I have a ton of work to do, but I'll save it for a snack."

"Where are you going?"

Tugging on my gloves, I turn around and walk backward toward the front door. "Time to muck some stalls. No rush, though. Finish your coffee and let yourself out when you're done."

Except he doesn't finish his coffee at all; he follows me outside and looks around. "I can help. Physical therapy isn't for another few hours, and if I go home, I'll just park myself in front of Coop's TV."

"Mucking stalls probably isn't on the list of activities you should perform with a shoulder injury. And Tess is coming out later to give me a hand."

Reaching toward his back, Rhett pulls off the sling. "I can do something else. Something less strenuous. It's strained, not destroyed."

"Funny, because I swear Coop told me it was torn."

Shaking his head, Rhett smiles. "Coop has a big mouth. There's a small tear. I can still move it; I just have to be careful. But the rest of me is fine." He holds his good arm out to the side.

"I'm sure there's something I can help you with that won't ruin my shoulder."

Pulling my bottom lip between my teeth, I look around.

"You could get the dogs some fresh water," I say, nodding to the green hose on the ground by the fence. "Pull it around back."

"Okay. I can do that."

I've never seen a man look so happy to be given a chore. With a smile on his face, Rhett grabs the hose and gets to work.

By the time I finish cleaning out the horse stalls and laying down a fresh bed of shavings, Rhett is standing at his car, adjusting the sling on his arm.

"You okay?" I ask, peeling off my gloves. "You didn't hurt yourself, did you?"

"No, I didn't hurt myself." He rolls his eyes. "You sound like my mother."

"Your mother is a very smart woman. I happen to be very fond of Vivian, so I'll take that as a compliment."

"She's fond of you too," he says.

We stare at each other as our history swirls around us.

I can't do anything but stare into Rhett's eyes and remember how it felt to be with him.

To kiss him.

To touch him.

To be loved by him.

But those feelings came with a heavy price, and I have to stay strong.

He finally clears his throat and breaks the spell. "I watered the dogs, gave them each a scoop of food, and let them run for a little bit."

"Thank you, that's a huge help."

Stuffing his hand in his pocket, Rhett retrieves his keys.

"I should get going. Don't want to be late for my first PT appointment."

"Good luck."

"Thanks."

He opens the car door and turns to look at me.

"Mo, I'm sorry about your dad," he says softly. "I knew he had a stroke, but I didn't find out until last night how badly he was affected. If I'd known, I would've come back, even after…"

His lingering words slice through me, hitting something deep in my gut, and I have to stop for a second to catch my breath. He doesn't want to say it out loud; I can tell by the heartache on his face.

"Even after I told you I slept with Charlie." I choose my words carefully because I promised myself that moving forward, I'd always speak the truth. No more lies, even if they're meant to protect myself or someone I love.

"Thank you, Rhett. That means a lot."

"See you tomorrow, Mo."

I tilt my head. "Tomorrow?"

"I told you I'd come by Friday."

"Oh, right." So much shit has happened in the last twenty-four hours, I completely forgot. "You don't have to."

"I know, but I want to."

CHAPTER
Eight

Monroe

I force myself to walk across the yard before I glance back toward Rhett. His vehicle nears the end of the lane and stops. I hold my breath, waiting to see what he's going to do, secretly hoping that he forgot something—me, maybe—and would have to turn around.

Unfortunately, that's not the case. Rhett flicks on his blinker and pulls onto the highway. A second later Tess's little red car turns down the lane.

Tess Walker moved to town a few years back. She runs the floral shop on Broadway, a few businesses down from Dirty Dicks, and volunteers here during her free time. And on Sundays so I can have a day off. So, pretty much, she's an angel. She's become an integral part of my life and she's a regular on the rare occasions Claire and I manage a night out.

Ruby whimpers at my side. Letting out a slow breath, I reach in my pocket to grab a treat. I squat down and hold out the bone shaped biscuit. Ruby snags it from my fingers. Her body might be slow but her mouth is not.

"I bet you never thought you'd see Rhett again did ya, girl?"

Her ears perk up at the mention of Rhett's name. "Yeah, I know. You always were a sucker for those Allen boys."

Gravel crunches under the weight of Tess's car as she makes her way down the lane. Tess parks, hops out, and stuff her keys into her pocket.

"You're early," I holler.

Tess shrugs. "I got tired of painting and decided to call it quits. Are my eyes playing tricks on me, or was that Rhett pulling out of here?"

"That was Rhett."

"Do you want to talk about what he was doing here, or will that require a case of wine? Because I'm not opposed to day drinking."

"You drink wine by the case?"

She gives me a look. "Don't most people?"

"No." I shake my head and chuckle.

"Don't knock 'til you try it."

Tess doesn't know much about my relationship with Rhett, the same way I don't know much about what brought her to Heaven three years ago.

"I'll tell you about Rhett if you tell me why you moved to Heaven."

Her smile fades. "If your story requires a case of wine, then mine requires several large bottles of tequila."

"I actually have a bottle of tequila in the office," I offer, curious to learn more.

"As tempting as that is, I'm going to pass. That's a time in my life I'd rather not think about let alone talk about."

"Maybe one of these days we'll confide in each other."

She doesn't look convinced. "Maybe."

"Well, I guess since we're not going to get drunk and spill all of our secrets we might as well get to work."

Tess laughs and falls in step beside me as we walk into Animal Haven. "It's a sad day when we'd rather shovel shit than talk about our past," I say.

She sighs. "Don't I know it."

———————◦———————

"Hey, sweet boy." I step into an enclosure and sit down next to an overweight black cat. Pickles lifts his head when I set a bowl of cat food in front of him. He sniffs his gourmet meal, takes a few bites, and then looks away.

"Come on, you have to be hungry." I lift the big ball of fur onto my lap hoping a little love might entice him. "You haven't eaten in three days. I'll make you a deal… If you clean your plate tonight, I'll give you some tuna tomorrow. I know how much you love tuna."

Pickles looks pleased with the offer. Hopping out of my lap, he winds his way around my ankles—the first time he's initiated any form of affection toward me—and my heart leaps with joy.

Rescues come and go, it's the part of the job, but some are hard to let go of. Pickles is one of them. Three times now I could've adopted him out. Who knew fat cats were a hot commodity? But, I couldn't do it.

"Meow."

"Fine, you can have wet food, but just this one time."

I grab a can of wet cat food from the supply closet and when I return, Pickles is creeping toward the door of his cage. "Oh, no you don't." I gently guide him back into the pen. "Tomorrow you're eating your dry food first," I say, peeling the top off. I plop the food into his bowl and when I turn around Pickles makes a mad dash for the open door.

Ruby barks and pickles skids to a halt.

Ears laid flat, he hisses and I scoop him up. "This is why

I can't let you roam free. You're mean to the other animals," I whisper, nuzzling his head. "One of these days you'll learn that there are perks to playing nice."

I've tried letting Pickles roam around Animal Haven the way Ruby does. My hope was that he'd get along with the other animals and I could make him a resident pet. Unfortunately, he failed each and every test. Not only does Pickles hiss and spit at every dog he sees, he doesn't seem particularly fond of the other cats either.

I set Pickles down next to his food bowl and rub his head. "Eat."

He plops down in front of his bowl. Craning his neck to the side, he sticks out his tongue and manages to snag a bite of food.

"Ruby, that's what we call lazy."

"Woof."

Using my knee, I nudge Ruby out of the way and shut the door to the cage, making sure it's locked before I turn away.

"Come on. One animal down, twelve more to go."

The closest humane society is over an hour away in Houston which makes Animal Haven the go-to when there's a stray or rescue animal. On average, we house anywhere from twenty to thirty animals although the facility is built to hold many more. A great turn out at the last adoption fair left us with the lowest census I've seen in a long time. Oddly enough, a lower number of mouths to feed doesn't make my job easier.

With Ruby by my side I let the friendly, well-adjusted animals into the fenced in yard to play. The grumpy ones aren't so lucky. They remain separated and I go from pen to pen giving each of them one on one attention.

"Mo?"

"Yeah?" I look up when Tess walks in.

"You've got someone here to see you."

CHAPTER
Nine

Monroe

Squirting sanitizer on my hands, I plaster on my best smile and pray I don't have animal feces visible on my clothes. There's a man standing at the edge of the drive talking to Tess. When I come around the corner, he looks up.

"You must be Monroe. I'm Jerry."

I take his offered hand for a quick shake. "It's nice to meet you, Jerry. What can I do for you? Are you looking to adopt a dog, because I've got several ready for a forever home?"

The pudgy man shakes his head. "Oh, no, quite the opposite." He takes a step back and turns for his car. "I'm here to drop one off." Jerry opens his back door and pulls out a large bird cage with a blanket draped over the top. "My father passed away a few weeks ago and left me his bird."

"I'm so sorry to hear about your father."

"I appreciate that. It was expected so we were as prepared as we could be."

I smile and nod, unsure of how to respond. "Are you here because you need to learn more about caring for your bird? I've got some great reference books you could borrow."

"No, you don't understand. I don't want the bird."

My eyes widen. "You don't?"

"My father was crazy and his bird is even crazier. Quite frankly, I don't have the time or patience to deal with the darn thing. I was told you take animals."

"Well, yes, but—"

"Perfect." Jerry sets the cage at my feet and grabs a giant bag out of the back of his car. "Here's all of his stuff—food, toys, and I tossed in a picture of my dad."

"Why would I need a picture of your dad?"

"I don't know, I just thought he might like looking at it from time to time."

"Oh, okay, so—"

"So that's it," he interrupts. "That's everything."

Before I have a chance to respond, Jerry hops in his car and peels out tossing up a cloud of dust.

Tess fans her hand in front of her face. "Does this happen often?"

"No. Most people drop their pet off after hours in a box on the front step."

She looks at the cage hidden under a white blanket. "Well, let's find out what's in there."

I pick up the cage and carry it into Animal Haven.

Tess lifts the hem of the blanket over the top of the cage, and we come face to face with the most gorgeous bird I have ever seen.

"It's a cockatoo," I breathe, leaning down to get a better look.

The bird is all white with a black beak, and obviously doesn't like my close proximity because he squawks, erects the lemon colored crest on top of his head, and fluffs his feathers.

"I don't think he likes us," Tess says.

"He's just scared."

"What do we do with him? I've never cared for a bird."

"I'm not entirely sure. I'll call the vet to see if he can stop by and check the bird out. Maybe he can give us some tips."

"It sounds like you've got a solid plan. Is there anything you need me to do for you, or should I get back to what I was doing?"

"I'm good."

Tess heads out back to finish up whatever she was doing. I grab the bag Jerry dropped off and pull out a container of food, two toys, and a picture of an old man who looks nothing like Jerry.

"Well, I don't know your name, but I know what your owner looked like," I mumble, staring into the now empty bag.

"Dave," he says.

The loud, screeching voice startles me. With a hand to my chest, I jump back and look at the bird. "You can talk?"

"Dave," he repeats.

"Is that your name?"

"That's my name, don't wear it out." His words are mumbled because, well, he's a bird, but I can still make out what he's saying.

"What else do you know? How old are you Dave?"

"That's my name, don't wear it out."

"Yes, I know that. How old are you?" I ask again.

"Shut up!" he yells.

"Excuse me?" Hands on my hips, I glare at Dave. He tilts his head to the side, starts laughing, and I'll be damned if it isn't the cutest thing I've ever seen.

"Shut up, Dave," he yells, bouncing on his perch in the cage. "Go to sleep, Dave."

"You want to take a nap? Now we're getting somewhere." I lower the blanket over the cage. "There."

"It's dark in here."

I peek under the blanket. "It's supposed to be dark, you're taking a nap."

"Shut up!"

I drop the blanket. There are a lot of things I'm willing to do in this job, but arguing with a cheeky cockatoo is not one of them.

"It's dark in here."

This is going to get annoying fast. "Goodnight, Dave."

"Goodnight, Dave," he says.

Dave sighs and doesn't make another sound.

"Just what I need," I mumble, walking out of the room.

I call the vet and leave a message to see if he can stop by to give Dave a checkup. Unfortunately, I'll have to keep Dave separated from the other animals until I get a clean bill of health from the vet.

Ruby bumps into my leg on her way to her water bowl and I reach down to pet her head. "You should probably stick with me today, girl. I'm not sure you're ready for the likes of Dave."

The next few hours fly by as I finish up the chores that Jerry interrupted. When I return to the office to check on Dave, I find him sitting on Tess's shoulder. She's thumbing through a book and he is looking over her shoulder as if he's interested in what she's reading.

"I take it you and Dave have become friends."

Tess and Dave look up and then she frowns at the bird. "You told me your name was Simon."

"That's my name, don't wear it out," he says, bobbing his head.

"I'm starting to think the bird doesn't know what he's talking about," I say.

"I'm not so sure about that. I've been doing some research

and cockatoos are incredibly smart," Tess says, raising a reference book she likely got from the book shelf in the office.

I pull out a chair and sit down. "What else did you learn?"

"Well, they like Kale, broccoli, carrots, sweet potato, and squash."

"Ew," Dave—or Simon—squawks.

Tess laughs and continues. "They also eat fruit in moderation, and should always avoid chocolate, avocado, caffeine, dried beans, pretzels, and alcohol."

"Grab me a beer!"

"Sorry, Dave, I only have Tequila," I reply.

"Simon says, shut up!"

My mouth drops open and Tess chuckles. "He's funny, isn't he?" she asks, clearly smitten with the bird.

"Sure, if you like being lied to and told to shut up."

Tess reaches up and pets the bird. He pecks at her hand with is beak and she yanks it back. "I think he's cute. If you don't have anyone else in mind, I'd love to foster him."

"What? Really? You don't know anything about birds."

"I can learn."

"Are you sure you want to?"

"Why not? I've got nothing else going for me. Simon can keep me company."

I rest my hand on hers. "You've got lots going for you."

She rolls her eyes. "Yes or no, Mo. Can I foster Simon?"

"Simon says, yes," the bird yells.

Tess smiles. "See, Simon says. You have to do what Simon says."

"Fine, but we have to get him checked out by the vet first."

"Speaking of the vet, he called why you were out back. He can't stop by, his schedule is too packed, but he'd be happy to squeeze us in if we can bring the bird to him."

"Oh, okay." I look around, unsure of when I'll have time to take him.

"I'll take him," Tess offers. "And then if everything turns out okay, I'll just bring him home with me. We'll even stop by the pet store on the way and grab a few more things."

I don't think I've ever seen Tess this excited, and who am I tell her no? "Fine. If you're sure."

"Did you hear that, Simon?" she asks. "You get to come home with me."

"Shut up!"

CHAPTER
Ten

Monroe

"Two days in a row? I don't remember you being such an early bird."

I came in to work early this morning to get a head start so I could leave a little sooner and have some downtime before my shift at Dirty Dicks tonight. Like every other day, I went around back to start with the dogs, and imagine my surprise when I saw they'd already been watered and fed for the morning.

There's a fenced-in three-acre patch of land behind Animal Haven that gives the dogs a place to run and burn off some energy. Right now it's occupied by six mutts and one very sexy cowboy.

Oh boy.

Rhett is leaning against the fence, his foot propped up on a rung, and when a lazy smile spreads across his face, I feel a rush of heat settle between my thighs.

"Couldn't sleep worth shit again last night."

"Dreaming of me, huh?" I tease.

I don't mean to flirt—it's not something I'm generally good

at—but when I'm around him, I can't help it. Things just come out of my mouth before I have a chance to stop them.

"Well, there's that." Rhett smirks, igniting a fire in my belly, and I have to look away before I combust.

Rascal, a Chihuahua mix I've been trying to home for the last year runs by, and I scoop him up—anything other than Rhett's blinding smile to focus on.

"But it's also my shoulder," he says, rubbing at the offending body part.

"The doctor didn't give you any pain pills?"

"He did, but I don't want to take them."

"Why not? There's nothing wrong with taking them if you need them."

"I know." He pushes away from the fence and walks toward me. Rascal lets out a growl but makes no attempt to nip at Rhett when he runs a hand along his back. "Pain pills fuck me up, and if I take them, I can't drive. If I can't drive, I won't be able to come help you."

"Rhett," I admonish. "I don't want you to be in pain just so you can come out here and help me. I'll manage on my own; I always do. You should go home and try to get some rest."

"I know you can manage on your own, but I wanted to see you."

Oh shit, there goes my stomach again.

"I remembered where your dad kept the spare key so I figured I'd help out and get you an early start. I also wanted to see my dogs. Where are they?" he asks, looking over my shoulder.

"They're running loose in the horse pasture. I was going to leave them there while I fed and watered the dogs, but I guess that's already done. Thank you, by the way. That saves a lot of time."

"You're welcome, and I'm yours for the day. Put me to work."

I give him a look. "I'm not going to put you to work when you just told me you're in pain."

"I didn't say I was in pain right now; I said I was in pain last night. My physical therapist worked my shoulder good yesterday. It was tight when I got up, but I did some of the stretches she showed me, and that took care of most of the ache. The anti-inflammatories help too."

"If you're sure. But any inkling of pain and you have to promise you'll stop."

"Cross my heart."

"Follow me."

Rhett tails me inside and down the main aisle past the dog kennels.

"We'll clean out the cages of the dogs that are outside, and once we're done, we'll bring them back in, let the others out, and clean those cages."

I unlock the storage room door and pull out the cleaning supplies and a large hose that's already connected to a faucet.

"I'll have you spray the floors down, and I'll come behind you and scrub. Then we'll rinse."

"I can scrub," he says, reaching for the brush, but I pull it back.

"No, sir." I shake my head. "You will not injure yourself further on my watch. Coop wouldn't let me hear the end of it."

Rhett's jaw clenches at the mention of Coop's name, and I scoff. "Oh, good grief, Rhett. I wouldn't sleep with your brother, and I'm not attracted to him in any way. Never have been; never will be."

"You used to be attracted to me, and we're identical twins."

Seriously? "That doesn't mean shit, Rhett. You two are polar opposites. You may look alike, but that's where the similarities end."

He smirks. "So, you *are* attracted to me?"

I shove his good arm. "Get to work."

Laughing, he takes the hose, and we spend the next hour working together to clean the cages. Once we get them clean, we round up the dogs and bring them in. Most of them are tuckered out from being outside and are anxious to curl up and take a nap. Then Rhett gathers the rest of the dogs and puts them in the fenced yard.

We wash and clean the remaining dog cages, then move on to the cats. We clean their litter boxes, give them fresh food and water and lots of love and attention, and when we're done, I go back into the storage room and pull out a can of tuna.

I peel open the container, and I can't help myself. I shove it toward Rhett. He hates tuna.

He makes a gagging sound and pushes me away. "Paybacks are hell," he warns.

"Ah, come on, tuna is good for you."

"Come near me with that stuff again and you'll be wearing it."

"Fine. Don't get your panties in a bunch." I walk toward the back of the cat kennels and unlatch the door to a walk-in cage. Rhett follows behind but stays outside the enclosure. "Will you shut the door? I don't want Pickles to make a run for it like he tried to do yesterday."

His eyebrows shoot up. "Pickles?"

"What?" I ask. "He loves his name."

"You're still addicted, aren't you?"

I've always had a deep affinity for dill pickles. Rhett used to make fun of me, because not only do I eat the pickles, I drink the juice. On more than one occasion back in the day, he brought me a jar of pickles rather than a bouquet of flowers.

"Don't judge me."

He holds up his hand and laughs.

Pickles is curled up in a ball in the back corner of the enclosure, and I take my normal seat next to him.

"Someone dropped him off here in a box. I think he was an inside cat because he's declawed and neutered. Poor little guy was scared to death."

"I'm not sure I'd call him little." Rhett keeps a hand on the cage, ensuring the door stays shut.

"Can you believe that, Pickles?" I ask, hoisting the twenty-pound cat onto my lap. "He thinks you're fat."

I have a bad habit of talking to the animals like they're people. Guess that's what happens when you spend your days with four-legged friends, but Rhett doesn't laugh or make fun of me.

Pickles looks up with sad eyes, but he makes no move to jump off my lap. Instead, he inches his way toward the can of tuna and takes a nibble.

"He doesn't eat much. I've had him checked by the vet, and he seems to be in good health. My guess is his owner fed him a lot of wet cat food or tuna because he won't touch the dry food."

"Or he's playing you."

I lift a brow. "You think a cat is playing me?"

"Sure. Cats are smart. He knows that if he refuses to eat the other food you bring him, you'll eventually offer his favorite. Tuna."

I look down at the wet cat food still sitting in his bowl from last night and frown. Damnit, maybe Rhett is right. I sit patiently while Pickles eats his fill, and then I give him one last pet and put him on the cat bed. "You aren't playing me, are you?" I whisper.

"Meow." He pushes his cold nose against my arm, arches his

back, and crawls off the bed. He curls up in the corner where I know I'll find him tomorrow.

I step out of the enclosure. "You hungry?"

Rhett closes the door behind me. "Starved. Want to run in town and grab a bite?"

A juicy burger and an order of fries sounds fantastic, but it'll put me out ten bucks, and I'm not willing to make that sacrifice. "Nah. Don't have time. I packed my lunch."

I grab my food from my truck and meet Rhett inside. He's sitting across from my desk, his long legs stretched out in front of him with ruby's head resting on his lap. He tugs his sling off, and my step falters when he reaches for the back of his shirt with his good arm and pulls it over his head.

It should be illegal for a man to do that move within a ten-foot radius of a woman.

Rolling my tongue up, I shove it back into my mouth and walk on in. "If I'd known you were providing the afternoon entertainment, I would've brought my dollar bills."

"Very funny." He slaps at my ass when I walk by, and I squeal, jumping forward. "It's muggy as hell out today," he adds, pushing his fingers into the fur on Ruby's head. The affection he has for her is so simple and familiar that it makes my heart ache for things to be the way they once were. "What did you bring for lunch?"

"Turkey sandwich, chips, granola bar, and an apple. Want some?"

He shrugs and stands up. Ruby isn't too happy about finding another spot to rest her head—because no other spot compares to Rhett's chiseled thigh—but she settles on her blanket in the corner of the room. Rhett goes through a series of stretches, each one pushing his shoulder further. I try to focus on my lunch, but it's damn hard with all those muscles flexing and winking at me. He's definitely beefed up over the years. And is that a V leading to his—

"Mo?"

"Yeah?"

"You're staring." He blinks. I search his eyes for frustration or amusement, but all I see is a desperate hunger.

"I can't help it," I whisper, and then I jam my apple in my mouth and take a bite before I do something stupid like beg him to bend me over this desk and have his wicked way with me.

He smiles, slow and seductive. "Maybe we should make it fair. I wouldn't be opposed to you stripping down so I can get in some ogling time of my own."

I toss my apple at his head. He catches it midair with his good hand and takes a bite.

"What did your physical therapist say? How long are they expecting for your recovery?" I ask.

"Nice subject change."

I smile.

He sighs. "You know, the normal shit. They can't give me a specific timeline, just said it takes time and patience for these things to heal. I'm hoping a few weeks, a month max."

"Good. That's good." I tear my sandwich in two and hand him half.

"You don't have to do that. Eat your lunch, Mo."

"There's plenty here. I don't mind. Eat it." I open the bag of chips and turn it toward him.

Rhett sits down, hands me the apple, and grabs his half of the sandwich.

He takes a hefty bite. "You still make a mean sandwich."

"It's funny," I say. "Not much has changed with me over the years, yet I don't feel at all like the girl I was when you left for the PBR."

"Mo, I—"

"I'm sorry." I frown. "I shouldn't have said that."

I can tell by the flat line of his lips that he isn't happy.

"Mo, we need to talk. I *want* to talk."

"I know. We will—"

"When you're ready, okay?"

I nod jerkily, focusing on the rest of my lunch. We eat in silence, and then I put Rhett on the riding lawn mower, toss him a can of sunscreen, and send him out to the back forty.

When we're finished with daily chores, I grab Duke and Diesel and put my lunchbox in my truck. Rhett hoses off the lawnmower, parks it back in the shed, and meets me by his car. The dogs fall at his feet. Rhett bends down, talking softly to them as he scratches and rubs.

"Thank you again, for today," I tell him.

"Don't mention it," he says, standing to his full height.

His sling is back on, and I hope all over again that he didn't do anything to strain it today. "The shoulder's feeling good?"

"The shoulder is fine, Mo."

"Okay. You should get home and ice it or put some heat on it or whatever it is you do for an injury like that. Oh, and take a pain pill, for God's sake."

"Mo."

"What?"

"Do you do this every day?"

"Do I do what every day?"

"This." He waves an arm toward Animal Haven, and Duke lets out a deep bark, turning toward where Rhett pointed. "All of it."

"I don't mow the back forty every day, no."

He frowns. "That's not what I meant."

"Yes."

God, I hate having this conversation. Everyone thinks I don't realize I'm working myself into the ground, but I do. I just don't have any other choice. I either take care of Animal Haven or I get rid of it, and the latter is not an option.

"Everything else I do almost every day."

He nods and tosses his shirt in the car. "You don't have help?"

His phone rings from inside his pocket, and Duke barks again, but Rhett makes no move to answer it.

"I have volunteers who come in from time to time."

"Let me rephrase. Do you have any regular help?"

"Yes."

"How often?"

Damn him. "As often as their schedules allow, and on Sundays."

"Right." His jaw clenches tight as his phone continues to ring.

"Your crotch is ringing."

He tries to fight it, but I see a hint of a smile.

"You going to answer it?"

"No." Shoving his hand in his pocket, he does something to silence his phone and opens his mouth, but I put a hand up.

"I get it, okay? You aren't going to say anything that hasn't already been said to me a million times. It's a lot of work for one person, yes. But it's necessary, and we have fewer animals right now, and I'm not willing to bend. I also won't argue about it or try to plead my case. I have volunteers who come when they can, and that's all I can ask for because they're volunteers. Now, stop shoving your nose into my business and get yourself home and take care of your shoulder."

"You lookin' out for me, Mo?" he asks, tilting his head away from the sun.

"Someone has to."

"And who's watching out for you?"

No one. God, Rhett, since you left me six years ago, no one has looked out for me. Except maybe Coop, but I've always wondered if that's out of courtesy to you.

With a deep breath, I look down at the ground. "I'm a big girl, Rhett. I watch out for myself." I look up and catch his gaze. "Now, if you're done assaulting me with questions, I have to get home and get cleaned up before my shift at Dirty Dicks."

Pinching his lips together, he looks away. "You're bartending tonight?"

"I am. You should come in for a drink if you don't have any other plans."

I climb into my truck and start it up, making sure to crank the air. Right before I shut the door, I hear him.

"Maybe I will."

CHAPTER
Eleven

Rhett

"What are you doing here?"

I'm exhausted. I didn't do strenuous work today, but my body is still healing, and I definitely pushed it too far. All I want is an ice-cold beer and my bed, which is why I'm not at all pleased to see Nikki sitting at the kitchen table, drinking a glass of wine with Coop.

But sure as shit, here she is.

She and Coop turn at the sound of my voice.

"Where have you been?" Coop asks, scrunching his nose. "You stink."

I glance down at myself. My jeans are covered in dirt—at least I think it's dirt. There's also a good possibility it's a combination of dog and cat shit. My boots are also covered, and there's a streak of something dark across my chest.

"I've been at Animal Haven."

Coop grins. "Animal Haven, huh? Decided to give Mo a hand?"

"Something like that."

"What is Animal Haven, who is Mo, and what in the world

is that god-awful smell?" Nikki asks, covering her nose with her hand.

"Animal Haven is a no-kill animal rescue shelter, Mo is the woman who runs it, and I'm going to go with dog shit."

Nikki takes a sip of her wine and turns around, giving me her back. "Why don't you go get cleaned up, and then we can talk."

"Or not." Coop jumps up from his spot at the table, grabs a beer from the fridge, twists the top, and hands it to me. "I'd much rather hear about you and Mo."

I take a swig. "There is no me and Mo." *Not yet at least.*

"Sure. Why else would you jeopardize your recovery?"

"I'm hardly jeopardizing my recovery. I used my right arm to wash out cages and sat my ass on a riding lawn mower for a few hours."

"And you just suffered a grade 3 concussion, and your doctor asked that you refrain from any strenuous activity for at least the next week," Coop says.

"I'm fine."

He smirks. "I'll bet you are after spending the day with Mo."

Nikki sits through our exchange with little to no interest.

I empty my beer and toss it in the trash. "I'm going to get cleaned up."

After my shower, I make sure to pull on jeans and a T-shirt before walking back through the house. If I was at home, I'd have no qualms about staying in the buff, and believe it or not, that's a hard habit to break.

Coop is standing at the sink.

"Where's Nikki?" I ask, looking around.

"She stepped outside to take a phone call." He turns around and wipes his hands on a towel. "That woman is hot, but she has to be the most pretentious, annoying person I have ever met. I don't know how you work with her without fucking her or plastering a piece of duct tape across her mouth."

It's awful of me to laugh, but I can't help it. "If you think she's annoying now, you should hear her in bed. '*Don't do that. Stop that. Faster. No, that's too fast. Just let me do it*'," I say, mocking her. "Hard to please, but even harder to say no to."

"Shut up." Coop stares at me, open mouthed. "You slept with your manager? Are you stupid?"

"She wasn't my manager at the time; she was my manager's daughter. And it wasn't exactly my finest moment. I was new on the PBR circuit, Mo and I had just broken up, and I was drunk."

"That's an awful combination."

"Tell me about it."

"Are things awkward between you now?"

"Mo or Nikki?"

"Well, both, but mostly Nikki."

I grab a few grapes from the refrigerator and pop them in my mouth. "Not really. We don't talk about it. I barely even remember it. As far as Mo, it's not awkward at all. In fact, things are really quite comfortable between us. We seem to get along as well as we always did."

"Have you had a chance to talk to her about everything yet?"

"Nah. The time hasn't been right. But I will."

"Talk to who about what?" Nikki asks, sauntering back into the room.

Coop rolls his eyes. "Nosy much?"

"I'm his manager. I'm allowed to be nosy."

"We were talking about Mo."

"Ah," she says, nodding slowly. "The woman who runs Animal Haven."

Coop clears his throat. "She also happens to be the first girl our boy here ever loved." He nudges my good arm.

"Is that right?" Nikki pulls a tight smile and plugs her phone into the charger. "Just don't get too cozy. You won't be here long, Rhett."

I could probably go home now if I wanted. I've only been here a few days, and I've already proven I can do most things on my own. It might take me a little longer, but I get them done. And as for the concussion, I think it's safe to say I'm back to my old self. I've had none of the symptoms Dr. Simpson told me to watch out for.

But it's funny—I was dreading coming back here, but now I'm in no hurry to leave.

"Too late for that. I've got Mo helping with the dogs and Coop cooking for me every night, so I'll probably never leave," I joke. "Speaking of food, let's hit up Dirty Dicks for dinner."

"Actually, you won't be going anywhere, handsome. I didn't come all this way to go have dinner at a bar," Nikki says. "I came here so we could talk about how we're going to handle your career."

I cock an eyebrow. "My career, huh? The way I see it, my career is on hold until I rehab this shoulder. And don't act like you drove across the country to see me, Nikki. It probably took you two hours to get here."

I grab Coop's keys, but Nikki snags them out of my hand. She tosses them to Coop. "Sit down, Rhett."

"I'm not a child, Nikki. Quit treating me like one."

"You know what?" Coop tosses a thumb over his shoulder. "I'm gonna head out, give you two some time to talk." He walks past me and leans in close. "She's not staying here."

"I know," I mumble, glaring at Nikki.

The door shuts behind him, and I pull out a chair and drop down, but I refuse to say a word. I'm so goddamn pissed at

Nikki for showing up unannounced and talking to me the way she did in front of my brother. If I open my mouth, I'll likely say something I'll regret. As much as I hate Nikki right now, she's the best manager in the market—aside from her father—and I can't risk losing her.

"You've been ignoring my calls." She pulls out a chair and sits across from me.

"I've been busy."

"You've had one PT appointment."

I lift a brow. "You checking up on me?"

"It's my job to check up on you." She sighs. "And you aren't making my job very easy. Cut me a break, Rhett. Your career is my business. Your *success* is my business."

I grit my teeth. "Fine. What do you want to talk about?"

"Give me a little credit; I'm not all business. I was calling because even though you're my client, you're also my friend."

She places her hand on mine, running her thumb along my knuckles. Her voice and face soften, and I start to feel bad for being such a dick because she's right; we are friends. She was my first friend when I moved away from home, and even after we slept together, we remained close. She might be a bitch most days, but she always has my back.

"I wanted to make sure you were doing okay, and when you wouldn't return my calls, I decided to come see for myself."

I pull my hand out from under hers. For some reason it feels wrong, like I'm cheating on Mo, which is absurd because she's no longer mine to cheat on. And anyway that's her department. Still, it doesn't feel right.

Running my fingers through my hair, I lean back in my chair. "I appreciate that. Thank you. And I'm sorry for not answering. I've been busy."

"Ah, yes, Animal Haven."

"I'm not discussing Mo with you, if that's what you're working toward."

She holds up her hands. "So quick to go on the defensive. I couldn't care less about your little friend Mo. Let's get down to business, shall we?"

I'm going to need a drink for this. "Want a beer?" I push up from the chair and grab a bottle from the refrigerator.

"A beer would be good."

My left arm is still in the sling, so I hold the beer bottle with my left hand and use my right to twist the cap. But the movement puts more pressure on my arm than I intended, and I wince.

"Shit," I hiss.

Nikki jumps up from her chair and takes the bottle. "Here, let me."

Cupping the palm of her hand over the bottle she manages to pop the cap on her beer and then mine. When she sees me looking at her funny, she laughs. "What? You've never seen a girl pop the top off a beer?"

"No, I've seen girls do it; I just wasn't expecting *you* to do it."

Nikki hands me my beer and sits back in her chair. "I'm not as prissy and stuck up as everyone thinks I am."

"No one called you stuck up."

Tipping her head back, she takes a drink. "Don't have to; they're thinking it."

I can't deny it—I've thought that a time or two.

"See," she says, pointing her beer toward me. "You've thought it before."

"Once or twice, but I don't think it *all* the time."

"You don't?"

"Not at all. I can't imagine how difficult it must be for you to work in a field littered with men. I think any woman would have to have some bite to her to do what you do."

"Thanks." She smiles and picks at the label on her beer. "I appreciate that."

A couple of seconds pass, and when she doesn't make an attempt to redirect the conversation, I do it for her.

"So, you wanted to talk about my career."

She looks up. "Yes. Your career." Reaching for her bag on the floor, she pulls out a file folder. "I think while you're rehabbing, this might be the perfect opportunity to get in one of those campaign ads. Your shoot for Rugged wasn't supposed to happen for another couple of months, but I talked to Jessica, and she's not opposed to moving it up."

I learned from Nikki that Christian Devonshire is a hot new designer with denim line called Rugged, and they sought me out to be the face of their brand.

"Awesome. As long as I don't have to do any heavy lifting or use my arm."

"No." She waves me off. "Nothing like that. In fact, your ad is with a female model." Nikki flips through her folder. "Molly Farris."

"I've never heard of her."

"Me neither. It'll be a couple shoot. They're aware of your shoulder and have agreed to work around it."

"When do I fly out?"

"Well…that's something I was going to talk to you about. When I was outside on the phone earlier, I was making a proposition to Jessica."

"What kind of proposition?"

"I've only been in Heaven for a few hours, but I'm already in love with this place. It holds a certain southern charm you can't find just anywhere, and I think it'll be a perfect location for the shoot. And it's a double win because you won't have to leave and interrupt your physical therapy schedule. If you're okay with it, all we'll have to do is find a location."

"I think it's a great idea, and I've got the perfect location."

Nikki and I down a few more beers as we talk about the ranch where I grew up. Nestled in the country, my parents' ranch is full of anything a western ad might require—animals, old barns, wood-post fencing. It's a photographer's dream, or at least that's what Beau tells me.

Once we've talked through the campaign, Nikki and I order a pizza and switch gears. Over dinner, we talk about my accident, which riders are putting up the highest scores while I'm gone, and what kind of numbers I'm going to need to pull when I come back. I'm confident that once I get my shoulder healed, I'll be a top contender for the championship, and Nikki agrees.

The longer we talk, the more comfortable she gets, kicking off her high heels and tugging her hair down from the fancy contraption she had it in, and for the first time in years, I see a side of Nikki that hasn't come out since she took over for her father. The chip on her shoulder seems to diminish, along with her sharp words. For a couple of hours, we're just two friends catching up and shooting the shit. It's nice, and a reminder that we were friends before any of the rest of this came along.

The clock in Coop's living room dings, and Nikki yawns. "What time is it?"

I glance at my watch. "Holy shit, it's after midnight."

"Tonight was fun."

"Don't sound so surprised. I'm a fun guy."

"It's just…we haven't hung out in a long time. We should do it more often."

My head is telling me to draw a line in the sand. The last thing I want or need is Nikki trying to rekindle what we had.

We've gone years without even acknowledging that night, and it needs to stay that way.

"We'll have to make a point of catching up a little during our weekly business meetings."

Her eyes widen a fraction, but she nods. "Right. Our meetings. Sure."

Pushing her chair away from the table, she slips her feet back into her heels and gathers her things. "I'm exhausted. I should really get going."

"That's probably not a good idea," I say, counting the beer bottles on the counter. I'm nowhere near drunk, but we've both had enough that neither of us should be driving.

"I heard your brother, Rhett. I'm not welcome to stay here, and for the record, I wasn't going to ask."

"I don't care what my brother said, you're staying."

"Rhett—"

"It's not up for discussion, Nikki. You've been drinking, and I'm not going to let you drive."

"You're sure? Because the last thing I need is your brother getting all pissed off at me. You two look way too much alike, by the way."

I laugh. "We're identical twins."

"I know, but I haven't been around him much. I thought I'd be able to tell you apart, but it's really hard. When he answered the door earlier, I cussed him up one side and down the other for not returning my calls before I realized it wasn't you."

"How'd you figure out it wasn't me?"

"He told me if I didn't shut my mouth, he was going to bend me over his knee."

Yup. That sounds like Coop. "Interesting."

She pulls at the collar of her blouse. "Tell me about it."

"You got a thing for my brother, Nikki?"

She mumbles something I can't quite understand and clears her throat. "Not at all."

"Good. Come on. You can have my bed tonight. I'll sleep on the couch."

"What? No." She shakes her head. "Your shoulder…I can't do that to you."

"It's not as bad as everyone's making it out to be. Plus, I won't sleep much anyway."

"If you're sure."

"I'm sure."

CHAPTER
Twelve

Rhett

I startle awake to find Coop hovering over me.

"What the hell, dude? That's creepy."

"Why are you on the couch?"

Honesty is always the best policy. That's what my mother says. In this case though, I'm exhausted, and it's way too early to listen to my brother piss and moan about Nikki, so I decide to tell him a little lie in hopes that he'll be long gone before she crawls out of bed.

"Must've passed out watching TV." I pull the cover up and roll over. "Thanks for waking me up, asshole."

"Where's Nikki?"

I don't answer right away, and Coop nudges me in the back.

"Don't know. Don't care," I mumble.

"I'm going to take a shower."

Coop walks down the hall. I hear the bathroom door shut, latch, and a few minutes later the shower turns on. A few minutes after that, the door to the spare bedroom opens and Nikki walks out. Her hair is an absolute mess—half of it plastered against the side of her face—and there's something about seeing her rumpled that takes away from her usual edge.

"You look like shit."

"Back at you, cowboy. Does Coop know I stayed?"

"Nope."

She purses her lips and shrugs. "What's for breakfast?"

"Whatever you're making, I guess." I wiggle the fingers of my left hand. "Can't do much with my good hand, remember?"

She grunts and disappears into the kitchen. I hear her rustle around in the refrigerator and then the cabinets, and within a few minutes the sizzle and smell of bacon and sausage fills the house.

I listen for the shower to turn off, and then a minute or so later the bathroom door opens.

Three.

Two.

One.

"It's about time you get your gimp ass up and cook me something for a change," Coop says, sauntering into the kitchen in all his naked glory. If he'd only looked over, he would've seen me on the couch, but Coop's always had a thing for food, so it's no surprise that his nose and belly led him straight to the kitchen.

I watch from my perch on the couch as Nikki turns around. "I hope you like eggs, bacon, and—" Her screech nearly pierces my eardrums. "Oh my gosh!" She flounders about, trying to look at anything except Coop's dick. "You're naked, Cooper."

Coop has no shame. "This is my house, darlin', and I wasn't planning on you being here. You don't like my sausage, get out."

Nikki's eyes drop down Coop's body and widen as he walks

toward the stove, his dick swinging back and forth without a care in the world. He eyes the breakfast Nikki was cooking.

"Maybe I was wrong. Looks like you're about to eat my sausage."

Nikki takes a deep breath and turns toward him. "It's a little small for my liking, but I can see that's a common thread in this house."

Coop's jaw tightens, and I realize I should probably intervene before they beat the shit out of each other.

"Everything okay in here?" I walk into the kitchen and grab some plates from the cabinet.

"Your brother is an asshole." Nikki pushes Cooper out of the way so she can rotate the bacon and sausage.

Coop shoots me a *she's crazy* look, and I sigh.

"Nikki, could you please play nice with my brother?" I'd swear I'm talking to a room full of four year olds.

She doesn't answer, just continues cooking the food. After a minute she plates the meat, along with scrambled eggs. She sets a plate on the table in front of Coop, and I frown.

"I want some."

Nikki ignores me and looks at Coop. "I was making you breakfast so I could apologize for the way I acted toward you yesterday and thank you for letting me stay the night. But I can see now you don't deserve the apology or the gratitude. Enjoy your breakfast, Coop."

Nikki turns away, wipes down the counter where she was working, and heads for the hallway.

I kick Coop in the shin under the table. "I think that was her way of saying I'm sorry. She's my manager, bro. At least play nice."

Coop rolls his eyes and looks at Nikki's retreating form. "Where do you think you're going?" he hollers.

She stops but doesn't turn around. "Don't worry, Coop, I'll be out of your house by the time you clean your plate."

"Shit." He looks at me like I somehow caused this. "Get your ass back in here and eat breakfast with us."

Nikki looks over her shoulder.

"Now's not the time to let your pride get in the way," I warn. "Get in here and eat. Whoever eats the fastest eats the most."

She ponders my offer but ultimately gives in. With a huff and a little quickness to her step, she comes back into the kitchen and makes herself a plate.

We eat in silence, which is totally cool with me, and once our plates are empty, Nikki starts to clean off the table.

Coop stops her. "You cooked; I'll clean."

"See?" I chastise. "Look at us getting along. That wasn't hard, was it?"

They both answer at the same time: Nikki with a rolled-up napkin aimed at my head and Coop with a *fuck off*.

"You got any plans today?" Nikki asks, looking at me.

"Umm…" I glance at Coop. He holds up his hands.

"Count me out. I've got to go to Dirty Dicks this afternoon and work on inventory."

"If you're not busy, I was thinking you could take me out to your parents' ranch and show me around."

"Yeah, I guess we can go out there, check out some spots for the shoot."

Nikki places her hand on my arm and smiles. "As long as you don't mind spending the day with an old friend." She winks.

Not at all. You're just not the old friend I was hoping to spend it with. "If I have to."

She slaps my arm and stands up. "I'm going to take a

shower. I'll be ready in an hour."

Coop watches her ass as she walks away.

"You got a thing for her?" I ask.

"Hell no," he assures me. "She's too prickly."

"Then why are you staring at her ass?"

"It's a great ass. Plus, it's not me she has a thing for."

"What are you talking about?"

"I always knew I was the smart one." He pushes away from the table, but before he stands, he levels me with his eyes. "And for the record, she remembers—everything, if I had to guess, and she's probably hoping for a repeat performance. Just make sure you think long and hard about saddling up for that ride."

"You're full of shit."

He lifts an eyebrow. "Am I?"

———o———

"Are you sure you don't need anything?" Mom asks, following Nikki and me to the car.

"Viv, leave the poor boy alone. He'll let you know if he needs anything," Dad says, rolling his eyes behind Mom's back.

"I'm good, Ma." I brush a kiss across her cheek as she wraps me in a hug. "Sorry I didn't call or come by sooner."

"That's okay. Just remember that I worry about you."

"I know."

"You're still my baby, even if you spend most of your time off riding bulls."

"I know—" I try to pull back, but she tightens her grip.

"And a call every once in a while would be nice. Since you're in town, you can come over for dinner and visit."

"Maybe next week sometime."

"I'd like that. Let me know what day, and I'll make your favorite."

Mom finally lets go of me and moves on to Nikki. "It was so nice getting to see you again."

"You as well, Mrs. Allen. And thank you again for agreeing to let us use the ranch for the photo shoot. I'll reach out to you as soon as I have some tentative dates."

"Anytime, dear."

I wave bye to my parents and climb into the car. Leaning back against the soft leather seat of Nikki's rental, I let out a deep breath. "My mother is exhausting."

"She loves you." Nikki pulls down the lane and turns onto the two-lane highway.

She lied this morning when she said it would take her an hour to get ready. It took her two. By the time we got to my parents', my mom was cooking lunch, and of course she insisted on feeding us. After lunch, we hopped on the Gator, and I gave Nikki a tour of the property. I took her along the bank of the creek, down by the pond, and we stopped at the various barns. We hopped off a few times to stretch our legs and enjoy the scenery, and when we made it back to the house, my dad insisted on getting Nikki on a horse.

There are some people who should never get on a horse. Nikki is one of them. The damn woman almost fell off a dozen times, but she loved every minute of it, laughing and carrying on as though she'd been born on a farm rather than a posh New York penthouse.

Several horrid childhood stories and five hours later, and we're finally on our way home. I'm hungry, I'm tired, I need a beer, and I want to see Mo. Most of all, I want to see Mo. My original plan had been to surprise her at Animal Haven with lunch, but Nikki put a chink in that.

"Now what?"

I look at Nikki. "Excuse me?"

"What do you want to do now?"

"I don't know about you, but I'm going to go meet Coop for dinner."

"Great. I'm starved. Mind if join you?"

Son of a bitch. "Sure."

CHAPTER
Thirteen

Monroe

I spent last night watching the front door, certain Rhett would come in. He didn't. Foolishly, I thought maybe he'd be waiting for me at work this morning with a hot cup of coffee. That didn't happen either, and now I know why.

"Who's the hot chick with Coop and his brother?" Sean asks, sidling up next to me behind the bar.

"No clue," I lie. I knew who she was the second they walked in the door. I'd recognize her face from a million miles away. That pretty little blonde is the reason I lost the love of my life, and I can't even be mad at him for bringing her here, because he has no idea the part she played in our demise.

"She's been cozying up to Rhett all evening. Do you think they're together?"

"Has she? I didn't notice."

Rhett and Coop walked in with her about two hours ago. They parked themselves in a corner booth—Rhett in the middle with Coop and *her* on either side—and they haven't gotten up since.

Several times I've caught Rhett watching me, and each time

he's offered me a smile that I've politely returned despite the urge to spit in his drink, which is absolutely absurd because the man has done nothing wrong.

There's no reason for me to be jealous. He and I aren't together—haven't been for quite some time—and my feelings for him are strictly platonic. Well, except for that fire in my belly I've been getting when he's in the same room—which I'll totally chalk up to indigestion related to my horrible diet—and the way my heart fluttered the other day when he took off his shirt. But any woman would react that way if she were staring at a half-naked Rhett, so I really can't count that one.

"You're a horrible liar," Sean whispers.

"So I've been told."

"He's not touching her," Sean adds. "Maybe they aren't together. You think I've got a shot at that?"

He might not be touching her, but she can't seem to keep her hands off him. Touching his arm while talking, leaning in close, brushing her thigh against his in the booth. That's why I insisted Sarah take their table. I couldn't watch it up close and not want to rip Blondie's hands off of her pretty little body.

And she does have a pretty little body.

"Well?" Sean asks. "What do you think?"

With my hand on the tap, I turn a dry look to Sean. "Really?"

"What?"

"Men," I mumble, grabbing the two glasses of beer for the ladies at the end of the bar. Once I check on all of my customers, I make a quick run to the bathroom. On my way back out, I spot Rhett sitting at my end of the bar. I'm shocked to find him alone. A quick look at the booth shows the woman talking with Coop, but her eyes are still very much on Rhett.

"What's your poison?" I ask, nodding to the empty glass in his hand.

"Bud Light." Rhett looks me in the eye. "You okay?"

"Yeah. Why wouldn't I be?" I ask, refilling his mug.

"I don't know. You just seem…off."

He's always been able to read me. Pisses me off as much now as it did when we were younger. "No, not at all."

He nods, accepting my answer, but the uncertain look in his eyes remains. "Long day at Animal Haven?"

"Always," I say, casting a glance down the bar. We're relatively slow tonight, and my customers all seem to be drinking happily, which makes me not feel so bad about stealing a few seconds to talk.

"I was going to stop by this morning, but I got sidetracked."

"I can see that." I look over his shoulder, and he follows my gaze. It's on the tip of my tongue to ask who she is, but I don't want to be too obvious. She must be important if she's been in his life for the last six years.

"Yeah," he says, looking me in the eye. "She made a surprise visit yesterday, stayed the night last night, and we spent the day at the ranch."

I spent the day shoveling manure while she spent the day at his parents' ranch. I love that ranch, and if I know Rhett, he probably took her to all his favorite spots—spots we used to sneak off to when we were wild, horny teenagers who wanted nothing but to be alone.

Oh God, what if they needed some alone time?

I grab a yellow rag and busy myself wiping down the top of the bar. "That was nice of Coop to let her crash on the couch."

Rhett smiles. "Nah, she slept in my bed."

"Oh."

He watches my face fall, and his eyes widen. "No. *No*, not like that. She didn't sleep in my bed with me. I offered her my bed because it was the polite thing to do. I slept on the couch."

I stare at him.

"She's my manager," he says, as if that will justify why she spent the night with him. And then he blinks, probably reminding himself that he doesn't owe me an explanation. "And she's a little drunk right now. I need to get her out of here."

She's the manager? "I thought your manager was a man?"

Rhett nods. "Bill Atwood was my manager when I joined the PBR; that's his daughter, Nikki. She sort of took me under her wing when I moved to Houston, and she eventually took over for her father."

Holy shit. I know she's the woman I saw him with at the anniversary party, but is she the woman I talked to on the phone? No wonder she wanted me out of the picture.

"Is that a normal thing, for managers to stay with their clients?"

Rhett's lips twitch. "She didn't stay *with* me. She stayed at Coop's because she had too much to drink and I didn't want her driving. And no, it's not a normal thing."

"That was very chivalrous of you."

"You jealous, Mo?"

"No, not at all. Why would I be jealous?" I say, not even believing myself. "Are, uh...are you two close?"

Rhett's playful smirk dies, and for a second I'm not sure he'll answer.

"Mo, table two needs a fresh round," Sean hollers.

I lift a finger to Rhett. "Hold that thought. I'll be right back."

I make quick work of replacing their drinks and take care of a few other people at the bar. When I make my way back to Rhett, he's sipping his beer.

"Sorry, where were we?" I ask.

"You asked if Nikki and I are close."

"Right. Are you?"

Rhett takes a deep breath, runs a hand through his shaggy hair, and nods. "We're friends, Mo. She isn't just my manager."

That still doesn't answer my question. Swallowing, I look down.

"That wasn't the answer you were looking for, was it?"

I look up. "No, it wasn't." *I want to know if you're still sleeping with her. But it's not really my business, is it?*

"Mo." Rhett shakes his head, and though he doesn't say anything else, it's written all over his face.

"It's okay." I push away from the bar. "I shouldn't have asked."

Leaning across the bar, he grabs my wrist. "She meant nothing to me. It was one time after you and I broke up. I was lonely and drunk."

"The night of your parents' fortieth wedding anniversary?"

Scrunching his brow, he tilts his head. "Yeah, how did you know?"

"Lucky guess."

"I'm not even sure she remembers it happened," he says, taking a swig of his beer.

Of course, she remembers it happened. How could she not? Every kiss, every touch, every promise Rhett gave is ingrained in my body. All I have to do is close my eyes, and I can remember the way his callused hands felt running up the side of my thighs, or the way the scruff on his jaw felt against my neck.

"Does it matter, Mo?"

The breath freezes in my lungs. A lie sits on the tip of my tongue. I want to tell him it doesn't matter, that the past six years don't matter, but they do. He matters. *We* matter.

"You're an extremely attractive man. I figured there have been women in your life."

"Now you're not telling *me* what I want to know."

Resting my elbows on the bar, I run my hands over my face. It's now or never. I promised myself I'd tell the truth moving forward. No more lies. "*You* matter, Rhett. You've always mattered. Everything I've done has been with you in mind."

"Mo." He nearly comes across the bar, wrapping my face in his strong, warm hands. "We need to talk, baby, so bad."

I press my hands to his. "There's so much you don't know, Rhett. You're going to hate me."

"I could never hate you."

Never say never.

"What time do you get off?"

"Your brother is a slave driver," I say. "I'm working until close."

Rhett laughs. "It's dead in here. Let me see if I can get you out early."

"You don't have to do that." My words fall on deaf ears because Rhett's already halfway across the room.

"Well," Sean says, sliding up next to me. "Is he bagging the blonde?"

I thump him on the arm. "Do you have to be so crass?"

He holds his arm as though I actually hurt him. "Damn, you're mean."

"And for the record, no, he's not." I grab a glass out of the full crate and stack it on the shelf. "But she's wasted, and she also happens to be his manager, so you're going to leave her alone."

"Damn." Sean walks off, leaving me to empty the crate.

Once that's done, I check on the customers at the bar and close out a couple of tabs.

"Haven't seen it this slow on a Saturday night in a long time." Coop leans up against the bar.

"I'll take your word for it." This is only my second weekend, so I can hardly make the call on what's normal. "Hopefully we're busier next weekend; I need the tips."

"Rhett said you worked all day at Animal Haven before coming in tonight."

I stop what I'm doing and look at Coop. "That's nothing new."

He takes a step forward and lowers his voice. "You told me you were going to get more help."

"Help is hard to come by, and I can't afford to pay anyone. I'm lucky I have the volunteers I do."

Coop rubs his jawline. "I can help."

My hands go to my hips. "When? You're the only person I know who works as much as I do."

"I'll make time."

"No, you won't." I place a hand on his arm. "Working at Animal Haven isn't a hardship. I love it out there. Don't worry about me. If things get too stressful, I'll let you know."

"Promise?"

I draw a cross over my heart.

"Good enough for me. Get out of here," he says, nodding toward the door.

I frown. "Did your brother put you up to this?"

Coop holds his pointer finger and thumb about an inch apart. "Maybe just a little, but we're slow, and you have to be exhausted."

"But what if we get a rush?"

Coop looks down at his watch. "It's almost midnight. I think we can handle it for a couple of hours."

"You're sure?"

"Go before I change my mind."

I close out my drawer, instructing my customers to let Sean or Sarah know when they're ready to settle up, and grab my purse from behind the bar. When I look up, I see Rhett and Nikki walking toward me.

Rhett has an easy smile on his face as I round the bar, and Nikki is oblivious to the world as she types away on her phone. She stumbles, but somehow manages to stay upright. How she walks in those damn heels, especially when she's been drinking, I'll never know.

"I see Coop let you off early." Rhett grins, and I feel that smile from my head to my toes. "You still want to talk?"

"Sure—"

My words are cut off when a perfectly manicured hand shoves between us. "I'm Nikki."

Sliding to the side, Rhett moves out of the way, and for the first time tonight, I get a good look at his manager. She's looks different from the first and only time I saw her before tonight. Her hair is longer, breasts bigger, and her lips look like they've had more than a few collagen injections.

I take her hand but don't introduce myself, because the last thing I want is for her to recognize me. Nikki wraps her delicate hand around mine. We do the obligatory handshake, but she doesn't let go. Instead, she blinks once, twice, and then a third time, recognition flaring behind her overly made-up eyes.

"Wait a minute, I know you." Her voice has the slightest hint of a slur.

I tug my hand out of her grip, intent on using her intoxicated state against her. "Um, no, I'm pretty sure you don't." How on Earth could she possibly remember me? She's seen me one time—one freaking time—and it was years ago.

Squinting, she takes a step forward, and I take a step back. Hoisting her purse up on her shoulder, Nikki hiccups and points a finger at me. "Yup. Pretty sure I'll never forget your face." She scrunches her nose. "Monica, right?"

"Monroe," Rhett offers, wrapping his hand around her arm. "Her name is Mo. Come on, Nikki. You're drunk. Let me take you back to Coop's."

"Oh my gosh, you're Mo!" She smiles brilliantly as she yanks her arm from Rhett's grasp. "I can't believe I didn't put two and two together when Rhett was talking about you earlier. You're the girlfriend who couldn't let go."

Oh shit. "You must have me confused with someone else." I fling the strap of my purse over my shoulder, prepared to leave before this bitch throws everything I hate about my past back in my face. Rhett needs to hear the truth, but he needs to hear it from me. "Rhett, I think I should—"

"No, I don't. I never forget a face; it's part of my job. You were the girlfriend," she says.

I shake my head, but it's too late, the words are already falling from her mouth.

"You were the one who wouldn't quit calling. Looks like you got your wish; Rhett's finally home, and from what I hear, he's been spending all his time with you."

Rhett looks at Nikki. "What do you mean she wouldn't quit calling?"

"The girl. You know the one," she mumbles.

"Enlighten me."

"Rhett—" I attempt.

He holds up a hand, quieting me.

Nikki slaps playfully at his chest, but his face is devoid of any humor. I take a step toward the door.

"I told her you were better off without her, but she wouldn't give up. She wanted to talk to you so bad, but I couldn't let that happen because I knew you'd run back to her. Persistent little bitch must've loved you more than I thought."

I hear a sharp intake of breath, but I'm not sure who it

comes from. Maybe Rhett, maybe me. Quite possibly both.

"You and I hadn't fucked yet, but it was only a matter of time, so I got rid of her. I did what was best for you and your career, and look at you—you're a star."

She shrugs and turns toward the bar as if she didn't just turn Rhett's life upside down.

Oh God, I think I'm going to be sick.

Anger and confusion blaze behind Rhett's eyes. "What do you mean you *got rid of her*?" His voice is low, gravelly, and holds a warning that I hope to God Nikki heeds.

"What I just said," she says, looking over her shoulder. "I got rid of her, told her to do whatever she had to do to push you away. You were better off without her, Rhett. We all know that. She was going to bring you down, and I couldn't let that happen. She didn't give up that easily though, which is why I made sure we gave her a damn good show at your parents' anniversary party."

Rhett's frantic eyes find mine. "She wasn't at the party."

"Yes, she was." Nikki's head bobs. "And she made it just in time for our performance." She runs a finger down the front of Rhett's shirt.

Every emotion from that time in my life comes flooding back. It's all too much, and I can't process the look of pain and confusion on Rhett's face. The air in the bar grows thick, stealing my breath, and I look desperately around the room. But my eyes seem to be drawn back to one person—one man.

Rhett is watching me. His eyes asking the question he can't get his mouth to say.

What is she talking about?

My heart jack-hammers in my chest, threatening to bust out as the burn of tears prickles behind my eyes.

Shaking my head, I turn toward the door. "I gotta go." And

then I'm out, making my way to the front door as fast as I can, ignoring Rhett and Coop as they call out for me.

I'm halfway across the parking lot when I hear the front door fly open, but I keep moving, desperate to get to my car.

"Mo, wait!"

Oh God.

"Mo!" Rhett yells.

His hand wraps around my elbow, and I whirl around. We're both breathing heavily. His eyes search mine, his expression shocked.

"What the hell was that back there? What was she talking about?"

"Please, Rhett." I look down, heat infusing my cheeks. "I need to be alone."

"No." He tugs my arm, pulling my body flush against his. I take a small step back, not wanting to hurt his shoulder, not sure I can handle being that close. His left arm is still in a sling, but that doesn't stop his right hand from sliding up my arm to wrap around the back of my neck. Using his thumb, he lifts my face to meet his. "I need to know what she was talking about."

"Then why don't you go ask her?"

"Because she's drunk, and I'd much rather hear it from you."

I squeeze my eyes shut, and Rhett brushes away the tears that fall.

"God," I whimper. "This is so embarrassing."

"What? Why are you embarrassed? You have no reason to be embarrassed."

"Yes, I do." I sniff and lower my chin to my chest. "Because she's right; you're better off without me." My voice cracks on a sob, and I pull away, but he reaches for me again.

He cradles my face and drops his forehead to mine. The familiar smell of him causes my heart to ache, and I cry for the stupid teenager I was and the foolish adult I've become.

"That can't possibly be true. Mo, I can't tell you how much I've missed you. Even after you cheated, I still wanted you in my life. But since that's not what you wanted, I've tried to move on. Why do you think I've stayed away from Heaven and threatened my family within an inch of their lives if they mention your name?"

I laugh, though it sounds like a strangled cry. "Don't you get it? That isn't what I wanted. I was doing it for you."

"Doing what? Mo, baby, I'm so confused. Please, tell me what you're talking about."

"I don't know where to start."

"The beginning, Mo. Start at the beginning."

The beginning. The beginning seems so long ago. I step away, out of Rhett's grasp, and tilt my head back. Hundreds of stars are scattered across the silky night sky. The moon is full and bright, sort of like my future with Rhett before it was ruined.

Despite all the revelations so far tonight, there's a good chance Rhett isn't ready for the truth. But I'm ready to give it to him.

I clear my throat. "Two months after you left for the PBR, and I left for college, my dad had a stroke. The doctors told me he'd never be the same again, and they were right. He was paralyzed on the right side of his body, and I had two options: I could either bring him home, where he'd require round-the-clock care, or I could put him in a nursing home—and you can bet your ass that second option wasn't really an option."

"Mo—"

"I was scared," I say, cutting him off. "Scared and alone, and all I wanted was you. I wanted you to wrap your arms around me and tell me everything was going to be okay, and selfishly, I wanted you to come home. I called you three times that night.

Left three voicemails begging you to call me back, but you never did."

"Mo, I—"

"Please, let me get this out."

Rhett nods, but he doesn't look very happy.

"I figured you were busy, and with our crazy schedules, we'd gone several days without talking to each other before, so I waited until the next morning and tried again, only that time a woman picked up."

"Nikki."

I nod.

"She said she was part of your team, but I didn't realize she was your manager's daughter. I told her who I was and that I desperately needed to talk to you. She said you were busy—an interview or something. She promised you'd call as soon as you were done, but you didn't, so I called back a few hours later. That time when she answered, I told her what had happened and that I needed you to come home."

Closing my eyes, I relive that horrible phone call, which resulted in a lie that forever changed the course of this relationship.

"She told me I was being selfish," I explain, keeping my eyes closed. "She told me how well you were doing, how hard you'd worked and all the sponsors you had. And she said that year was your chance—that you could win the world championship."

I take a deep breath and open my eyes to look at Rhett in the dark. "But she said if you left to come home, you might never get it back. Your chance would have passed, and I'd have done nothing more than ruin your dreams right along with my own."

Even now I remember how her words swirled around my grief-stricken brain. I'd felt so alone in that moment, so overwhelmed by the decisions I had to make.

"She told me to figure it out, to find a way to solve the problem," I whisper.

Rhett's jaw ticks, his hands clenching into fists at his side, but he doesn't say a word.

"I didn't know what to do." I take a deep breath, remembering how bad it hurt to sit there, coming up with a lie significant enough to push Rhett away. "I wanted you with me, but she was right. You would've walked away from the tour to come home, and I couldn't let you do that. I had to make sure one of us captured our dream, and I knew it wasn't going to be me."

The steady sound of the crickets chirping fills the silence while I gather my thoughts. "You called me the next morning. It was the first time we'd talked in a week—"

"Son of a bitch. She was screening *all* my calls." Rhett pushes his fingers into his hair and turns away for a moment. He takes a few deep breaths and turns back. "Coop finally called the arena, demanded to talk to me, and told me about your dad. I ran straight to my truck, wondering why *you* hadn't reached out to me, and when I called, you told me you couldn't handle a long-distance relationship and you'd slept with Charlie Dixon," Rhett says, his voice strained. "You said I needed to forget about you. Worst day of my life."

I shudder at the memory, at the sound of his voice when he begged me to tell him it wasn't true, and then again when he yelled out to me as I hung up the phone.

"After that call, I spent the next hour throwing up in the bathroom. I hated myself for what I'd done. I picked up the phone a hundred times to call you back and tell you it was all a lie, but I couldn't get myself to do it. And then after a while I realized it didn't matter—"

Rhett takes a step forward, his face twisted in pain. "Come on, Mo, didn't you know me at all? You weren't thinking about me, about us, because if you had been, you would've known my future meant nothing to me if you weren't a part of it."

"I'm sorry," I say, my voice breaking. "I was just so confused…"

He pushes his fingers into his hair and turns away. "You lied to me." He stops and turns back, the disappointment in his eyes hitting me square in the gut. "You didn't sleep with Charlie Dixon."

I shake my head and watch the look on his face transform into anger. "You took what we had, and you let someone manipulate it. You made a choice about what was best for me without consulting me, and then you lied about sleeping with another man!" he yells, his voice getting louder with each word.

"My father had just had a stroke!" I shout back. "I didn't know what was going to happen to him, and I had no one. The life I'd planned for, yearned for, was gone. You were so far away—and then suddenly I had someone telling me what I needed to do. I know now I made a mistake, but I was drowning! I wanted you to be happy."

"Happy? Do you know what that did to me?" In three giant steps, he has me backed against the side of my truck. "Do you know how bad that screwed with my head? It's all I thought about. Every time I closed my eyes, I pictured Charlie Dixon sinking his dick inside of you. I saw him holding you and touching parts of your body only I had touched."

"I'm sorry." Tears flow down my cheeks. "I was wrong."

"Finally, something we agree on."

I flinch, wishing I could rewind time and take back my lies.

"You broke my heart, Monroe. I was in love with you. We may have been young, but we'd talked about our future, and I wanted that more than anything."

"I did too." I reach for him, but he takes a step back.

"Don't," he warns. "Don't touch me."

"It was a terrible time for me, Rhett. I made a mistake, and I'm sorry."

"A mistake?" He rears back as though I've slapped him across the face. "You lied to me, and you call that a mistake? God, Mo, do you know how hard coming home has been for me? Since that day, I've dreaded every trip back to Heaven for fear that I'd see you with Charlie. I've avoided my family, I've secluded myself from my friends, I've fucked nameless, faceless women because I couldn't fill the gaping, black hole you left in my goddamn heart."

"You have to understand—I was trying to do what was best for you," I cry, my words turning into sobs.

Rhett hangs his head. He takes a breath and blows it out slowly. "When I saw you the other day with my dogs, something sparked inside me—something I hadn't felt since our last phone call—and I knew right then that no matter what I told myself, every attempt I'd made to put you in my past had failed. It's felt so good to have a friendship with you again. I convinced myself I could look past what you'd done if it meant having you as part of my life, but I'm not sure I can get past this."

"Yes," I plead, stepping toward him. "Yes, you can, because there's more, Rhett. God, there's so much more you need to know."

His eyes grow wide, his lips turning up in a sardonic smile. "How much more could there possibly be? I'm not sure I want to hear what else you have to say, Mo. I don't know how much more I can take."

My mouth drops open. He has to hear me out; he has to know I tried to fix us. "You have to try, Rhett. This matters. *We* matter."

He shakes his head and gives me his back, walking toward

the front of Dirty Dicks.

"Where are you going?"

"I need some space, Mo. I need to think, and I can't do that here. I can't do that when I'm around you."

"You can't leave," I beg. "You can't walk away without letting me finish."

When Rhett's eyes meet mine over his shoulder, I feel like my insides are being ripped out. "I'm not walking away, Mo. You did that six years ago."

CHAPTER
Fourteen

Monroe

"You want some more bacon?"

I hold the plate out toward my father, but he lifts the fingers on his good hand and shakes his head. "N-no. Th-thank you."

He never ceases to amaze me. After all this time, he's still making progress. The doctors told us his speech might never be normal, and it's not, but it's pretty darn close. His words come slowly, but they're getting clearer.

"More coffee?"

He shakes his head.

Dad's eyes track me while I move about the kitchen, washing the breakfast dishes and putting them away. Times like this, I wonder what he's thinking about. Does he see my mom in me? Does it hurt him to think of her the way it hurts me? Or maybe he's thinking I'm a shit caregiver and he'd be better off at a home.

Draping the towel over the sink, I look at my dad. "Can I ask you a question?"

He nods toward the seat. I pull it out and sit down.

"What are you thinking about right now?" I ask. "Sometimes you watch me, and I wonder what you're thinking."

His brow dips low, and after a few seconds he looks over my shoulder with a blank stare. Eventually he speaks. "Th-that I'm so p-proud of you."

I wrap my hand around his good one so he can feel my touch. "I'm proud of you too."

Dad squeezes his eyes shut, and I scoot my chair closer to his wheelchair. "You okay?"

He tries to shake his head. It's more of a jerky movement, but one I understand. "I w-wish I would've d-died."

"What?" I gasp. "No. No, Dad, don't think that."

His jaw tightens. "Th-this isn't the life I w-wanted for you."

"Dad—"

He squeezes my hand tight. "I want you t-to close the sh-shelter and go b-back to school."

"No." I shake my head. "Absolutely not."

"That was my d-dream, not yours, M-Monroe."

"Dreams change, Dad. That's the thing about life—it's constantly shifting and rearranging itself, and with that comes new perspectives. Animal Haven might not have been my dream in the beginning, but I love what I do, and I love those animals. I'm not keeping it for you; I'm keeping it for me."

Dad's eyes well up with tears. "What about s-school?"

I don't bother telling him I'll likely never go back—or that even if I wanted to, they wouldn't accept me. My advisor made it clear that getting accepted into the program to begin with was difficult, and once a seat is given up, it's virtually impossible to reclaim. I could always apply to a different program, but there are only so many in the United States, and I don't want to move away from Heaven. Not anymore.

"You let me worry about that, okay?"

He doesn't look happy with my request, but he squeezes my hand to tell me he'll oblige. For now.

I kiss his cheek. "Want to go in the living room and watch a movie? Or we can take a walk. It's beautiful outside."

With sad eyes, my dad shakes his head. "I would l-like to lay back d-d-down for a while."

Tilting my head, I frown. "You just got up an hour ago."

"Haven't b-been sleeping well."

My mind goes on red alert. "You aren't getting a bedsore, are you? Maybe you should let me check."

"No. N-no bedsore. I hear you c-crying."

"Oh, Dad." Shaking my head, I look down.

"Wanted to c-come check on you, b-but I couldn't g-get up. Hate that, M-Mo."

Damn. Most days I'm able to stay strong, to shoulder the stress of my life, but this last week—since that night after leaving Dirty Dicks—has been increasingly tough. Everything has piled up, and all I've been able to think about is the look on Rhett's face and the lies I told to cause it. I've been over and over how I could have let Nikki manipulate me like that, and I don't have an answer. I think only now do I realize the depth of my despair in those days after my dad's stroke. Anyway, I certainly didn't mean for anyone to hear me breaking down, particularly my father.

Six years of pain and frustration, six years of thinking it had to be for the best. Six years of running my ass off day after day—and seven days since I've seen Rhett. Seven days since he refused to let me tell the rest of my story.

"I'm okay, Dad. I've just had a bad week."

"When those d-dogs were here, you were s-so happy. I haven't seen y-you that happy in y-years."

It wasn't the dogs that made me happy; it was their owner.

There was a warmth in my heart, knowing Rhett was back home.

Coop showed up the morning after my argument with Rhett. He didn't ask what happened and he didn't make small talk, he simply took Duke and Diesel and left a bigger hole in my life than I'd woken up with.

"I'll get back there, Dad. I promise."

"W-want you to be h-happy."

"I know you do."

He pats my hand and nods. "I'm here f-for you."

"I know you are." I kiss his cheek again, thankful he's still with me. "Want me to help you back to bed?"

"P-please."

Getting my father into bed isn't as hard as it could be. He's lost a lot of weight over the years, which makes it easier on my back. I keep a gait belt wrapped around his waist, so all I have to do is push his chair next to the bed and make the transfer. He's got enough strength on one side to help steady himself as I turn him toward the bed.

Once I get him situated, I put the bell on his nightstand. "Ring whenever you're ready to get up."

His eyes are closed in a matter of seconds, and I shut off the light on my way out. I close the door and lean my back up against it. With my head in my hands I slide to the ground. I've just pulled my knees to my chest when there's a knock on the front door.

I groan, dropping my head back against the bedroom door.

The front door opens, and Claire pops her head in. "It's just me." She spots me on the floor, shuts the front door, and drops her purse on the couch. "What are you doing on the floor?" she asks, sliding down the wall across from me.

"Thinking."

"That'll get in you in trouble."

"The way I see it, a little thinking might've kept me out of it."

"Ahh." She nods. "We're talking about Rhett. You should go talk to him." She says this as though it's the simplest thing in the world.

"I can't."

"Why not?"

"I don't know." I shrug. "Because everything is ruined. I broke his heart, Claire. He doesn't want to hear what I have to say, let alone see me."

"You didn't break him, Mo."

I give her a look, and she smiles.

"What? You didn't. Yes, you may have done some damage, but that man is anything but broken. He's had an amazing career, made tons of money. He's a freaking model, for God's sake, and he could have any woman he set his sights on."

"That doesn't make me feel better."

"Lucky for you, he doesn't want just any woman; he wants you."

"Ha! He wants me to go away maybe, but that's the only thing he wants from me."

"I wouldn't be so sure about that."

"What are you saying, Claire?"

She purses her lips. "You made a mistake, and now it's time you make it better. It's not his job to come after you so you can stop staring at your phone and waiting for him to call. If you want to be heard, make him hear you."

Her words spur something inside of me. Maybe she's right. Whatever else was happening around me, I made this mess, so I'm the only one to clean it up. I've been giving Rhett time, waiting for him to come to me when he's ready, but why should he after what I did?

"Do you have any plans today?" I ask.

"It's Sunday. Do I ever have plans on Sunday?" Claire smiles and pushes up from the floor. She pulls me up alongside her and says, "I don't even know why you're still here. Go."

"Thank you." I wrap her in a quick hug and grab my purse from the kitchen. "I'll try to be back soon."

"Take your time. I've got nowhere to be."

"You sure you can handle Dad if he wakes up?"

"Go! Stop worrying about everyone else for a change."

CHAPTER
Fifteen

Rhett

"Want to grab a burger?" Coop asks.

"Nope."

"Pizza? I could go for a slice of Dewey's."

"Not hungry."

"Come on," he sighs, kicking my legs off his coffee table. "You've gotta get up and do something, brother."

"I have. I went to physical therapy four times this week."

"That's all you've done."

My phone rings from the table, but I don't bother checking it. It's probably Nikki, and she's about the last person I want to talk to right now—right behind the Woman Who Shall Not Be Named.

"You gonna answer that?"

"Nope."

I look at the phone when it stops ringing and see a missed call from Mo. It's the first time she's called. I should answer it, give her the chance to explain, but I don't because I'm an asshole.

"That the first you've heard from her?"

"Yup."

"You don't want to hear what she has to say?"

"Doesn't matter."

"We both know that isn't true." Coop grabs the remote from my lap and presses pause on the TV.

I exhale a sharp breath. "You really want to do this, Coop? Should we paint our toenails, have a pillow fight, and talk about our feelings?"

His lips twitch. "Sure, if it means getting your ass off this couch. You're starting to stink."

"Screw you."

Duke stretches out next to me, rolls over, and farts.

"Your damn dog stinks too." Coop groans, fanning the air in front of his face.

Duke lifts a lazy eye to see what all the commotion is about and then rolls back over. My fingers slip through his soft coat, rubbing at the sweet spot behind his ear. Coop pissed and moaned about getting the dogs from Mo, said I should let her keep them a few more days, but I needed to remove the temptation to see her.

"Don't worry, we won't be around much longer."

"What're you talking about?"

"Come on, Coop. This isn't permanent. I'm over a week into physical therapy, and my shoulder feels good." There's still a tight pain when I try to lift my arm, but it's getting better by the day. "It's been two weeks since the accident. I need to start focusing on my career and getting back on the bull."

"You and that damn bull," Coop says, shaking his head. "What about that photo shoot you were telling me about? I thought Nikki wanted to do that out at Dad's."

"I fired her."

"Figured as much."

I didn't fire her that night at Dirty Dicks; she was way too drunk to understand what was going on. Coop and I put her up in a hotel, and I was there waiting for her in the morning when she woke up. I delivered the news and walked out—nothing she could've said was going to make a difference. Her breach of trust still takes my breath every time I think about it. Poor Mo. I mean, I have my own set of issues with Mo, but Nikki interfered in my life, manipulating my relationship to get what was best for her and her father without any thought about me as a person, and messed up my future in the process.

"Now what? Do you have another manager lined up?"

"Not yet, no. I contacted my lawyer. He's drawing up paperwork to sever my contract with the Atwood Agency. I'll wait until that goes through and then figure something out."

My phone rings again. Coop and I look down at the same time to see Mo's name flash across the screen.

"Must be pretty important if she's calling back."

"She doesn't give a shit about me."

Scowling, Coop stands up from the couch. "Is that really what you think?"

"You don't know what she did, Coop. Trust me, if you knew, you would agree."

"Maybe you're right, maybe not, but you won't tell me, so…" He looks at me meaningfully. "As things stand, I believe that woman cares about you." Coop digs in his pocket, pulling out his phone.

He taps the screen a few times and drops it on my lap.

"What is this?" I ask, ignoring the pounding in my heart.

"Watch that and then tell me Mo doesn't care about you."

I drop my head, my eyes locked on Coop's phone. The picture is shaky but clear as his face comes into view.

"*Hey, brother.*" He smiles into the camera before turning

toward the bar. *"Everyone is piled in at Dirty Dicks to watch the show. We're all rooting for you. Everybody say hi,"* he yells.

The camera scans the room, and there are several familiar faces. They all hoot and holler, each one fading out of the picture to make room for the next, and then the camera lands on Mo, and I stop breathing all together.

She glares at the camera before flipping it off, and then I'm left with another view of the room. The picture on the TV is faint, but I can make it out through the video. Everyone cheers as the announcers rattle off a series of statistics. Everything seems to happen much faster now that I'm watching it from Coop's phone, and I gasp for air along with everyone in that room when I'm thrown from Lucifer. But what happens next nearly brings me to my knees.

Mo flings herself over the bar and rushes to the TV as though she wants to reach through it and be the one to help me. The camera on the phone shifts, the sound muffling, but I'm able to make out what Mo says.

"Why isn't he moving?" She's crying, and as morbid as it sounds, I'd give anything to see her face. *"He should be moving, right? Dammit, Rhett,"* she cries. *"I need you to move. Fucking move already. He's so still. Why aren't they helping? They need to do something."*

Mo comes back on the video. The view is slanted to the side, and there's too much white noise to hear what she says, but the wild, desperate look in her eyes tells me everything. I swallow hard, waiting to see what she'll do next. There's a pause, followed by her frantic cry for Cooper. *"Coop!"* After a loud thud, the video goes black.

I look up to find Coop. He's standing in the doorway between the kitchen and living room, his hip propped against the frame.

"She was scared to death. We both were. I don't know what happened between you two all those years ago—other than Nikki clearly helped make a mess of things—and frankly, I don't need to know, but Mo cares about you. Probably even loves you, if I had to guess. She hasn't dated anyone since you two broke up. Not once."

Pressure builds behind my eyes. I'm not sure what to think about that. Why didn't she date? Because of me? Was she hoping I'd come back? Because that's pretty twisted after the lie she told.

I look away, taking a second to get a hold of my emotions, although I'm finding it difficult because they're swirling all over the damn place.

"You've seemed happy since you've been back in Heaven, and I'd say it has something to do with seeing Mo. If there's still something there, you owe it to yourself to figure out if you two can sort through the past. A girl like her won't stay single forever." Coop grabs his phone from my lap and slides it into his pocket. "I've gotta head down to the pub, check on a few things. When I get back, you better be off this couch, and for the love of God, take a damn shower."

I stare at the front door for a long time after Coop leaves, wondering what in the world I'm supposed to do about Mo. I'm relieved that she didn't cheat on me with Charlie Dixon, but I'm not sure I can get over her lie, mitigating circumstances or not. She's had six years to come clean, and she never chose to do that until she had to.

I groan, and my head falls into my hands. Duke shoves his wet nose against the side of my face.

"I'm okay, bud," I say, giving him a pat. "Just trying to figure out what to do about Mo." His ears perk at the sound of her name, and I laugh. "She's gotten to you too, huh?"

Sitting up, he lets out a deep bark.

"Now you sound like Coop."

I glance at the sweats I've been wearing for two straight days. No woman is worth this. Surely it won't kill me to talk to her, if that's what she wants.

Mind made up, I take a quick shower and get dressed. I slip my feet into a pair of Nikes, grab my keys, yank open the front door, and plow straight into a body. Grabbing Mo's arms, I make sure she's steady.

She blinks up at me. Her puffy eyes are red, lips swollen. My stomach twists in knots. I get a whiff of her strawberry shampoo and without fail, I'm reminded of a blanket, a six-pack of beer, my favorite country song playing on the radio, and Mo's soft moans as we made love under the stars. My heart flops around in my chest, and I have to take a step back. It's too much, and without the cover of anger, I'm not ready to be this close to her.

"What are you doing here?"

"I was hoping we could talk." She bites her lower lip and glances at the keys in my hand. "I can come back if this is a bad time."

"Mo—"

"Just so you know, I'm not going to let this go."

"I know." I rub the back of my neck. "I was actually coming to find you."

She shifts on her feet, a nervous habit that she's had for as long as I can remember. "You were?"

I nod. "I told you I wanted you to start from the beginning, and then I walked away before you could finish. That wasn't fair to you, and I apologize."

She looks down at her feet, and I follow her gaze. Mo's toes peek out from the tips of her sandals. They're painted a pale aqua color—odd choice if you ask me, but what do I know? The corners are chipped and worn—the way my heart has felt this past week. It's time to move forward.

I clear my throat, catching Mo's eye, and gesture over my shoulder. "Would you like to come in, or we can stay out here?"

"I don't care where we go, Rhett, just somewhere quiet where we can talk."

Coop lives off of Route 143. His closest neighbor sits a mile down the road, and the only sounds are birds chirping and the light rumble of thunder off in the distance. And, if we stay out here, the smell of the impending rainstorm will distract me from the smell of Mo.

I motion for her take the chair while I prop myself up on the banister of the front porch.

"Okay, Mo, you said you had more to tell me. I'm listening."

CHAPTER
Sixteen

Monroe

Rhett's eyes are ringed by dark circles, the dark strands of his hair are sticking this way and that, and the stubble across his jaw looks like it hasn't seen a razor in days.

I hate seeing him like this.

"You told me you slept with Charlie, hung up on me, wanted to call back and tell me it was all a lie, but you couldn't make yourself do it. That's where you left off."

His voice cuts through the air, along with a sharp gust of wind, and I look him in the eye.

"It took a few weeks, but my head finally cleared enough to catch up with my heart, and I knew I had to come clean. I knew I couldn't live the rest of my life with you thinking the worst of me, and I shouldn't have let Nikki tell me what to do; I just didn't know how to go about telling you. It couldn't be over the phone. I wanted to talk in person, show you how sorry I was. Then Coop called one night and told me you'd be in town for your parents' fortieth wedding anniversary party."

Rhett's face pales as I speak.

"I spent the last of the money in my savings account to buy a dress—"

"And I showed up with a date."

I'll never forget the pain that ripped through me when Rhett walked in with a beautiful blonde. "I couldn't believe you'd moved on so quickly."

"I hadn't," he says softly.

"At the time, I didn't know who she was, but I recognized her the second you two walked into the bar last week. It was Nikki."

"Shit," he groans. Pushing his fingers into his hair, he steps off the porch to pace alongside his truck. "We weren't together," he says. "She was the daughter of my manager, learning her father's trade, and I didn't want to show up alone and risk seeing you there with Charlie."

"When I saw you out on the dance floor with Nikki, I realized I'd already lost you."

He shakes his head, confused. "You hadn't lost me. I was hurting, but I would've forgiven you. I would've taken you back."

"I lost you long before I broke up with you, Rhett. One look at you and I could tell your time away from home had changed you. Your shaggy hair was gone, styled in one of those preppy spikes we always made fun of, and you were wearing a suit. Every other guy at the party was in flannel and denim, but not you. You were in a tailored suit, Rhett."

"I was still the same person."

I shake my head, swallowing hard as the memory passes through me. "It didn't seem that way, and I didn't fit with you at all. I was so proud of you, though—proud that you'd gotten out of this town and made something of yourself, and proud that you looked happy, even if your happiness wasn't shared with me."

"God, Mo, why didn't you come talk to me? Slap me across the face and force me to listen to you?"

"I was going to…" I tell him. "I was waiting until you were alone, so I hung back from the party, watched from afar. But she wouldn't leave your side. At one point she spotted me watching you, and I thought for sure I'd been caught, but then she smiled, wrapped her hand around your arm, and pulled you onto the dance floor. She kept touching you and pressing herself close to you, all while keeping an eye on me. Looking back, I think she knew exactly who I was. I've never wanted to punch someone so badly in my entire life. I wanted to rip her away from you, scream that you were mine, but I'd already made sure that wasn't the truth."

I take a deep breath and let it out slowly. "Finally you stepped away, and I followed you."

"Jesus Christ," Rhett huffs, stepping back onto the porch. "Mo, I don't know what you saw, but—"

"I saw everything."

His head falls.

"She followed you into the woods. I saw the surprised look on your face when you realized she was behind you."

If I close my eyes, it'll put me right back there in the trees—the smell of grassy earth, pine needles, and my dime-store perfume. So I keep my eyes open.

"You reached for her hand, and it felt like you were tearing my heart out of my chest." My voice cracks as I sob, and I put a hand over my mouth, trying to hold it in. "God, Rhett. I watched you pull her close, push her up against a tree, and—"

"Stop. I get it; I was there," he growls. "Jesus, Mo, why did you watch that?"

"I had to," I whisper. "It was the only way to keep from

throwing myself at you down the road, from begging you to forgive me and take me back. I had to let you go, Rhett."

The clouds roll in, bringing some much-needed rain. The first drops fall, offering nothing more than a slight drop in temperature.

"Shit, Mo, I—"

"Seeing you with Nikki was awful, but it was my fault. I'm the one who pushed you toward her, so please don't apologize. If I hadn't lied to you, I know you wouldn't have slept with her."

"I don't even know what to say. This is all so screwed up."

"That's the whole story. I needed you to know I'd planned on making it right."

Lips pressed together, he nods. "I'm really sorry you saw that. I'm still processing how you got to the point where you thought you were protecting me by pushing me away. I'm trying to get there, Mo. And I'm relieved you didn't cheat on me, but you still destroyed us, destroyed me, and I don't know how to get past that."

"What would you have done if you'd found out I had to sell dad's business and quit school so I could take care of him?"

"I would've come back."

"Exactly." I stand up and take a step toward him. "You would've dropped everything to come back and help me."

"Of course I would've, Monroe, because that's what people do for those they love. They don't push them away or create irreparable damage, they support them and love them, even if it costs them something in return."

I flinch at his words but refuse to let them tear me down. Look at him now—all he's achieved. Of course I did the right thing. "And what would you have done? Gone to work at your dad's ranch?"

"I would've made an honest living—"

"You know as well as I do that you wouldn't have been happy here," I argue. "Your life is out there, riding bulls and chasing the buckle."

"My life was you, Mo. That dream I was chasing was supposed to have you in it." His breaths come out in harsh pants, as though he just ran a mile, which is pretty much how I feel.

Several seconds pass as we stare at each other, neither one of us making a move, and I know this might be my last chance to lay it all on the line.

"Rhett." I reach for his hand, and he doesn't pull away. I lace our fingers together. "I'm still in love with you. A lot has changed over the years, but my love for you has remained constant and steady. However you feel about me now, I hope you can find it in your heart to forgive me. I would never do anything to hurt you again."

Curling his fingers around mine, Rhett tugs me forward until my body is pressed against his. I can feel his heart beating against my chest. The soft patter of rain pings against the gutters. There's a gust of wind and a couple of raindrops hit my face.

Rhett lifts his finger, wipes them away, and leans his forehead against mine.

"I want to believe you, but I'm not sure I'm there yet."

I nod, laying my head on his shoulder. I take a deep breath, inhaling his warm, spicy scent, trying to catalogue everything about him that I can.

"I don't know if I'll ever get there, Mo."

Swallowing, I shift and kiss his cheek. He sighs, moving his face a millimeter to the left. I press my lips to the corner of his mouth. His warm breath fans the side of my face, and I pull back before I push him too far.

His hand curls around the back of my neck, and he brings

my mouth to his for a gentle kiss. There's nothing passionate about it, and all too soon he opens his eyes and steps back.

"I'm sorry, Mo."

I lay my finger against his lips. "You have nothing to be sorry for. This is on me, and I'll just have to live with it."

A tiny sliver of my heart had hoped he'd grant me forgiveness—and if I was real lucky, another shot at his heart. Disappointment races through me. Walking away from Rhett after coming clean feels even more final than hanging up after telling a lie.

Hands shaking, stomach twisted, I take step after step toward my truck. A crack of lightning streaks through the sky, followed by a roll of thunder. Rain drips from my hair, seeping through my clothes and shoes, and I have to fight the urge to look back at Rhett. I can't. If I do, I'll drop to my knees and beg for any crumble of love he can salvage for me, and we both deserve much more than that.

This is it. We're finally done.

CHAPTER
Seventeen

Rhett

I should think about this more, sleep on it for a few nights, try to determine the next step. But I'm damn tired of thinking, and each step she takes causes a sharp pain along the left side of my chest, leaving me feeling like I just screwed up the best thing that ever happened to me.

I know now I can't fuck her out of my system, like I thought I could when I first got back, and I don't know what option that leaves me. But I can't get myself to focus on any of that.

Just as she makes it to her truck, I step up behind her. I push the door shut, spin her around, and press her back against it. Here she is: Monroe Danielle Gallagher, the only woman I've ever loved—soaking wet, chest heaving, and body tight with restraint.

We lunge for each other at the same time.

Our mouths slam together as her fingers slide into my hair. She turns my head and plunges her tongue into my mouth. I reach for her shirt, my hands slipping under the hem to find her soft, warm curves. We move together effortlessly, as though this is something we've done every day for the last six years.

She moans into my mouth, her body melts against mine, and any and all control is lost. We're a frenzy of hands and lips and teeth, grasping at each other, trying to get closer. My right hand slides down her back and along her hip, and when I grip her ass, she wraps her legs around my waist. My left hand rests at her lower back, holding her to me without putting too much stress on my shoulder.

"Shit," she huffs, trying to wriggle loose, but no way am I letting her down. "Your shoulder—"

"Is fine. I just need you to hold on, Mo. Tighten those pretty legs around me and don't let go."

Her arms and legs cinch around my body, and she's latched onto me like a spider monkey. Fingers curled in the hair at the base of my neck, Mo guides my lips to hers as I move toward the front door.

The cool rain falls in waves, soaking us to the bone, but it does nothing to calm the heat radiating from our bodies.

"What about Coop?" she asks against my lips.

"Not here." We fumble our way into the house. My mouth slides down her throat, and Mo's head falls back, exposing the milky skin of her neck.

"We should talk, right?" she pants, holding my head to her neck as though she's terrified I'll move.

Not a chance, sweetheart.

"No." I nip at her skin while kicking the bedroom door open, and once we're through, I nudge it shut and flick the lock.

"I don't want you to regret this in the morning."

"Mo." I lower her onto the bed, and she scoots to the center, propping herself up on some pillows. Her eyes are bright as she watches me with naked vulnerability. "The only thing I'm going to regret is if I let you walk out of here. I forgive you for what happened. I know it wasn't entirely your fault. Nikki took advantage of your pain."

Her chin drops to her chest. I imagine she's waited six years to hear me say that, and if she asked, I'd repeat myself over and over until she believed the words.

I tip her chin up to look at me. "I need you to promise me something."

"Anything."

"No more lies, baby. If we're going to move forward in any capacity, there isn't room for anything but the truth."

She nods, moisture pooling in her eyes, and I kiss her. This time isn't hurried like the last. This time I slow it down a notch, promising with my mouth all the things my heart has yet to say.

"Rhett?"

"Hmm?"

"Make love to me."

"Plannin' on it." Pushing up from the bed, I kick off my shoes and slip her sandals from her feet. Her eyes follow my every move. Careful not to lift my left arm too high, I reach behind my head and pull my shirt off. When I reach for my sweats, she sucks in a sharp breath, her eyes glued to my cock as I let my pants fall to the floor.

"Your turn." I crawl onto the bed, her eyes searing through me. When I undo the button of her shorts, she lifts her hips, allowing me to pull them off, along with her white cotton panties. Sitting up, she reaches for the bottom of her shirt, lifts it over her head, and flings it off to the side.

"You are so beautiful, Mo."

The last time I looked down at her like this, sprawled out in front of me, I was too young to appreciate her—too young to understand the depth of what she was giving me. But that's no longer the case. I've dreamed of her many times over the last six years, but my fantasies didn't do her justice. Nothing compares to having her in my bed—hair fanned out, chest heaving, creamy skin begging for my mouth. I have to reach out to touch her to make sure she's real.

I slide my fingers over her abdomen. The muscles contract beneath my touch.

She looks down, but I shake my head. "No, sweetheart, keep your eyes on me. You have nothing to be embarrassed about. I've seen every inch of you, remember?"

Her cheeks turn the prettiest shade of pink. "It's been a long time. My body has changed."

"Hasn't been that long, and trust me, your body is perfect."

With a flick of the front clasp, her bra opens, her beautiful breasts spilling out. She shrugs out of it, and I lower my body to hers, scarcely able to believe this is happening.

———————o———————

Monroe

"Rhett," I breathe, my eyes rolling back in my head as his lips wrap around my nipple. His hand finds my other breast, rolling the nipple between his fingers while his other hand slips between my folds.

Oh, God. I've been touched by men over the years—a few guys here and there who weren't significant enough to tell anyone about—but no relationships or sex, because no one has been able to light my body on fire the way Rhett does. His fingers work with a practiced skill—coaxing me toward bliss.

I've wondered several times over the last six years whether—should this ever happen—things would be as easy and good between us as they once were. Now I have my answer.

It's better.

So much better.

We move together like skilled dancers, never missing a step.

His tongue is relentless, swirling and suckling first one breast and then then other, not stopping until they're swollen and heavy. I close my eyes, only to have them to fly back open a second later when his mouth locks onto my clit.

Unable to do anything but watch, I prop myself up on an elbow and look down. Rhett's broad shoulders look even bigger between my thighs, and his tanned skin is a stark contrast to my pasty white, but we look good together. Like two pieces of a puzzle that fit in the most glorious of ways.

Threading my fingers through his soft hair, I grip it tight. Lifting my hips, I hold his face while I grind against him.

"Oh, Rhett," I moan, feeling his tongue dip inside of me before pulling out and swirling around my swollen clit. "That feels so good."

He runs a finger down my slit, slipping it inside while his lips continue to move. My legs start to quiver, a slow burn igniting deep in my gut. Rhett must notice the shift in my body because a moan rumbles from his chest, the vibrations hitting me in all the right spots. With his face between my legs, I toss my head back against the pillow and let go. My body flies apart. A kaleidoscope of colors bursts behind my eyelids, and I tighten my knees around his head, my hips bucking against his face.

He rides the wave with me, only pulling back when I'm limp beneath him.

"I think you broke me."

He grins, kissing my inner thigh and slowly making his way back up my body.

Sitting on his haunches, Rhett works his cock from base to tip. His hooded eyes smolder as he looks down at me.

"Are you on birth control?"

I bite my lower lip and shake my head.

"That's okay." Leaning across the bed, he grabs a condom from his wallet and slides it over his cock. Then he positions himself at my entrance. "Are you ready?" he asks, rubbing his cock along my slit.

"You cannot even imagine."

Rhett lowers himself over me, his body pressing me against the mattress. With his hands cradling my face, he pushes inside, inch by inch, until by my body is stretched around him.

He blows out a harsh breath and buries his face in the crook of my neck. "So tight, Mo."

I shift my hips, easing him out and then back in, and he presses his hips to mine, pinning me against the mattress.

"Give me a second, sweetheart, or I'm going to get off before we even get started."

I run my fingers along his back from the base of his neck to his ass, exploring the tight ripple of muscles as he holds himself above me. A few seconds pass, and then he rocks his hips. I moan, loving the way our bodies fall into a familiar rhythm.

"Feels so good, Mo."

I've waited for this moment for so long, thought about it for years, and now that we're here, my words seem stuck in my throat. But that's okay, because suddenly Rhett has enough for both of us.

"God, baby, I missed this so much. I missed you so much."

"I missed you too."

Our hips move together. His cock grows impossibly thick inside of me, creating a delicious friction, and when my body tightens for the second time, I dig my nails into Rhett's scalp and guide his mouth to mine.

Our tongues duel, twisting and sliding, mimicking our bodies, and I unravel at a beautiful pace, with Rhett following shortly behind.

His muscles flex beneath my hands, his hips slamming into mine as he groans through his release. He slows to lazy movements, and it takes everything I have to keep my eyes open. But I do because I love the look on his face, and even more, I love knowing I put it there.

CHAPTER
Eighteen

Monroe

The afternoon sun pours through the window, casting a blanket of warmth across my body. Rhett's heart beats steady beneath my ear, which is pressed to his chest while my fingers draw slow, lazy circles over his abs.

"What are you thinking about?" he asks, running his fingers through my hair.

"I'm thinking your ab muscles are unreal. How does one even get this defined?"

"All I do is work. If I'm not at the arena, I'm at the gym."

"Maybe you work too much. What do you do for fun these days?"

Rhett chuckles, kissing the top of my head. "I ride bulls."

"That's your job. What do you do for fun?"

"It's not a job if it's something you love."

I look up at him.

"And you really want to lecture me on working too much?" he continues. "Pot meet kettle."

"Touché." I flop back on his chest, situating myself until I can hear his heartbeat again. Being close enough to feel his body against mine is a much-needed balm to my tattered soul. "I'm also wondering how pissed Claire is going to be."

The last thing I want is to leave Rhett's bed, but I should probably get home. With an exasperated sigh, I kiss his chest and push myself up. I don't make it far before he pulls me back down.

"Why would Claire be pissed?"

I rest my chin on his chest. "She stayed with my dad so I could come see you." I glance at the alarm clock on the nightstand. "And I've already been longer than I intended." Not that she'll mind, but I appreciate everything she's already done for me, and I don't want her to feel taken for granted.

"Mo." Rhett's eyes soften, and he cradles my head, his other hand settling at the small of my back. "I need you to know something; if I'd known you wanted me, needed me, I would've been here in a heartbeat, because I needed you just as bad. I didn't move on. Nikki was a one-time thing."

I flinch at the mention of her name, and Rhett brushes a strand of hair out of my face.

"She meant nothing to me."

"I know," I say softly. "But I hate myself for pushing you into her arms."

"Don't. Don't shoulder all the blame. She took advantage of you. She played with your emotions. I can't imagine how awful those weeks were for you. And I hate that you've struggled so much over the last six years, and I haven't been here to help." He sighs. "We've got a mountain of regrets and what-ifs between us, Mo, but if we're going to move forward, we've got to start letting go of the past."

Knowing he wants to move forward puts a smile on my face, but it quickly dies because… "I'm not sure how easy that's going to be with her as your manager. A constant reminder day in and day out—"

"I fired her."

My eyes widen. "You did?"

"Yes," he breathes. "My lawyer is working on severing my contract with her family. I couldn't stand to look at her after what she did. I swear to you, Mo, I never got one voicemail or message. Not one. If I had, you can bet your ass I would've been right here with you. I never would've let you go through all of that on your own."

"I know." Sliding my hands up his chest, I cradle his jaw. "I know you would've been here. I just don't understand how she was able to intercept all those calls and messages. It doesn't make sense."

Rhett shakes his head and pushes himself up in the bed, bringing me with him.

"I know, but you have to understand that in the beginning, I was so busy—in and out of interviews and meetings, not to mention all the damn training I was doing. Bill and Nikki were around all the time those first few months, and she had access to my phone. I wasn't allowed to take it in with me during interviews, and when I was training, it was always in my locker."

"Which she could get to."

He nods. "I will never forgive myself for not being here after your father's stroke."

"Don't." I press my cheek to the palm of his hand. "No more, okay? We let go of those regrets today."

"Deal." Rhett pulls me in close.

His warm, spicy scent wraps around me, and I hold on for dear life, because this is everything I needed and everything I missed.

"Maybe we should revisit the better parts of our past by taking a trip back in time," he suggests.

"Oooh... I like where this is going. What are you thinking, Mr. Allen?"

"Mr. Allen. I like that. Let's use it more often."

I giggle when he grabs my ass.

"I'm going to my parents' for dinner this week. Come with me. We can hop on the horses and take a ride down by the creek."

"That sounds amazing, but I'll have to find someone to stay with my dad." I start scrolling through my head for possible contenders. I know Claire's mom and her aunt would do it in a heartbeat, but they're his full-time caregivers while I work, so I hate to ask them to put in more hours. And I could ask Claire, but—

"Bring him."

"Really?"

"Yes." Rhett laughs. "My parents would love to see him—I would love to see him."

With a flutter in my chest, I return his smile. "Okay. Let me talk to him about it, and I'll let you know." I swing my legs over the edge of the bed, and Rhett moans.

"Do you have to go?"

My clothes are still damp from the rain as I slide them on, and when I slip my feet into my sandals, they make a squishy sound.

"I wish I didn't."

I lean across the bed to give him one more quick kiss, but he has other ideas. His fingers slide into my hair, and he holds me in place. My lips part, and in a matter of seconds my body is at his mercy, fired up and ready to go.

"I have to leave." I rest our foreheads together. "Thank you," I whisper, my lips grazing his.

"For what?"

"For forgiving me. For coming home. For being you."

"You're welcome," he says, kissing me between each response. "Let me get some clothes on, and I'll walk you out."

"No. Stay here. You look comfortable. I can let myself out." I bend over to grab my phone—which somehow ended up on the floor—and Rhett growls.

"You're teasing me."

I shake my ass, and he growls again.

"You better get out of here before I drag you back to this bed."

"We do have six years of make-up sex coming our way."

He grins. "I like the way you think."

"I'll talk to you soon." I press my lips to his one last time and walk out through Coop's house. I reach for the handle at the same time the front door flies open.

Coop nearly rams into me, and then smiles like the Cheshire cat. "Hey, Mo."

"Coop." Cheeks flushed, I duck my head and try to step around him, only to have him step in front of me.

"Your shirt is on backwards."

What? I reach for my neck and look down at my shirt. *Liar.* I scowl. "I hate you."

"No, you don't."

"Yes, I do. Now move so I can go."

"Not until you tell me what you were doing here."

"She was doing me, asshole." Rhett's voice, thick and warm, floats down the hall, and I turn around. He's not wearing a shirt, and his body is a sight to behold. His broad chest tapers to a trim waist—his abs cut to perfection with that chiseled V everyone loves to dream about. His light gray sweats once again hang low on his hips, and his bare feet pad against the floor as he walks toward me.

What is it about a barefoot man that's so damn sexy?

"You're drooling," Coop whispers.

I elbow him in the side, and he lets out a soft *oomph*.

"Your brother is harassing me," I pout, reaching for Rhett because I can, and that's a damn good feeling.

Coop smiles as Rhett pulls me against his chest. "About damn time." He claps Rhett on the shoulder as he walks by. "But if I hear you two bumping uglies, I'll send you back to Houston."

Back to Houston.

Coop may as well have thrown a bucket of ice water in my face. What happens when Rhett goes back to Houston? Because he will inevitably go back. He has to. That's where he trains. He has a house there, for crying out loud.

"I've gotta go." I wave to Coop, kiss Rhett one last time, and walk out of the house.

I climb into my truck and drive home on autopilot, trying to figure out how all of this is going to work, how I'm going to fit into the equation. Do I fit into the equation? What is the equation? Rhett and I talked about moving forward, but I don't know what's going through his head. Does he mean while he's here or long term, because there's a huge difference, and I'm not sure how I feel about him going back and me staying here. We'll be a couple of hours apart, which isn't bad, but I won't be able to commute to see him, not with taking care of Animal Haven and my dad.

The high I felt just minutes ago deflates, and by the time I pull into my driveway, I feel about the same as I did when I left—only with a tingle between my thighs, and I choose to focus on that for now.

It's all I can do.

CHAPTER
Nineteen

Monroe

"Hey, Ruby," I say softly, running my hand down her back. Her chest moves up and down as she breathes, but Ruby makes no attempt to open her eyes and acknowledge me.

She's sleeping more and more in her old age and I know my time with her is limited which is why I soak up as much of it as I can.

"I love you, sweet girl." I place a kiss on top of her head, my lips lingering for a few extra beats before I pull back.

Ruby opens one eye and looks at me as though to say *I love you too.* Then she looks around the room, probably hoping to see Rhett.

"Sorry, Rhett left earlier for a physical therapy appointment."

Rhett and I spent three hours on the phone last night after I left Coop's house. Much to my surprise, he was once again waiting for me at Animal Haven when I arrived this morning. He had an easy smile on his face and I noticed that a lot of the tension I had been carrying around with me was gone.

My phone rings and I pull it out of my pocket and smile

when I see Tess's name. "Hey," I say, answering my phone. "Are you ready to give the bird back?"

"Heck no. Simon is the best company I've kept in a long time. I was actually calling to tell you that I could come in tomorrow for a few hours and help if you'd like. I know I wasn't on the schedule, but I had an appointment get cancelled and figured I could spend the extra time at Animal Haven."

"I can always use the extra help."

"Perfect. I have a few things to do in the morning and then I'll be in."

"You talk too much," Simon says, his squawk piercing through the phone.

"Sorry about that," Tess says. "He has a huge vocabulary. He also talks way too much and loves to play Simon Says."

"Simon says, shut up!"

Tess growls. "No, Simon, I'm not playing with you right now."

"Shut up!"

"Sometimes it gets a little annoying, but I've gotten used to it. His incessant chattering is better than silence… I think," she says, ignoring Simon's high-pitched voice in the background.

"Shut up!"

"Will he eventually stop telling you to shut up?" I ask, secretly thankful that she offered to foster the bird because there's no doubt he would've driven the other animals here crazy—myself included.

"Oh yeah, when I get off the phone and actually play his little game."

"Shut up!"

The phone muffles but I hear Tess talking to Simon. "Simon if you don't stop telling me to shut up, I'm going to put a blanket over your cage and make you take a nap."

"Ew!"

"That's the only way to get him to stop."

"Threaten him?" I ask.

"Pretty much. He hates taking naps," she says, unapologetically.

"Nice. You're learning fast."

"I'm going to be the best darn cockatoo mom this world has ever seen. And now I have to go because Simon just fell off his swing."

"Oh my gosh, is he—" Tess hangs up before I get a chance to finish asking if he's okay, but a minute later she sends a text.

Turns out he knows how to play dead, too. Damn bird.

I smile and type out a quick reply. ***Want me to take him back?***

Not a chance in hell.

Thank God.

After shoving my phone in my back pocket, I check on the other animals, saving Pickles for last. There's just something about him... He's special. Okay, they're all special, but Pickles has a unique grip on my heart.

I open his cage and rather than waiting on me to come to him, this time Pickles comes to me and it's a welcome surprise. There's a purr thick in his throat as he rubs against my leg.

"Did you miss me, or are you just hoping for more Tuna? Because I'll be honest, I think Rhett is onto something. You're playing me," I say, scooping the cat up.

Moving his head along my chin, Pickles continues to purr and I find his sweetness deceptive because I know he's ornery as hell.

"I have paperwork to do and I could use some help if you're up for the task."

Pickles stares up at me lazily and blinks twice before closing his eyes, unaware that I'm about to give him another chance at becoming an Animal Haven regular.

"Your eyes might be closed, but I know you can hear me, so listen up. You're going to sit with me while I go through some files and you're not going to pick on Ruby. Absolutely no growling, hissing, biting, or slapping. If I see any of the above you're going right back to your cage. Got it?"

Instead of responding, he yawns. As gently as possible, I lower Pickles to a makeshift bed on the floor near my desk. He lays there for a minute and then gets up. Pickles inches his way around the room sniffing every nook and cranny before walking toward Ruby. He sniffs her tail and then works his way up her body. When his nose meets hers, he nuzzles her and I imagine he's saying *come on, girl, get up and bark at me*, but Ruby doesn't move.

Pickles kneads at the floor beside Ruby, turns in a circle, and curls up in a ball, his back resting against Ruby's belly.

I knew it, Pickles. I knew you were a big softy. Welcome to family.

Relieved at how well that went, I turn my attention back to the task at hand.

A typical day's work may begin with mucking stalls or cleaning out cages, but there's so much more to running a shelter than caring for the animals. I have to keep track of each animal, updating their progress and social skills, and it's imperative I keep their files up to date. On top of that, I keep track of vet appointments, foster applications, adoption applications and volunteer applications. It's tedious work, but someone has to do it.

I'm an hour into my work with files spread out in front of me when Pickles pushes up on all fours and arches his back in a giant stretch. He meanders across the room, winds his way between my ankles a few times, and curls up in a ball at my feet.

"I knew you could listen if you wanted to," I whisper, grabbing a tuna flavored treat from my pocket and handing it to him under the desk. "Good boy."

My cell rings, but I let it go to voicemail because this work won't do itself. A second later I get a notification for a voicemail and then the office phone rings and I pick it up.

"Animal Haven."

"Hey, beautiful. I just tried calling your cell."

I smile at the sound of Rhett's sexy voice. "Sorry, I didn't even look to see who was calling. I'm trying to catch up on paperwork."

"Do you need me to come back out there? I can help."

"No, I'm good. You helped me a ton this morning. This is just boring stuff."

"Are you sure?"

"Positive."

"Are we still on for tonight?" he asks.

I smile at the thought of seeing him again. "Of course."

"And we're still on for dinner at mom's tomorrow?"

"I wouldn't miss it for the world," I say.

"I'm glad you were able to talk your dad into coming."

"It didn't take much to convince him. He is thrilled to see your family."

There's a long pause and then Rhett clears his throat. "He's probably not too thrilled about seeing me."

It's the first time Rhett has shown an insecurity about Dad's feelings toward our break up, and I don't like it. I want us to have a great time and enjoy everyone's company without him being nervous or uncomfortable. "He doesn't know everything that happened between us, Rhett, and I never made you out to be a bad person. It's going to be fine, I promise. My dad loves you."

I can almost hear Rhett relax through the phone. "Thank you. I can't tell you how much I needed to hear that."

"You have nothing to worry about."

"Okay, sweetheart. I'm going to let you get back to work. Call me if you need anything. I'll see you tonight."

"Bye, Rhett."

I hang up the phone and smile. This time last year if you would've told me I'd be having dinner with Rhett and his family, I would've called you crazy. And if you would've told me that I would be back in Rhett's bed, my eyes would've bugged out of my head. But, here I am, happier than I've been in a long time.

My gaze drifts across the room toward Ruby. She's still curled up on her bed and it isn't lost on me that she's watched me go full circle. She watched me fall in love and subsequently break my own heart, and now she's here to witness me get it put back together.

If dogs could talk, Ruby would have a million things to say.

CHAPTER
Twenty

Rhett

"She's here." Mom flings the dishrag over her shoulder and makes a beeline for the door. My hand on her arm stops her.

"Where do you think you're going?"

"To get that wonderful girl."

My mom has been so excited since I told her Mo and Phil were coming for dinner. She's spent the last few days stewing over what to make and finally settled on chicken and dumplings—Mo's favorite.

"Slow down," I laugh. "You're going to scare her away."

Mom palms the side of my cheek, her eyes going all misty. "I'm so happy. You haven't stopped smiling since you got here, and you know how much I love Monroe."

"Yes, I know," I say, gently pulling her hand from my face.

"Can I go now?" she asks, a sparkle of hope in her eye.

"Fine." I sigh. "Go."

"I haven't seen your mom move that fast since she walked down the aisle," Dad says, stepping up beside me as we watch Mom barrel through the front door to greet Mo and Phil.

I look at Dad. "She walked fast down the aisle? Don't most women go slow?"

He shrugs. "Your mom isn't most women. And according to her, I was a flight risk."

No way. My dad is the most stable, loyal person I know. "You were a flight risk?"

He nods and pats my back. "Yup, and so are you. Your mom says it's in our blood. We chase the bull, and in your case, the buckle. Lucky for you, you've got a good head on your shoulders, and you know a good thing when you find it—you get that from me." He smiles proudly.

"I'm not a flight risk."

"I know you're not, but she doesn't know that," he says, nodding toward Mo. "It's never about what we think; it's always about them—what they're thinking, what they want. It'll do you good to remember that. Your mom was worried about everything under the sun: how we would make it work, what would happen when I went on tour—the women, the temptation, everything. And all I could think about was her barefoot and pregnant in a home I built just for her."

I step to the side and watch Mo help her dad out of the car. Mom holds the wheelchair in place, and when Phil is seated, she wraps Mo in a hug.

"I'm not following."

Dad laughs. "It'll make sense one of these days when you know you've found the one. She'll be coming up with a million reasons why you can't work, or she'll worry about losing you to some buckle bunny, and all you'll worry about is finding a way to make her yours before she realizes she can do so much better."

I shoot Dad a look.

"Hypothetically speaking, of course, because no one is

better than my son."

"Damn right," I say, turning my gaze back to Mo.

Dad's words filter through my head as I watch from the porch. Mo's dark hair hangs over her shoulders in loose waves. She's wearing a pair of jeans, a pink blouse, and cowboy boots. When she looks up, her eyes catch mine, and for this one moment in time, everything seems right in the world. My heart slams inside my chest as though it's trying to throw itself at her, and I have no choice but to follow its lead.

"You might be closer than you think," Dad mumbles as I step off the porch.

Mo watches me walk across the yard. The closer I get, the bigger her smile grows, and when I'm close enough, I reach for her hand. I tug gently, pulling her against me to kiss her cheek.

"You look beautiful," I whisper, as though I haven't seen her in days. Only it hasn't been days, it's been hours. It's been two days since our *reunion*, and we've spent as much of them as we can together. I've helped her at Animal Haven, and in the evenings after Phil is in bed, we've cuddled together on his front porch, looking at the stars and reminiscing about old times.

Her bright smile shines up at me, a pink tinge infusing her cheeks. She bites her lower lip, and I have to step away or risk getting a chubby in front of my parents and Phil.

When I turn to Phil, one side of his mouth is lifted up in what I believe to be a smile. It's hard to tell, because the other side has a slight droop.

Phil was always larger than life. He had a big heart and an even bigger frame, and if he hadn't showed up with Mo tonight, I'm not sure I would've recognized him. This is the same man who taught me how to shoe a horse and bopped me upside the head when he caught me ogling his fifteen-year-old daughter in her bikini. I have almost as many memories of Phil as I do of my own parents, and I have to swallow past a lump in my throat when I step toward him.

Unsure what he's capable of, but not wanting to insult him, I hold out my hand and return his smile. "It's good to see you, Phil."

It takes a bit of time, but he manages to lift his hand. His grip isn't nearly as strong as it once was, but I can tell he appreciates the gesture.

"It's b-been way too l-long."

"I know it has, sir."

"Guess that's n-not a problem anymore?" He glances up at Mo.

She blushes.

Mom smiles.

I laugh.

"No, sir, I suppose it isn't. And I hope you're hungry, because Mom made enough food to feed an army."

He nods jerkily and pulls his hand back, resting it in his lap. "W-what are we w-w-waiting for?"

Mom scurries around to the back of Phil's wheelchair and pushes him toward the house. I wait until they're a few steps ahead of us and grab Mo's hand. Her fingers lace with mine.

"How was it getting him here?" I ask.

"Good. It's not hard to transport him. He's able to help me out quite a bit, and I owe most of that to his therapists."

"How many does he have?"

"Just physical and occupational. They come in a couple of times a week, and his caregivers are good at working with him too. Where's everyone else?" she asks, looking at the empty driveway.

"Mom didn't want to overwhelm your dad by inviting the whole tribe over on his first trip here."

She looks up at me. "First trip, huh?"

"If I play my cards right, I'm hoping there'll be some more family dinners, and a few dates scattered in there, too."

"Rhett." Mo stops and tugs my hand. "My life isn't normal. I can't just pick up and go out on a date with you or come to one of your shows, and I don't want you to feel like—"

My mouth on hers stops everything. Her words melt away, and all the jumbled mess of feelings I've had lately seem to work themselves out as I lose myself in this kiss. Her hands dip into my hair, and she grips it tightly, pulling me close. My tongue pushes into her mouth, and off in the distance, I register the sound of someone clearing their throat.

Shit. We have an audience.

Mo must hear it at the same time, because she pulls back. Her eyes are hooded, lips swollen. When she places her fingers over her mouth, I pull them away and kiss her again.

"We're going to finish that kiss later."

"And the conversation," she adds softly.

"Would you give the girl some room to breathe?" Dad chides, shouldering past me.

Mo steps into his embrace—a testament to how close our families have been over the years. And probably to how close she's remained to mine.

"It's great to see you again, sweetheart."

"You too, Mr. Allen."

Dad scoffs. "What did I say about calling me that? It's Sawyer."

Putting his arm around her shoulders, he leads her into the house. I follow, and when she tips her head back and laughs at something he says, I can't help but feel like this is right where she belongs.

CHAPTER
Twenty-One

Monroe

After dinner, Vivian insists we eat dessert outside. She grabs the plates and forks, along with a pitcher of tea. Rhett picks up the apple pie, and I push my dad outside.

"Here you go, Daddy." I situate his wheelchair as close to the table as it can get. Vivian serves the pie on paper plates, pushing one over in front of my dad.

Out of habit, I grab his fork, and Dad glares at me as best he can. "I c-could've gotten th-that."

"I know you could've."

Rather than putting the fork in his hand, I hold it out and wait for him to take it. Then I step back.

"Here you go, dear." Vivian hands me a plate, but I politely decline.

"Oh, no, thank you. It looks fantastic, but I'm stuffed from dinner."

"Well, then, more for me." Rhett takes my plate from his mother, and we sit down at the table.

Eating out—or at another person's house—isn't something

Dad and I do. In fact, I can count on one hand the number of times we've done this in the last six years. A million scenarios float around my head as I watch Dad guide an unsteady hand toward the pie.

What if he spills his food or drops his fork—which he often does—and gets embarrassed? Or worse yet, what if the chicken and dumplings goes right through him and I can't get him to the bathroom in time?

I clearly didn't think this through when we agreed to come over.

As best as he can, Dad scoops a chunk of pie onto his fork. It wobbles precariously, and I reach out, wrapping my hand around his to steady it. Together we guide it to his mouth.

I wait for him to chew, and when he reaches for another bite, I scoot closer. Only this time, Dad shakes his head and pulls the fork away.

"N-no, Mo," he says with as much authority as he can muster.

"I'm just trying to help you, Dad."

"I d-don't want your h-help."

"Dad—"

His sharp gaze causes the words to die on my tongue.

"A-all through dinner you h-hovered over m-m-me."

"I don't hover."

"Yes, y-you do. It's embarrassing, M-Mo."

His soft-spoken words settle low in my gut, causing a ripple of nausea. *Is that what I do?* I think back over all the times I've fed him or taken over after he's tried so hard to do something on his own, and tears fill my eyes.

On the edge of losing my shit in front of everyone, I excuse myself from the table and walk toward the house. For the first time since his stroke, I don't go to my father when he calls out for me.

The door shuts quietly behind me—either that or I just can't hear it because of the blood rushing in my ears. Bracing my hands on the counter, I lower my head.

Dad's therapists have told me before that I enable him, that I need to let him be more independent and do the small things he's capable of doing—like feeding himself.

Shit.

I blink up, looking out the window over the sink. My dad is talking and eating with Vivian and Sawyer as if nothing happened.

"You okay?" Rhett asks.

Pressing a hand to my chest, I gasp. "You scared me."

He brushes the hair off my shoulder and kisses the side of my neck. "Sorry."

"That's okay."

He follows my gaze out the window. Snaking his arms around my waist, he props his chin on my shoulder. "What's going through that head of yours?"

I take a deep breath and blow it out. "I've hindered my father's recovery."

"What do you mean?" He leans against the counter so he can look me in the eye.

"For the last six years I've treated him as if he were my child, and for the longest time, that's how it was. But he's gained so much strength. He can do a lot on his own now, and I've continued to treat him like a child."

"You've taken care of him. Do you know how many people would do what you did? What you continue to do?"

He runs his fingers down my arm to my hand.

Tilting my head, I look at him. "Most people would do this for someone they love."

"I disagree. There are a lot of selfish people in this world, and you are definitely not one of them. You put your entire life on hold to keep him out of a nursing home. You need to cut yourself some slack."

Easier said than done when regret is involved. "He can feed himself, but it takes a while, and sometimes I get impatient. Or I'm stressed and it's just easier to do things myself than wait for him. He's never complained, until today."

"Maybe it's because you're here. Maybe it's us that's making him uncomfortable."

I shake my head. I know for a fact it's not. I've spent an incredible amount of time with my father since his stroke, and I've learned to read him. I could see it in his eyes. He's been wanting to say something for a while.

"I think he's tried to tell me; I've just never listened."

"Sounds like you need to sit down and have a talk with your dad."

"Maybe you're right," I say, turning back toward the window. "He looks happy, though, right?"

"Yes. But are you happy?"

I sigh, resting my head back on Rhett's shoulder when he steps up behind me. "More than I have been in a long time." Turning in his arms, I splay my hands out across his chest, slide them over his broad shoulders, and push up on my toes to kiss his lips.

"Now, I have a surprise."

I smile against Rhett's mouth. "You're sweet for planning a surprise, but I'm not sure I should leave Dad."

"Too late. He's already insisted that you come with me. I think his exact words were 'That girl could use a few surprises in her boring life'. He'll be here with my mom and dad."

"He didn't say that." I laugh.

"Oh, yes he did. Come on." Rhett pulls my hands, leading me toward the back door. "We won't be gone long, an hour or two tops."

"An hour or two? What are you planning to do?"

He winks. "You, if I'm lucky."

———◇———

A little while later, I squeal in delight as Shadow jumps over a log. It's been years since I was on a horse. I can hardly believe I let Rhett talk me into it now, but he promised to bring back the best memories of our time together, and how was I supposed to say no to that?

Rhett is on Sadie, a few paces ahead of us. "Duck!" he yells, and I have just enough time to lower my head before it gets taken off by a branch.

My hair whips around my head, the warm sun beating against my face, and for the first time in a long time, I feel free. I push Shadow faster as Rhett picks up speed.

I know exactly where he's taking me. I knew it the second we started down this path, and there isn't a doubt in my mind that the horses still remember where to go. The overgrowth on the trail indicates how long it's been since anyone was out here, and that makes my heart both happy and sad.

As teenagers, Rhett and I would ride out here to watch the sunset. It was our secret spot, and the memories this little chunk of land holds are immeasurable.

Shadow slows to a trot when the brush clears and we hit the meadow. Rhett glances over his shoulder and nods to the left. I can't fight the smile that creeps across my face when a giant oak tree comes into view. It sits about ten feet from the pond and represents so many firsts for us.

With my back against the bark, he kissed me for the

first time.

On a blanket in the sun on a warm summer day, he made love to me for the first time.

Wrapped in each other's arms on a cool fall evening, we said goodbye for the very first time.

He was off to be a professional bull rider. I was off to college. That was the last time I was out here, and I can still feel the stabbing pain in my chest that began as we walked away from the tree all those years ago.

Before I have a chance to stick my emotions back into perfect little boxes, Rhett hops off of Sadie and grabs Shadow's reins. I swing a leg over the side and slide off while he ties the horses up.

My feet lead me toward the tree, and when I see the familiar red-and-white plaid blanket spread out over the grass and a picnic basket, I laugh and spin around.

"When did you do all this?"

He smiles shyly. With his hands stuffed in the pockets of his jeans, he shrugs. "Earlier. Before you and Phil showed up."

"It's amazing."

I turn back around and head toward the edge of the pond. Closing my eyes, I tilt my head to the sky, allowing the warm summer breeze to take me back to a simpler time. The air is fresh and clean, with hints of lavender from a field I know sits adjacent to the pond.

"Do you remember the first time you brought me here?"

"How could I forget?" Rhett smiles and pulls me to his side.

CHAPTER
Twenty-Two

Rhett

"It was my sixteenth birthday," I tell her. I still remember how excited I was. "Jake and Christopher wanted me to pick them up so we could go cruisin', but all I could think about was getting you alone."

Mo buries her face against my shirt. "That was a great day," she says, smiling up at me.

"It was." I grin. "If memory serves, I made it to second base."

"Pretty sure it was third."

I know for a fact it wasn't third. "Nope. Third base came on *your* sixteenth birthday when I took you to see *Dirty Dancing* at the drive-in."

"Oh my God, that's right! How did I forget about that? We spent the entire night in your truck. By the time we thought to leave, the movie was over, your windows were fogged up, and the entire place was empty."

"When I dropped you off, your dad asked what we'd thought of Swayze's performance, and I said—"

"Who's that?" we both say at the same time.

Mo tosses her head back, laughing. "He was so pissed! He

thought we'd lied about going to the movies, and he grounded me."

"Worst punishment ever. I didn't get back to third base for another month," I scoff.

"And then you made it there, like, every day after that." She swats my chest, and I catch her wrist, holding her to me.

I smile as I remember the first few days after she got ungrounded. We couldn't keep our hands off each other. "Not long after that, I hit a home run."

"Right over there on that exact same blanket. Only I don't remember a picnic basket."

"That's because there wasn't one. I'm older now, you see, and a lot wiser. I know how to wine and dine a girl before I get up to bat."

"Oh yeah?"

Our fingers entwined, I walk Mo to the blanket. She sits down and crosses her legs while I pull out a bottle of wine and two Solo cups. I pour us each a glass and have her hold mine while I reach in for my other surprise.

"Whatcha got there?" she asks, trying to peer inside the basket.

"I knew the second my mom made apple pie that you wouldn't eat it. You've never been a pie lover. You always said if you were going to inhale calories, it had better be something better than pie."

"You remember that?" she asks, her eyes going soft.

"I remember everything, Mo." I pull a small, pink container out of the basket.

"Is that from Sweetie Pies?"

I open the box, and Mo nearly swallows her tongue at the sight in front of her.

"It is. Apparently they removed their double chocolate

fudge brownie from the menu a few years back—replaced it with a different brownie—but once I explained why I needed it, Sweetie insisted on making one."

Carefully, Mo sets both glasses of wine down in the grass and reaches for the brownie. She closes her eyes and gives a soft little moan as she takes a bite.

"There are no words for how amazing this is."

She holds the brownie up for me to taste, and we go back and forth like this until the entire thing is gone.

"I think we just ate our weight in brownie." She picks up her wine and takes a hefty sip. "But it was so worth it."

Seeing the look of contentment and pure happiness on her face—over a brownie no less—was worth the money I had to pay the bakery to dig up their old recipe and make the damn thing.

"It was." I finish off my wine, tossing my glass next to hers before I scoot back on the blanket and pull her between my legs.

I lean back on my hands, her back to my front, enjoying the way she settles against me as though it's her favorite place in the world to be.

The sun has begun its decent, casting a warm glow across the pond.

"Do you really remember the first time we…" her words trail off.

"The first time we what?"

"You know…had sex."

"Made love." I turn her face toward mine. "We may have been young—and in the beginning, we had no clue what we were doing—but make no mistake about it; every time I was inside of you, it was pure love."

"We were right here, on this blanket with the sun setting,

when we made love for the first time," she says, turning in my arms.

It's a memory I've pulled up several times over the years. "You crawled into my lap and told me you couldn't wait another second, that you needed me more than you needed your next breath."

"When we were done you…" She pauses, crawling out of my lap and over to the tree. It takes a few seconds for her to find what she's looking for. "There it is," she whispers, brushing her fingers over the carved bark. "When we were done, you carved our initials into the tree."

I can hardly breathe in the intensity of this moment. I wish things were still that simple, that I could hold her and tell her nothing has changed, that I still love her. I want that to be possible, but it feels like a lifetime ago. Still, I'm happy to be with her now.

Several seconds of weighted silence pass, and when she stands up, my stomach sinks. I knew we wouldn't be able to stay out here long, but I'd hoped to at least get through the sunset. Stacking the cups, I toss them in the basket, and when I look up to see what Mo is doing, all of the air disappears from my lungs.

There are a few moments in my life that have left me breathless—falling off a bull for the first time in competition, getting kicked by a bull, the day Mo broke my heart, and subsequently, the moment she stole every piece of it back.

This moment.

She's an angel, brought to Earth for the sole purpose of torturing me, and like the devil I am, I enjoy every minute of it.

Pulling her hair over one shoulder, Mo peeks at me. Her cheeks are stained the most delicious color of red as she slowly, deliberately lifts her shirt over her head. The flimsy material falls to the ground as she reaches behind her back to unhook her bra. The straps slip down her arms before joining her shirt on the grassy bank of the pond, and when she shimmies out of her panties and jeans, I nearly lose it.

Her body is breathtaking, a work of art meant to be examined and explored, and I'm the lucky son of a bitch who gets the privilege of doing just that.

I've seen Mo naked more times than I can count, but not once has it been like this. Not once has she seduced me with the soft sway of her hips or this hungry look in her eyes.

She's no longer the girl I knew all those years ago. She's turned into a beautiful, confident woman who I want to lay before me again. She's all-consuming: the rise and fall of her chest as she turns to face me, the goosebumps that scatter over her arms when my gaze traces her body, and the vulnerability in her eyes as she comes over to join me on the blanket.

I hold out my hand. Her fingers lace with mine as she straddles my legs and lowers herself to her knees.

Her hand, gentle and steady, cups the side of my face. "There might be six years of pain between us, but nothing has changed. I feel the same way today as I did back then." She hooks her fingers under the hem of my shirt, dragging it over my head, being extra careful with my shoulder. "And I can't wait another second to be with you, Rhett." She smiles. "In fact, I need it more than I need my next breath."

"Mo." I push my fingers into her hair, pulling her face to mine, and I kiss her with everything I have. Her tongue pushes between my lips, and we kiss until we're both panting and breathless.

With her forehead pressed to mine, she searches my eyes. I let her see everything—all the pain and love and happiness she's brought me. With her hands on my chest, she gently pushes me back onto the blanket. Her hair falls forward, brushing against my chest, creating a curtain. She kisses me once, twice, and then a third time before scooting back. My boots and socks are the first to go, followed by my jeans.

I reach for my cock, stroking from base to tip, watching the heat flare in her eyes. Mo always did love watching me touch myself.

"You were right," she whispers, slipping her hand between her thighs. "You remember everything."

Oh fuck. She slides two fingers into her pussy, drags them out, and circles her clit. And I am fucking screwed. I'm going to blow my load before I even get my dick wet. Head back, eyes closed, and pussy glistening, Mo torments me, one stroke of her fingers at a time.

My dick swells in my fist, my balls cocked and loaded for release. She moves her fingers out of her wet pussy and positions herself over my cock. Inch by inch, she wraps me in her body until she's fully seated.

My hands curl around her hips, guiding her. Nothing has ever felt this good. It's like a bonfire on a crisp fall night, a cold beer after the best ride of my life…it's like coming home.

Her body is soft and warm in my hands, and for the life of me, I can't remember it ever feeling this good. I look down at my cock sliding in and out of her pussy.

My bare cock.

Shit.

"Mo, baby." I still her with my hands.

She blinks heavily and follows my gaze to look at where we're connected.

She presses her knees to the ground next to me, slowly lifting herself off before lowering back down.

"You feel so good, Rhett."

Oh, God, I should tell her to stop, tell her to let me get a condom, but I can't. I fucking can't. *I have to.*

She repeats the movement, but this time I don't let her come back down.

"Baby, we forgot a condom."

The hazy lust clears just a bit from her eyes, and she glances at my wallet sticking out of the back pocket of my jeans.

Pulling her lips between her teeth, she says, "I haven't been with anyone since you, Rhett." Her eyes drift away from mine the second the words leave her mouth.

I grab her chin and turn her face to look at me. "You haven't slept with anyone?"

She tries to look away, but I don't let her.

"Why?" I breathe, my heart in my throat.

I wish I could say the same. I would give anything to turn back time and erase every nameless face, just to be able to give her what she's giving me.

"I—" She gasps when I shift my hips, pushing inside of her again.

"Why, Mo?"

"I didn't want anyone else. No one else can make me feel the way you do, and I didn't want to settle for anyone other than the man who owned my heart."

"Oh, sweetheart." My hands slide up her thighs, gripping them as she rocks back and forth on my cock. "I—I wish I could—"

"It's okay." She places a finger over my lips. I nip at the pad, and she smiles. "You thought I'd cheated on you. I didn't expect you to stay celibate."

"I'm clean. I have to get tested regularly with the organization, and I haven't been with anyone in a while anyway. As soon as you get on the pill, I promise there will be nothing between us ever again. Until then…" I reach for my wallet, grab a condom, and slip it on.

My cock slides back into her easily. It doesn't feel the same as it did before, but it's still amazing.

"Did you think of me—of us—when you got yourself off?" I ask, surging my hips forward. Her grunts grow louder with each thrust, her pleasure just beyond my grasp.

"Yes! Every night, you're all I thought about," she admits. "Oh, God, Rhett. You're all I think about."

I pull her down on top of me so I can kiss her. "That's so hot, baby. I want to watch you—watch you get yourself off the way you did when I wasn't around."

My movements speed up, along with Mo's breathing. She loves the dirty talk more than any woman I've ever known.

"Will you let me watch, Mo? Can I watch you finger this tight little pussy?" I squeeze a hand between us, press my thumb to her clit, and she bucks against me.

"Yes! Yes! You can watch. Oh, God." She moans loud and long as her sweat-soaked body slides against mine, her breasts swinging in front of my face.

I capture a tight nipple with my lips, sucking it deep into my mouth. I flick the bud with my tongue the way I know she likes, and Mo's body explodes atop mine.

Her pussy contracts, tightening around my throbbing dick. I continue to move in and out of her, relishing the way it feels to be connected once again.

"Rhett," she breathes, her husky voice causing a tingle at the base of my spine. It swirls upward through my stomach and explodes through my chest, radiating to every inch of my body.

My orgasm slams into me with enough force to blur my vision. I bury my face in Mo's neck, breathing her in as I moan through my release.

She collapses on top of me, and we lay like this for several seconds.

Eventually she pushes herself up, brushes the hair out of her face, and grins, sending my heart into a frenzy.

"You take my breath away," I whisper.

Tears fill her big, beautiful eyes. "I don't deserve you." Her voice cracks, but she continues. "I don't deserve your forgiveness, or your heart."

"Stop." I shake my head. "Mo—"

"Let me finish," she pleads. I shut my mouth and nod, unsure of where this could be going. "I don't deserve a second chance at your heart, but if you give it, I won't turn it down. I'm still madly in love with you, Rhett Allen."

Mo Gallagher is sitting on top of me, naked, begging for a second chance at my heart, and for the life of me I'm trying to remember what it was like to hear her say those three little words.

"Say it."

"I love you," she whispers.

I look down at her hand on my heart and place mine over it. We're really here together. Somehow this has happened...

"It's okay if you're not there yet," she says. "I don't need the words. But I do need you to know how I feel."

The words sit on the tip of my tongue. I feel them in every fiber of my being, but fear keeps me from pushing them out. Everything between us is happening so fast, and while I want it, I'm not sure Mo fully understands what she'll be getting in to. She hasn't been a part of my professional life. She doesn't realize the time constraints it puts on my personal life—how much time I spend traveling and interacting with my fans. What if it's too much for her, and she decides she can't do it? Her life hasn't been fully her own in six years. It isn't even now.

I love her—of course I love her. It was silly of me to ever pretend otherwise. But once I say it, it's out there, and I'm totally exposed again. We have so much more to talk about, to live through. I need to be sure she's certain before I give her this last sliver of myself.

Reaching for her face, I curl my hands around her neck, pull her to me, and pour every emotion I feel for her into our kiss. The sun dips below the horizon, bringing with it a blanket of stars as I make love to Mo for a second time, showing with my body what I'm still afraid to say.

CHAPTER
Twenty-Three

Monroe

The bell above the door rings as Claire breezes into Animal Haven.

"Mom said you were working late," she says, holding up two containers of Chinese food. "Thought you could use some fuel, and selfishly, I was bored at home by myself."

"I'm starving," I groan, reaching for one of the containers she sets on my desk. "I hope you brought some forks."

She digs around in her purse. "I came prepared." She tosses me a set of utensils, and I tear through the plastic and open the container.

The scent of pepper steak makes my mouth water. "You are too good to me," I say.

She sighs as she takes her first bite.

The door flies open again and Rhett walks in, wearing nothing but a pair of low-slung Wranglers and brown boots. His cell is wedged between his shoulder and ear, and beads of sweat drip down his chest. Ruby is a few steps behind him. Her arthritic hips make it hard to keep up, but if Rhett's around, she wants to be next to him.

Can't say I blame her.

"I want to lick him," Claire whispers.

"I *have* licked him."

"Bitch."

I grin and take another bite. Claire and I eat silently as Rhett finishes his call. He tucks his cell in his pocket and gives us an easy smile.

I swallow hard. This man is going to be the death of me, and Claire too, for that matter.

She clears her throat. "I didn't know you were here or I would've brought more food."

"That's okay." He pulls out the shirt he had tucked in the back of his jeans and wipes it over his face. "I'm going to have dinner with Trevor and Coop. It's Thursday, which means five-dollar wings."

Claire perks up at the mention of Trevor, and I make a mental note to ask her about that after Rhett leaves.

"You ladies are more than welcome to join us, if you'd like."

"Woof!"

Rhett looks down at Ruby and smiles. "Don't worry, pretty girl, I'll bring you left overs."

Ruby's tail thumps against the floor as Rhett pats her head.

"Where is Pickles?" he asks, looking around the room.

I shrug. "Who knows? He's been in feline heaven since I gave him free reign of the place. Knowing him, he's probably in the back prancing in front the dogs, taunting them."

"So, he's officially an Animal Haven house pet?" Claire asks.

"For now, unless he does something wrong. I warned him that he's on a ninety-day probation period."

Claire grins. "I'm sure you did."

"So, what do you say, wings tonight?" Rhett asks.

"We'd love to," Claire answers immediately.

What I wouldn't give for the freedom to say yes. But that's not my reality. "I can't."

"What?" Claire pouts. "Why not?"

"Come on, Claire. You know I can't leave my dad by himself."

"My mom will stay with him, or we can call my aunt. You know they won't mind."

I shake my head. "It's not fair to ask them to do more than they already do. But you should still go." I hate the idea of her going without me. It's silly. I know she doesn't really have a thing for Rhett, but that doesn't make it any easier knowing she gets to spend time him while I'm stuck at home.

Stuck at home.

Fuck.

I've got to stop thinking like this, or I'll drive myself insane.

"That's okay," Rhett offers. "I don't even have to go. I'd much rather hang out with you anyway."

"Awwww," Claire croons.

"No. You should go," I tell him. "You haven't gotten to spend a lot of time with Trevor."

He tilts his head. "You sure? I can come by afterward."

"I'd like that."

"I'll call you when I'm on my way." He leans down to give me a kiss and looks at Claire. "Dirty Dicks at seven, if you'd like to come."

"Thanks for the invite, but I was only going if Mo went."

I could kiss her.

"Your loss," Rhett says, turning toward the front door.

"Tell me about it," Claire mumbles.

She drops onto her chair as Rhett walks out the door. "He really is gorgeous."

"Don't I know it."

We lean our heads to the left, watching the way his jeans hug his ass as he walks to his truck.

"Please tell me his ass is as tight as it looks."

"Tighter."

"I hate you."

"We need to get you laid."

She takes another bite. "Tell me about it."

"Maybe you could get laid by Trevor."

Claire sputters, inhaling a chunk of her food. I slap her back when she starts coughing, and I can't help but laugh.

"You do want to get laid by Trevor, don't you?"

"Why would you think that?"

"Really? Every time his name is mentioned, you get this dreamy look in your eyes. I can practically see cartoon hearts floating above your head."

"I do not."

"Do too. And I guarantee I'm not the only one who's noticed."

"I don't have a thing for Trevor Allen. That would just be silly."

"Why? Trevor is a great guy."

"He's also four years younger than I am."

"So?"

"Plus, he's a firefighter. I don't date firefighters."

Claire's father ran into a burning building and never came back out.

"Well, if you did date him, no one would blame you."

"I'm not going to date him. Can we not talk about my love life, or lack thereof? Tell me what's going on between you and Rhett, and don't leave out a single juicy detail."

"There isn't much to tell," I lie.

"Have you slept with him?"

"Three times, although he would call it making love."

Her fork drops on the desk. She fans her face and lets out a dreamy sigh. "Of course he would. And there is *so* much to tell. Spill your guts, you lucky bitch."

So I do.

We spend the next hour laughing as I give her a rundown of all the sweet things Rhett has said and done. I even give her a hint of the sexy stuff—but not too much, because those memories are mine.

Claire picks up the empty containers and her napkin and dumps them in the trash. "I'm happy for you, Mo. Just take things slow, okay? You've got a lot going on in your life, and I don't want to you see you get derailed when he leaves."

"I told him I love him."

She freezes. Her eyes widen, and she lowers herself back into the chair. "Well, that's not taking things slow."

"I couldn't *not* tell him," I admonish. "I don't want any regrets where he's concerned. We were in the moment, and it felt right, so I just said it."

"And..."

"He didn't say it back."

Claire furrows her brow. "Did you expect him to?"

"Yes... No." I shake my head. "I don't know. I mean, of course I hoped he would, but I should've known he might not be there."

"After everything you've told me, it sounds like he still has feelings for you."

I nod. "I think so too. He didn't give me the words, but I could feel it—he still cares about me."

"Of course he does; you two have been through a lot together. Does it bother you that he didn't say he loved you?"

I take a breath and think for a second. "No. He'll say it when he's ready—when the time is right. Things are still fresh between us, and I told him I love him because I promised myself I'd always be honest with my feelings."

"What if he doesn't get there? What if this thing between you crashes and burns?"

"Well, geez, thanks for the vote of confidence, Claire."

"What? I'm just trying to help you think this through. You two just got back together, and you're throwing yourself into it full force because that's what you do—and I love that about you—but you're my best friend, and I don't want to see you get hurt."

I place a hand on her arm. "I'm doing this the only way I know how. It's going to be okay. I promise."

"How do you know?"

"I can't explain it, Claire. I can just feel it. When I'm with Rhett, it's like the stars align and there's a calm to my world I haven't felt since we were together before."

"It's called lust."

"It's called *love*." I laugh. I love Claire, and I adore her even more for looking out for me. "You've never felt it, so I wouldn't expect you to understand."

She scoffs. "I've been in love before."

I roll my eyes. "Noah Cunningham doesn't count. We were in seventh grade."

She pouts. "He gave me his dessert every day for a year."

"And when you fall in love, that man will give you his heart every day for life."

The easy look on her face fades. "Rhett hasn't given you his heart."

"I think he will. Just you wait and see."

CHAPTER
Twenty-Four

Monroe

"He's already been bathed, and he's in bed. Probably not asleep yet if you want to talk to him."

"Thank you, Sharon."

"You're welcome, sweetie." She gives me a hug, grabs her purse, and slips out the door.

I tiptoe down the hall, trying to be quiet in case Dad is already asleep, but when I pass by his room, he calls to me.

Closing my eyes, I stop outside his door. Part of me wants to keep walking, get into the shower, and act like I didn't hear him. But that's not fair to either of us.

We haven't talked much since the other night at the Allens' when he told me I was hovering. We've been living around each other, neither one of us ready to break the ice. I'm not sure I'm ready now, but I might as well get it over with.

"Hey, Daddy." I push his door open. "Everything okay?"

He taps the side of his bed with his fingers. The floor squeaks beneath my feet as I move across the room. Lowering the bedrail, I place my hands under his arms, stuff a pillow behind his back and sit down.

"You w-worked late t-tonight."

"I had a horse come in today. Palomino. She's real pretty."

"W-w-was she spooked?"

"A little. I stayed until she was settled. Sorry I wasn't home for dinner."

"That's o-okay." He places his hand over mine. "I'm s-sorry about the other d-day—" Dad's words turn into a cough. I grab the glass of water from his nightstand. Tilting it to his lips, I help him take a sip.

"Better?"

He nods.

"You don't have to apologize, Dad. I didn't mean to embarrass you."

"I know y-you didn't. I sh-shouldn't have said anything."

"Yes, you should. I do too much for you. I need to let you be more independent." Swallowing, I look at our joined hands.

"T-talk to me, M-mo."

"It's all just so overwhelming sometimes," I admit, tears blurring my eyes. "I get up at the ass crack of dawn, work all day, come home and take care of you, and sometimes it's easier to do things for you than wait for you to do them on your own, because all I can think about is taking a hot shower and crawling into bed."

I hate the words coming from my mouth. They make me feel weak and like a horrible daughter, but they're the truth. "I'm so sorry, Daddy."

He tugs my hand. A wave of heat washes over me as I lower myself onto the bed. I curl up next to my dad like I did as a young girl. He tries to quiet me, running his good hand over the top of my head, but it's useless. Pressing my face into his shirt, I cry. My shoulders heave and sobs burst from my throat. Only when my tears begin to dry does he speak.

"We need t-to talk about Animal H-Haven."

"What about it?" I sit up and wipe the tears from my face.

"It's t-t-time."

"I don't understand. Time for what?"

"To c-close it."

"What? No!" I gasp, scooting back on the bed. "No way. Why would you want to do that?"

"You can g-go back to school, and I can go t-t-to go to a nice h—"

"Don't say it," I hiss. "Don't you dare say it. There's no way I'm putting you in some shady nursing home."

"It's not your ch-choice, M-mo. It's m-mine. It's also m-my choice whether or n-not to c-c-close Animal H-Haven."

"I can't believe you're doing this. Jesus Christ, Dad. I can't get back into the vet program. It's too late. They'll never accept me, and I'm not sure I'd even want to go back. Animal Haven is my life. If you take it away, what will I have left?"

"It isn't your l-life. It *stole* your l-life. I only w-want you to be h-happy."

Emotion clogs my throat. "I am happy," I whisper, a fresh wave of tears falling down my face. "I'm happy," I repeat, unsure who I'm trying to convince.

Even I can hear the uncertainty in my voice, and if I can't convince myself, there's no way I'll convince him. "Let me think about it. Promise you won't do anything until we have more time to talk."

Pinching his lips together, he nods.

My emotions are running high, and I need to get out of here. "I'm going to take a shower." I pull the pillow from behind him, help him lie down, and kiss his forehead. "We'll talk tomorrow."

Emotionally and physically spent, I walk down the hall,

stripping out of my clothes along the way. In the shower, steaming hot water flows over my body, easing my aching muscles. I stand under the spray for far longer than normal, taking my time as I wash my hair and scrub my body—and only because I'm hopeful Rhett will come over, I shave my legs.

My body is refreshed, but my heart is still bruised as I climb out. The soft cotton of the towel feels good when I wrap it around my body. I stand in front of the mirror until the fog clears, and then I stare at my reflection.

Somewhere along the way, I lost myself. I lost Mo Gallagher, and as much as I want to find her again, I don't know where to start. If Dad decides to shut down Animal Haven, I don't know what I'll do. I can't imagine an existence that doesn't involve those animals day in and day out.

Visions of a bitchy cat pop into my head just as a knock sounds at the front door. It could really only be one person, so I don't bother putting on my clothes. With water dripping from my hair and a white towel knotted between my breasts, I pad down the hall. I peek through the blinds to make sure it's Rhett before opening the door.

"Hey."

"Jesus Christ, Mo. You can't answer the door like this." He pushes his way into the house and shuts the door. "Please tell me this isn't a thing for you."

"Gotta be honest, Rhett, I didn't expect you to be so upset about it."

"Trust me," he breathes, pulling me into his arms. "I'm anything but upset. Intrigued? Yes. Horny as fuck? Hell yes. Upset? Not one bit."

"Shhhh," I laugh, covering his mouth with my own. "My dad is sleeping in the other room."

"Sorry," he whispers, pulling me in for another kiss. "Guess that means I can't have my way with you."

"Is that what you were hoping for? A quickie?" Not that that sounds bad—I'm just not sure it's something I can do with my dad in the other room.

Wrapping his hand around the wet strands of my hair, he tugs, forcing me to look up at him. "You and I will never be a quick fuck. Understood?"

I push up on my toes, sealing my lips over his. "Understood."

"I feel like a teenager sneaking into his girlfriend's house while her parents are gone." He makes a face. "Only your dad is home. I'm thinking we should sit at least three feet apart on the couch, and you better not touch me, Mo Gallagher." He pushes me away from him.

I laugh, reaching for him. "This is exactly what I needed. You are what I needed tonight."

"Bad night?"

I shrug, not wanting to rehash everything. I just want to cuddle up with Rhett and enjoy being in his arms. "Long day."

"What can I do to make it better?" He rubs his hands up and down my arms. "You know what? I've got an idea. Follow me." He kicks off his shoes and leads me down the hall. "Is your room still on the right?"

"Yeah. Why?"

"You'll see."

He pulls me into my room and locks the door behind us.

"You do realize my dad can't get out of bed on his own."

"Right." He furrows his brow but leaves the door locked as he drags me to the edge of my bed. "You are way overdressed, Ms. Gallagher." Dipping a finger in the top of my towel, he tugs it down until the knot loosens and it falls around my hips.

Goosebumps scatter across my body as his eyes sweep over me.

"You're so beautiful, baby." Snaking his arm around my waist, he hauls me in close. He cradles my jaw while his eyes search mine. "I would kill to make love to you right now."

"No need to commit a felony." Wrapping my fingers around his, I guide his hand away from my face and press it between my legs.

"Mo," he hisses, sliding two fingers along my slit. He pushes them inside, and I buck my hips against his hand. "This isn't why I brought you in here." His voice is thick—strained—and the gritty sound settles between my legs, creating a rush of moisture.

"Maybe this is what I want."

"Not tonight, baby. Tonight, I've got other plans." He drags his fingers out of my pussy, circles them along my clit, and pushes back in.

His touch lights my body on fire. I moan, rotating my hips, a silent plea to keep going. "Please, don't stop," I pant.

Rhett's mouth captures mine in a heated kiss. His teeth bite lightly on my lower lip before sucking it into his mouth, making me shudder. I grasp his wrist, encouraging him to push harder, faster.

"You like that?" His lips move down my neck. He sucks at the soft spot behind my ear as he curls both fingers deep inside me.

My stomach clenches tight as waves of electricity shoot through my body.

"That's it, baby, let go for me," he coaxes, and like the good girl I am, my body follows his command.

Rhett slows his hand to an aching pace, riding out the remainder of my orgasm, but when I reach for his cock, he shakes his head.

"Nope. Tonight is about you, and I've got plans. Follow me."

With my hand in his, Rhett leads me to the en-suite bathroom. After my mom left, and I hit puberty, Dad switched rooms with me so I could have my own attached bathroom. And on a night like tonight, I'm so grateful. I try not to be self-conscious about the state of my house, but it's difficult when I'm here with Rhett. He probably has one of those big fancy tubs with a walk-in shower, and all I've got is a stained vinyl tub, accented by eighties floral wall paper.

But he doesn't seem to mind. He leans into the tub, twists the stopper, and turns the knob. He keeps his hand under the water as he adjusts the temperature, and when he gets it just right, he turns to me.

"Where's your girly shit?"

"What makes you think I have girly shit?"

"Every girl has some sort of girly shit."

"Under the sink."

He leans down and starts pulling things out, setting them on the counter one by one. Lavender oil. Bubble bath. Three peony-scented candles. Taking the bottle of bubble bath, he dumps a solid stream into the water and adds a few drops of lavender. I almost ask how he got so good at drawing bubble baths, but then I remember it probably involves another woman and I'd rather not know.

"Lighter?"

I disappear from the bathroom, coming back a few seconds later with the lighter. By the time he lights the candles and places them around the room, the tub is almost full.

He turns off the water. "Your bubble bath awaits," he says, motioning toward the bathtub. It's overflowing with bubbles, and when he flicks off the bathroom light, we're surrounded by the smell of lavender and the faint glow of the candles.

"But I already took a shower," I say, flicking the ends of my still-wet hair.

"Fine, suit yourself." Rhett tugs off his shirt, followed by his jeans, boxers, and socks. "I'll get in."

"Not without me you won't." I scurry across the tiny space.

Rhett climbs in first. He stretches his legs out as far as they'll go, but they're still bent, and he can't be at all comfortable.

"Come here." He holds out a hand, helping me into the tub.

Bubbles encase my body as I slip into the warm, sudsy water. Gripping my waist, Rhett situates me between his legs. Pooling water in his hands, he lets it fall over my shoulders and down my back, and then those amazing hands follow the same path.

His fingers work their way over my muscles at a slow, methodic pace.

"Oh, God," I moan, dropping my chin to my chest. "That feels so good."

Sliding the palms of his hands up my spine, he curls his fingers over my shoulders, kneading them over and over, working out all the knots before moving his way down my back.

"I feel like I should be massaging *your* shoulder, not the other way around."

"My shoulder is good, Mo, getting better every day. Let me take care of you right now."

How can I say no to that?

"We need to talk about Animal Haven," he says after a moment.

"What about it?" I ask, wincing as he works his hands along my lower back.

"Does that hurt?"

"Just a little." I wince again, and he stops.

"What happened?"

"I had to haul bags of shavings to the barn for that horse I got in today. Think maybe I pulled something."

"Why didn't you have me do it?"

"You weren't there yet, and it needed to be done. Plus, I won't chance you reinjuring your shoulder. It's not a big deal."

He sighs. "It is a big deal. Who helps you out when you have big loads like that?"

"Usually it's nothing I can't handle."

"And if it is?"

"I call Coop or Sean."

"Not anymore. Now you call me. Got it?"

"I'll do whatever you say as long you promise to keep massaging." I roll my head to the side. Rhett moves his hands to knead the area I just opened up.

"Mo, you really need to get some extra help at Animal Haven. I don't know how you've managed all these years by yourself—"

"I haven't been completely by myself. I have volunteers."

"No," he corrects. "You have Claire and Tess."

"I have a couple more, but they've been busy lately and haven't been able to help out as much."

"That's a start, Mo, but you need someone more regularly. I hate to think about you out there doing all that shit on your own when I go back to Houston."

My heart stops, along with my breathing. It's the first time either one us of has mentioned Houston. What's going to happen to us when he leaves? What happens to me?

Swallowing, I blink back tears, grateful I'm facing away from him. "I, uh…I can't afford to hire anyone. All the money we make from donations and adoptions goes straight back into the business. I don't keep a dime for myself."

His hands pause for a second on my shoulders, then pick back up again. "How do you pay the bills?"

"I just told you; all the money goes back into the business."

"I mean at home. How do you pay the bills at home?"

"The house is paid off; so is my truck. Dad gets Social Security, and we have the money he made from selling Ruff Times, along with what he draws from his retirement. I also make a decent amount in tips on the weekends. Why all the questions?"

"I just worry about you, that's all."

I rest my head against his shoulder, melting into him as he wraps his arms around me. We sit like this until the suds start to fade and the water cools. I'm not ready to leave our little cocoon, so I pull the plug, drain some of the cool water, and refill the tub with hot so I can relax back into Rhett's arms.

"Have you ever thought about going back to school?" he asks, his voice echoing off the walls.

That's a tough question to answer. "I gave up on that a long time ago. The money isn't there, and I've grown to love Animal Haven."

"What if the money was there? Would you go back?"

"They probably wouldn't let me into the program since I gave up my seat."

"Christ, Mo, this is a what-if situation. Play along, would ya?"

"Fine. Yes, if I didn't have Animal Haven and the money was there, I would go back to school. Happy?"

"Yes." He kisses the side of my head. "Sorry for pushing you; I just want you to be happy."

"I am happy, Rhett," I say, turning in his arms. I feel like I'm having the same conversation I just had with my dad, only with Rhett I can be brutally honest. "I haven't always been, but I'm getting there, and you play a big part in that. Before you, I had nothing to live for. I worked, took care of my father, ate and slept, and on rare occasions, I'd hang out with Claire. I was depressed and lonely. Now I have moments like this to look forward to. Quiet bubble baths, family dinners, someone to share my day with—it's the small things like that I didn't realize I was missing."

Rhett kisses me softly, brushing a strand of hair from my face. "We need to talk about what we're going to do when I go back to work."

"Have you been cleared?"

"Not yet, but it won't be long. I have an appointment with my orthopedic doctor next Friday. I want you to come with me."

"Back to Houston? Rhett—"

"I already know what you're thinking, and I've got it figured out. My appointment isn't until the afternoon. It's an hour and a half drive. We'll get up early and take care of the animals, drive to Houston, and go to the appointment. We'll be able to make it back to Heaven in time for evening chores. And if we have a few minutes to spare, I'd love to show you my house."

I open my mouth, and Rhett takes it as an invitation to kiss me. "Just think about it," he whispers against my lips. "Don't say no; just think about it."

"Okay."

"Okay?"

"Yeah." I'll figure it out this time; I'll find a way to make it work—possibly even make it an overnight trip—but it's going to be difficult to do anything like this on a regular basis, and I wonder if that's something Rhett will be willing to put up with.

"It's always going to be like this," I whisper. "Are you sure this is what you want?"

He cups my jaw. "What are you talking about?"

"If I am who you want, you need to understand that you aren't just choosing me; you're choosing my father too. We're a package deal. I will take care of him as long as I'm able, and that's going to make it difficult to have a normal relationship. I can't just pick up and go when you travel, or even come see you at home. I need you to think about this before—"

"I don't need to think about it, Mo. I want this to work."

He rests his forehead against mine.

"And I know that means you and your father and Animal Haven and Ruby and that damn cat—"

"Pickles."

He smiles. "That's the one. But what about you, Mo? What happens when I go back on tour and I'm gone for weeks at a time? Are you going to be okay with that? What if it's too much and you change your mind about us—about me?"

I take a deep breath and close my eyes before I look up. "That's not going to happen. I let you get away once, and I won't make that mistake again. You'll see."

He stares at me for a long moment, seeming to absorb my words, and I can't decide if he's trying to convince himself I'm telling the truth or trying to stop himself from telling me how he feels.

"Can we make love now?" My hand dips under the water as I run it down his stomach. I curl my fingers around his cock, swirl my thumb around the head, and revel in the way his eyelids droop. "I really want that."

"You think you can be quiet?"

"I guess we'll find out."

With an arm around my back and another beneath my legs, he lifts us both out of the tub. I don't even care that we leave a trail of water as he moves out of the bathroom and drops me on the bed, because all I can think about is how he looks crawling toward me and how his big, strong body feels pressing me into the mattress.

"I love you," I whisper.

CHAPTER
Twenty-Five

Rhett

I wake as the first rays of sunlight slip through the blinds, making it hard to open my eyes. My body feels rested, the pain in my shoulder not as pronounced as it has been, and I wonder if maybe it has something to do with Mo and her bubble bath, or the full body massage she returned after we made love.

With a lazy smile on my face, I look over to see her asleep next to me. Dark hair fans the pillow beneath her head, a few pieces sticking to my beard when I roll over to get a better look at her. She looks so peaceful with her hands tucked under head, her lips parted as though they're just waiting for mine.

Last night was the best sleep I've had in a long time. After I lifted her from the tub, we made love. She lay in my arms for several long minutes afterward, and about the time I was ready to doze off, she rolled me onto my stomach, straddled my hips, and gave me the best damn massage I've ever had. Her hands rivaled any masseuse I've ever paid for. Or maybe it's just that it was her.

It was well after two in the morning before we finally pulled the covers over our naked bodies and succumbed to sleep. I lift my head, glancing over Mo to get a look at the alarm clock. Unable to resist her perfect lips, I kiss her gently as I lay my head back on the pillow. She smiles before she opens her eyes, and it's the sexiest thing in the world. Her lashes flutter open as she blinks up at me.

"Good morning, beautiful."

"Good morning." Shifting her body closer to mine, she tangles our legs together.

I nearly sigh in contentment when she lifts a hand, threading her fingers through my hair.

"Why did you wake me up?" she rasps, letting her eyes drift shut.

"I wanted to see those beautiful eyes before I leave. And maybe steal a kiss or two."

Her eyes pop open. "Why are you leaving?"

Resting my hand over her hip, I squeeze. "I wasn't sure what time your dad gets up, and I figured you might not want me here when he does."

Her sleepy eyes watch me. "I want you here."

If that doesn't about kill me, I don't know what will. "You do?"

She yawns. "Always. I don't want to hide us."

"I don't want that either."

"Good." She smiles and presses her face in the pillow.

"I'm going to go make breakfast. What does your dad like?"

"No," she whines, peeking at me with one eye. "Don't leave. You're nice and warm."

"I'm also a growing boy who's starved."

She threads my fingers with hers under the covers and draws my hand to her thigh, positioning it between her legs. She's soaking wet.

"I've got something you can eat," she says in a raspy voice.

"No." I pull my hand away and kiss her bare shoulder. "First I feed you; then I eat you."

I hop off the mattress before she can use her seductress ways on me. I pull my jeans on. "You didn't tell me what your dad likes for breakfast."

"Don't worry about him. He usually doesn't get up until ten, and it's only—" She cranes her neck to look at the alarm clock. "Five," she moans, flopping her head back down on the pillow. "Sharon will make him breakfast when she gets here."

"You sure?"

"Positive. Just hurry back; it's cold in here without you."

"Yes, ma'am."

Mo is sitting up in bed waiting for me twenty minutes later when I return with a bowl of scrambled eggs and a plate of jellied toast. The sheet is tucked around her, but I can see the outline of her breasts and the tight peaks of her nipples.

"Gimme." She holds out her hands, taking the bowl and plate.

"What would you like to drink?"

"Milk would be good."

I head back to the kitchen and pour each of us a glass of milk, taking the time to add chocolate syrup to hers because I remember how much she loves chocolate milk.

"Your milk, madam."

She takes the glass and looks down at it, her eyes smiling when they find me. "You remembered."

I can barely understand her words with the food in her mouth, and we both laugh. She covers her mouth and swallows before taking a drink.

"I told you before," I remind her, "I remember everything."

"Thank you." She takes another sip, sets her milk on the

nightstand, and digs back into her eggs. "These are delicious. I can't remember the last time I had scrambled eggs."

I frown. "What do you normally eat for breakfast?"

She shrugs. "If I eat breakfast, it's usually a Pop-Tart or a bag of chips in the truck on the way to work. I'm not about to get up earlier just to cook myself a meal."

I manage to work my fork into the bowl and steal a bite. "Breakfast is the most important meal of the day. You need to take care of yourself, Mo."

"I know." She sighs. "I just don't always have the time."

"We're going to work on that."

"We, huh?"

"Yes."

Her smile is thoughtful. "I like the sound of that."

We each take another bite, and then Mo hands me the bowl and grabs her milk. "Will you tell me more about the PBR and your life away from here? I feel like we're always talking about me."

My life seems to have shifted quite a bit over the last few weeks—to the point that I hardly remember what it was like before my accident.

"There isn't much to tell. I wake up, train, and spend time with my buddies. Most of the time I'm on the road, traveling from city to city for events. It's not very appealing."

"Do any of your friends have an old lady?"

I lift a brow. "And old lady? What are we, a motorcycle club?"

She laughs. "You know what I mean. Are any of them married?"

"A few are, but most are single. Why?"

"I'm just curious. I feel like nothing in my life has changed and everything in yours has."

"Does that bother you?" I ask, taking a bite of eggs.

She picks at a piece of toast, eventually tearing off a chunk and putting it in her mouth. I want to say something, get into her head and get her talking, but I decide to wait her out.

"It bothers me that I don't know anything about you anymore. I used to know everything."

"What's my favorite color?"

She rolls her eyes. "Red."

"My favorite meal?"

"Sirloin, garlic potatoes, and fried okra."

"What did I do on my eighteenth birthday?"

"You went skydiving."

"And what happened when I got in the air?"

Monroe snorts with laughter. "You chickened out. Realized you were scared of heights."

"It's not funny." I give her a pointed look.

"It was at the time."

"I've cried twice in my life."

The smile falls from her face. "I miss your Grandma Allen."

"I do too," I reply.

"I also miss Mugsy," she says, referring to my beloved dog.

I take her hand, running my thumb over her wrist. "You know the important things. You know what makes me smile, what makes me mad. You know my soap boxes—those haven't changed. You know I'm a stickler for punctuality."

"It's a virtue," she whispers.

"It is a virtue."

She smiles. Turning her hand over, she links our fingers together, pulling them to rest on her thigh.

"You know how hard I worked to get where I am today. You were with me through all of my amateur rides. I could go on and on, Mo, but it all boils down to the same thing. You know me better than anyone else. Yes, there are things in my life that have changed. There are things you don't know, but you'll learn them over time."

"You're right. I guess I just want to know other things—like who your best friend is, where you hang out after an event. Who's there with you, watching out for you when you get on a bull? What do you do on a lazy Sunday when you don't have to train?"

"Lincoln Bennett. He's a surly son of a bitch, but you'll love him, and he'll think the world of you. The Broken Boot is about the best bar in town. My dad is always with me, and if he can't make it, I've got Linc there to watch out for me. On Sundays, I do what I've always done…"

"Watch movies," we both say.

"See? Not much has changed. I've spent the last six years passing time."

"Passing time, huh? What were you waiting on?"

"Didn't realize it at the time, but I was waiting on you."

"Thank you," she whispers.

"For what?"

Monroe leans across the bed and kisses me. "For being the guy I fell in love with all those years ago. For giving me a second chance. Should I keep going?"

"You should probably kiss me again."

"I can do that."

CHAPTER
Twenty-Six

Monroe

"Honey, I'm home." I shoulder my way through the front door, only to come to a freezing halt when I look across the living room and see my dad and Sharon sitting at the kitchen table. Dad's wheelchair is pressed as close to Sharon as it can get. Their joined hands rest on the table and—*are they kissing*?

It's a soft kiss, the mere touch of her lips against his, but it's still a kiss. I didn't even know my dad could kiss. He can barely smile. Feeling like a third wheel in my home, and unsure what to do—because they clearly didn't hear me come in—I kick the door shut with enough power to make a loud thud.

Sharon's head pops up, but my father's a little slower to react. Her eyes are wide as she slides away from the table, easing her hand out of my father's.

"Hey, Monroe," she stammers, wiping her hands down the front of her shirt.

"Y-you're home early," Dad says, backing his electric wheelchair away from the table. "It's S-Saturday. I thought y-you had to b-b-bartend tonight."

"I do."

Sharon looks like she's going to be sick, and my dad is acting as if nothing happened.

I set my purse down on the table. "I wanted to take a quick shower before my shift, but I can do that at Coop's if I'm interrupting something." I wave between the two lovebirds.

Clearing her throat, Sharon excuses herself. "I'm going to give you two some privacy." Her fingers graze the top of my dad's hand on her way out of the room, and I can't help but smile.

Eyebrows raised, I turn to my dad, giving him a silent *what's up with that* look.

"Rhett s-stayed the n-n-night the other night."

"Oh no," I laugh. "You are not turning this around on me. I haven't been hiding Rhett from you. I've been open and honest about us getting back together. But this...what is this? Are you and Sharon..."

I leave my words hanging in the air because I don't even know what to say to my father. *Are you dating? Are you sleeping together?*

Can he even have sex?

Shit. I shake the thoughts away before I give myself a heart attack.

"You know what? It's none of my business. You are a grown man capable of making your own decisions." With my hands raised in the air, I turn to go down the hall, only to stop when my dad says...

"I'm h-happy."

With a resigned sigh, I turn around and walk back to the table, sitting down next to my father.

"She m-makes me h-h-happy," he says, his voice cracking on the last word. "Haven't h-had that in a l-l-long time."

Well, shit, if that doesn't make my heart smile, I don't know what will. "When did you two…start dating? Is that what we're calling it here? Because I'm a little confused. You're gonna have to help a daughter out."

Dad laughs, and I realize that's a sound I haven't heard in way too long. "We're n-not dating."

"Wow. Okay. Not gonna lie, this is a little awkward. So, you're…sleeping together? Is this a physical thing?"

The words sound worse coming out of my mouth than they did in my head, and all I can think is *Abort! Abort!* "Forget I said that. If it's a physical thing, I'd rather not know." A little lost and a lot confused, I rub a hand over my face.

"No. N-not sleeping together. She just m-makes me happy."

I stare at him, confused. "So, you're not dating and you're not…you know…sleeping together. What are you?"

"F-friends."

"Friends don't kiss."

Dad's brows furrow. I can tell he's getting frustrated as he tries to explain.

"Maybe I can help," Sharon says, walking back into the kitchen. She retakes the seat she vacated, rests her hand on my dad's, and looks at me.

"Your mother has been gone for a long time, and so has my Jack. Life gets lonely sometimes, which is why I offered to take over as your father's caregiver. It's also why I don't mind letting you go do extra things while I stay here with him. Your dad is a wonderful man, Mo, but I don't have to tell you that." She smiles at me and then looks at him. "I've spent the last six years taking care of him, every day. You don't spend that much time with someone and not grow close to them."

I guess I didn't look at it like that. To me, Sharon is my best friend's mom and a nurse who takes care of my dad. Sure, she's always been special to me, but I guess I failed to consider her as a widowed woman who still wants to be cared for and loved.

"I don't want to get married—Jack was the love of my life—but I've realized over the years that it's okay for me to love another man. It's okay for me to find comfort with another man's touch, even if it's just the touch of his hand."

"Do you love my father?"

She answers without hesitation. "Very much."

Dad squeezes Sharon's hand, and she bends down so he can kiss her cheek. The move is so fluid I'd swear they've been doing it for years.

"How long has this been going on?"

Sharon shrugs. "I can't answer that. It's been organic over the last several years. Your father and I have shared many stories over many meals. We've laughed, cried, watched movies, done all the things a normal couple would do, and one day, it just happened."

"Is this why you want to go into assisted living?" I ask, looking at Dad. "Because you want more privacy?" I'm not sure how much more privacy the two of them could get. I'm usually only home long enough to sleep.

Sharon frowns at Dad, clearly unaware of the talk he and I had the other day. "You're not going into assisted living, not as long as I'm around," she declares. "You might need help, but you're too independent for a nursing home."

"That's exactly what I said. See? You're out numbered, Dad."

"No," he says. "I want t-to give y-you more priv—acy. You and R-rhett or whomever y-you might date."

"Dad." I close my eyes, hating that he feels this way.

"Move in with me," Sharon tells him, a little too eagerly for my liking.

"No." I shake my head.

"Why not?" she challenges. "I'm with him all the time anyway. This way you'll save some money. You can stop paying me to come over, and I can enjoy my retirement with your father and take care of him at the same time. It's a win-win."

"It's a full-time job," I remind her.

"Mo, sweetheart, taking care of your father isn't a job or a chore. I enjoy it the same way I enjoyed taking care of Jack. Sure, it's a little more work, but I don't have kids running around anymore or a job to take up my time."

Dad is watching me, but I can't decipher his expression.

"Is this what you want?" I ask.

"I want t-to be h-h-happy and enjoy the l-life I have l-left."

"Jesus, Dad, you make it sound like you're ancient and dying—which you're not, by the way. You're still young and have a lot of years ahead of you."

"I k-know, and I want t-to enjoy them."

My mind is spinning right now. For so long, it's just been the two of us. What will happen if he leaves? He's been my motivation for the last six years—the reason I get up every morning and work my ass off. What will I do when I don't have that anymore?

You'll do all the things you've dreamed about.

"You're not happy here?" I hate to ask the question, but I need to know. "Did I do something wrong? Did I upset you? I know I'm gone all the time but—" I choke on the words, and Dad raises his hand from Sharon's to place it on mine.

Time and life and stress show on his aged skin, his hands not as thick and powerful as they once were. But they're still the hands that took care of me, the hands that gave me a good life. Bending down, I kiss his knuckles.

"You did n-nothing wrong, Mo. I couldn't h-have asked f-for a b-b-better daughter. Now it's y-your turn t-to be happy and l-l-live your life. I want to g-give you your l-life back."

I swallow past the lump in my throat, but I'm unable to stop the tears from forming. Squeezing my eyes shut, I feel them on my cheeks as he continues.

"I want you t-to be able t-t-to go out to d-dinner with Rhett without w-worrying about who is g-going to stay with me. I-I want you to go b-back to school, if that's something you w-want to do. I want you to b-be young, Monroe. Young and h-happy."

Swiping at the tears, I lower my head to Dad's shoulder. "We'll talk about it, okay? If this is what you want, we'll talk about it. Me, you, and Sharon. We'll find time to sit down and work things out. But I want you to be sure." I give Sharon a firm look. "He's my life, and I need to know you're ready for this."

She nods, tears in her eyes, and I can tell from the look on her face that I have my answer. Somewhere along the way, they fell in love, and who am I to judge that or stop it from blossoming?

"Okay." I kiss both of them on the cheek and stand up. "I'm gonna leave you two alone. I'll grab my clothes and take a shower at Coop's. I told Rhett I'd stop by before my shift anyway."

I walk to my room and collect my uniform and brush, and when I get to the front door, Sharon is waiting on me. As soon as I'm within reach, she pulls me into a hug.

"Thank you," she whispers.

Pressing my face against her hair, I breathe in her familiar scent and relax, knowing my dad couldn't be in a better set of hands.

"For what?" The way I see it, I should be thanking her for making my father happy in a way I can't.

"For sharing him with me."

CHAPTER
Twenty-Seven

Monroe

"I thought you were working tonight," Coop says as I blow through his front door.

"I am. Just dropped by to see Rhett before my shift and grab a quick shower. He in his room?"

"No, he's in the shower."

"Lucky me," I tease.

"I better not hear any funny noises coming from the bathroom," he hollers.

I wink and stride down the hall. The bathroom door is cracked, so I sneak in, strip out of my clothes, and step in behind Rhett.

He doesn't even startle when I slide my hands around his soapy body and reach for his cock. It's half-mast but grows quickly in the palm of my hand.

"Is this a common occurrence, women joining you in the shower? Should I be worried that you didn't even flinch when I touched you?"

"You should be worried that your stealth skills are waning with age," he says, wrapping his hand around mine, guiding it over his cock as he shows me the rhythm he likes. "You should also be worried that you won't make it to work on time."

"Oh no." Releasing his cock, I steal the loofah from his hands. "I'm already running late."

Rhett whips around. "You touched my cock, babe. Now it wants you." We look down at his straining erection. It's covered in suds and bobbing heavily between us.

Rhett grabs his cock, working it while I watch. "Why are you running late?"

Dammit. I squeeze my thighs together to suppress the growing ache, but it's useless.

"Mo, I asked you a question."

"Huh?" Peeling my eyes away, I blink up at his face. "I can't concentrate when you touch yourself."

He lets go of his cock, his soapy hand finding my hip. "I asked why you're running late. Something happen at Animal Haven?"

"No. More like something happened at my house."

He tilts his head, and I sigh, dropping my forehead to his chest.

"I walked in on my dad and Sharon kissing." Several seconds pass, and I look up. "Say something."

"That'll kill the mood."

Laughing, I reach for his cock and sure enough, it's shrinking.

"If we're going to talk about your dad kissing your best friend's mom, I'm going to need you to let go of my dick, babe."

"Sorry." I let it go, but not without one final squeeze.

"Tell me what happened."

"I don't have time," I say, soaping the top half of my body. "It's going to have to wait until after my shift."

Rhett takes the loofah back. "You talk; I'll wash."

Nothing in this world is better than a naked, wet Rhett kneeling between my legs. I'm tempted to latch onto his hair and shove his face between my thighs.

"Talk or I'll stop." He runs the loofah up the inside of one leg and then other.

"Right. Sorry."

Rhett does as promised, washing my body first and then my hair as I replay everything that happened with my dad. I finish the story about the same time he finishes rinsing the conditioner from my hair. With his hands on my shoulders, he turns me to face him.

"It sounds like this could be a good thing."

"I know. But my feelings are so jumbled, I don't know how I feel about it. I want him to be happy, and it would be nice to be able to do a few things I want to do, but who will I come home to? Who will eat cinnamon rolls with me on Saturday mornings and listen to my sad animal stories?"

"Me."

My knees go a little wobbly. *Did he just say that*? "But your job…you said you're traveling all the time."

He puts his face right in front of mine. "I do travel all the time, but I'm home a few days during the week, and we have summers off," he says, kissing me.

"But you train in Houston."

"Are you trying to find a reason to keep me away, Mo?" he whispers.

"No. That's not it at all. I'm trying to figure out how we fit into each other's lives."

Taking my hand in his, Rhett brushes wet hair from my face. "I can train anywhere. My life isn't in Houston."

"But your home is."

"Home is a figurative word. My home isn't where I lay my

head at night."

Oh my. We're doing this. We're really doing this. "It's not?"

"Relax, Mo. Take a deep breath," he instructs, running his hands up my arms. I follow his command, allowing the oxygen to seep into my body and carry the doubt away. "Home is where I find peace when I'm stressed, happiness when I'm sad, balance when life gets crazy—and trust me, it gets a little crazy."

"And where do you find peace and happiness and balance?" *Please say in Heaven. Please say in Heaven.*

"It's not where, Mo; it's who."

My heart fills with warmth as his words soak in. We're in our own little world, the hot water beating against our bodies as his eyes hold mine. I wait for the words, wait for him to tell me I'm his home, but I can see the hesitation in his eyes.

He still doesn't trust me with his heart. He wants to trust me, but I have to show him. He has to see that I'm here to stay and I'll never hurt him the way I did before.

"You're my *who*, Rhett Allen." Cupping his jaw in my hands, I kiss him gently. "I've got to get ready for work, but this conversation isn't over. Not by a long shot."

I yank open the curtain and have one foot out of the shower when I'm hauled back against a large, warm, wet chest. His lips mold to mine in a bone-melting kiss. I allow myself a moment to drown in his arms.

"I'm getting there," he whispers.

"Take your time. I'm not going anywhere."

It takes all of my self-control to step out of the shower and leave him behind, but I have a job to get to and bills to pay. I'm pulling up my pants when Rhett's phone rings from a pile of clothes on the bathroom floor.

"Can you grab that, babe?"

I shuffle through his clothes, but by the time I pull his

phone out of the back pocket of his jeans, the call has ended.

Missed Call: Nikki Cell appears on the screen.

I glance at the shower and back at the phone. Why is she calling? I thought he fired her. A second later his phone beeps with an incoming text from Nikki.

I know we left things on shaky ground, but I'm glad we got to talk the other night, and I can't wait to see you. Next Wednesday is perfect. I miss you.

Stuffing his phone back in his pocket, I sink onto the toilet seat, feeling like someone reached into my body and pulled my guts out. I swear I don't breathe for an entire minute as I run through all the things that text could mean.

Is he talking to her again?

Is he planning on seeing her next Wednesday?

Why would he see her next Wednesday?

Was he going to tell me about it?

Does he miss her too?

Adrenaline pumps through my veins, along with a rush of anger and confusion.

Sometime between finding out the truth of what Nikki did to us and having our lovely shower talk about home, he talked to Nikki and made plans to meet up.

I stand on wobbly legs, tug my shirt over my head, and brush through my tangles. Twisting my hair into a pile on my head, I secure it with a ponytail holder and wait for the water to shut off.

"Who called?" Rhett asks, yanking the shower curtain open. He reaches for a towel, runs it over his head and looks at me expectantly. "Mo?"

"Yeah?"

"Who called?"

"Nikki."

His gaze jumps from the phone to me. "Mo."

"I have to go."

I walk out of the bathroom as he stumbles from the shower, reaching for his boxers. "Mo, wait. It's not what you think."

Flinging my purse over my shoulder, I pull open the front door, slamming it shut as I walk out. I'm halfway to my car when it flies open again.

"Mo, wait."

"We'll talk about this later. I'm going to be late for work."

I slam the truck door shut and stick the key in the ignition, but I don't have the strength to crank it over. Dropping my head to the steering wheel, I blow out a long breath. Today has been a crazy day. My emotions are running high, and I'm afraid if I go back into the house, I'll say things I'll regret. But worse yet, I'm afraid if I leave without working things out, I'll ruin the delicate foundation we've begun to build.

I trust Rhett, which is why I reach for the handle at the same time a soft knock taps the window. I kick the door open and get out of the truck.

Rhett has one hand propped against the door, the other against the body, caging me in.

"I was just getting out to come talk to you."

"Good. I was hoping you weren't going to leave without letting me explain what her text was about. We don't walk away mad, okay?"

I nod, but it isn't good enough.

"We talk through our shit, no matter what it is."

"I know," I stress. "Why do you think I was opening the door?"

A smile threatens his scowl. "Nikki called the other day and left me a voicemail."

"You didn't answer?"

"Hell no. I have no place for her in my life. She wanted to tell me that Jessica, the woman from Rugged, is planning on coming to the ranch next Wednesday for the shoot. I texted her back and said thank you, that Wednesday would work, and that's it."

"Then why did she say she can't wait to see you?"

"Not a clue. I saw that message right after you walked out. I'll text her back and make sure she knows she isn't invited to the shoot."

Well, don't I feel like an ass. "I'm sorry." I sigh. "She just brings up terrible feelings for me. We can't trust her, Rhett. She's going to be a hard limit for me."

"Babe. At least let me get you naked if we're going to talk about hard limits."

I roll my eyes, unable to suppress a smile. "You know what I mean."

"I do." He curls his hand around my neck, presses his lips to my forehead, and lingers there a few seconds. "And you're my who, Mo. Always have been."

"You can't say that to me right before I leave."

"I can't let you leave without saying it." He presses a kiss to my lips.

CHAPTER
Twenty-Eight

Monroe

A s promised, that following Wednesday, Rhett and I pull up to his family's ranch at ten sharp. I wasn't sure I'd be able to make the shoot, but I put out an emergency call to my volunteers and one of them picked up the rest of the day for me.

Thirty minutes later, two vans roll up, followed by a sleek silver BMW. A slew of people pile out of the vans and begin unloading: lighting, cameras, clothing racks, jeans, jeans, and more jeans, and every shade of flannel shirt known to man.

"Do you have to wear all of that?" I whisper.

"God, I hope not. It's hot as hell out here today. They better pick an outfit and stick with it." Rhett pulls off his Stetson, wipes the sweat from his forehead, and puts it back on. "We're still good to go to Houston on Friday?"

"Yup. What time is your appointment?"

"Two o'clock."

I smile to myself, because I'm keeping a secret—a surprise of sorts—and I can't wait to tell him. But not today.

I bite my tongue, and we watch patiently as two women and

a man climb out of the BMW. One I instantly peg as Jessica. She's tall, lean, and dressed in a slate gray pencil skirt with matching pumps and white silk blouse. Her hair is pulled back in a bun at the nape of her neck, and she looks every bit the business woman. I'm assuming the man is the director or photographer, and last but not least…

"That must be Molly."

She's blond and blue-eyed with a tan that rivals Rhett's. Together they'll look amazing.

Rhett grunts, but doesn't say much more than that. I already know he hates that he has to pose with someone he doesn't know. He hates it even more that I'm here watching.

"It's fine, Rhett. I'm fine. You're making this into so much more than it needs to be."

We've come a long way since our *who* conversation. Both of us know what we want and what we're working for, and it's an amazing feeling. He and I have also alternated having dinner at each other's houses since then. Some nights we eat with his family, other nights with my dad and Sharon, and it was over a plate of steak and potatoes last Sunday that he tried to talk me out of coming to the shoot.

It seems he's about to try again.

His eyes narrow on mine. "We've gone over this, Mo. I don't think you should be here. This is where shit gets screwed up in relationships. I've had several buddies lose their girl because she couldn't handle seeing him wrapped around another woman."

"First, I'm not just any girl. Second, I trust you. And third, I'm going to see the ad eventually anyway. This is a photo shoot. Nothing more, nothing less. It's not like you're going to take her home when it's all said and done." I pause. "Right?"

He scrunches his nose. "Hell no."

I push up on my toes and kiss his cheek. "And that's why I

trust you. Relax. You look way too uptight. I'm here because I want to help."

Jessica approaches us, her eyes warm and friendly.

"You must be Monroe," she says, embracing me. "It's a pleasure to meet you." She turns to Rhett. "And how are you?" She pulls him in for a hug and air kisses both of his cheeks.

He rolls his eyes as she steps back.

"This is our photographer, Pilar De Luca, and I'm sure you're familiar with Ms. Farris."

"Actually, I'm not," Rhett says.

His words are a bit too cool for my liking, and I nudge him in the ribs. He glares down at me, and I do my best to give him a *be nice* look, which he must understand because his shoulders relax, and he plasters on that panty-dropping smile I know and love.

"It's a pleasure to meet you."

Molly's crimson red lips part in a coy smile as she takes his offered hand. Her slender fingers wrap around his, and a twinge of jealousy forces me to look away.

Clearing my throat, I turn to Jessica. "We've got the horses ready to go. There are some old, distressed fence posts along the ridge as well as a red, wooden barn. Everything up here toward the front of the ranch is going to be modern and updated."

Pilar's eyes light up as he looks around, taking in all the beauty that is Allen Family Ranch. Around us, several people start setting up along the edge of the barn. A woman steps up to Rhett with a tape measure. He takes a hasty step back when she lowers herself between his legs.

"Hold still, honey," she instructs. "I won't bite."

Trevor steps out of the barn, a bale of straw balanced on his shoulder. He stops to look at Rhett, grins, and walks away.

Rhett doesn't look at all amused. He flips his brother the

bird, but gives the woman room to do her job.

After a moment she looks up at Pilar. "32-34." She studies Rhett's face.

He hasn't shaved for a couple of days, so he's sporting a scruffy jaw, which is what I assume she's looking at.

"His beard growth is a little thick," she says. "Would you like me to shave it?"

Pilar shakes his head. "No. I want him edgy and raw. What's a handsome cowboy without some scruff?" he says, winking at the woman.

Jessica turns toward Rhett and Molly. "For the fall campaign, we're looking for something sweet, but sexy, and we need hot, raw chemistry."

"I'm not sure our man is going to deliver," Pilar muses.

I follow his gaze to Rhett and Molly a few feet away.

"That won't be a problem," Molly hollers. She's all smiles and hands, chatting Rhett up, and he looks seconds away from growling.

"He'll loosen up," I assure them. "I'll talk to him before you start."

"Perfect." Pilar nods. "Let's get them into wardrobe and head out to the red barn. We can start there."

Thanks to Rhett's dad, we have the Gators to haul everything to the location, although walking wouldn't be bad. It's only a half mile out. Once they've loaded up the clothes and equipment, everyone else piles into their vehicles—everyone but Rhett and me. We head for Shadow and Sadie, who are saddled up and waiting in the pasture.

Rhett and I mount the horses, and that's when I see Molly whisper something to Jessica and climb out of the Gator. With her hands in her pockets and a sexy little smile that makes me uneasy, she approaches Rhett.

"Mind if I ride with you? I've never been on a horse before."

Rhett's stares at her, totally indifferent, and then cuts me a look. Rolling my eyes, I give Shadow a little kick and take off through the field, allowing him to make the call. It's a bitch move, considering I promised I'd be fine watching the two of them and said I was here to help, but I wasn't expecting her to look at him as if he were a piece of meat she wanted to consume.

He's my piece of meat, dammit, and it's that thought that has me looking over my shoulder. Rhett is only a few paces behind me, and the knot in my stomach loosens when I see that he's alone. He smiles, winks, and flies past me, along with a Gator carrying an annoyed-looking Molly Farris.

I slow Shadow to a walk so I can take a second to clear my head. Being a supportive girlfriend is important to me, and I can't let the green monster inside rear his ugly head again—not if I want Rhett to relax and cooperate for his shoot.

By the time I make it to the barn, the crew is nearly finished setting up. Rhett and Molly are getting their clothing, and each walks off to get changed—Rhett in the barn, and Molly behind a set-up dressing curtain off the side of the van.

When everyone is ready to go and the makeup artist has swept her brush along their faces, erasing any imperfections, Pilar starts barking orders.

I stand back, not wanting to get in the way, and watch everything unfold.

"Rhett, up against the fence. Yes, that's good. Prop your boot on the rung and drape your arm along the fence."

Rhett follows Pilar's commands to a T, and when he's situated just perfectly, with his Stetson pulled low, Pilar turns to Molly. So do I, and holy shit.

My jaw nearly hits the dirt. How they transformed her into a cowgirl goddess in such a short amount of time, I'll never know. She's wearing a pair of faded jeans that hang low on her hips and a flannel shirt tied below her breasts, showing off her tiny little waist. Her hair is in a loose braid hanging over one shoulder, and her Ariats are scuffed to perfection—although I'd bet just about anything she had nothing to do with that.

And it's settled: I hate her.

Pinching at the roll that hangs over my jeans, I frown. Okay, I don't hate her as much as I do myself for letting my own health go. Frustrated, I focus my attention on Rhett.

"Molly, I want you to start over there and slowly walk toward Rhett. Rhett, when she hits this post, your gaze is going to slide up her body. I want to see chemistry. I want to see the connection. You're the cowboy, and she's the bull you're about to mount," he says, using a terribly inappropriate analogy, if I do say so myself. "You two stare at each other. It's intense, and after a few seconds, you push away from the fence and walk toward her. That's where we'll cut."

Rhett's face tightens, but he nods his understanding.

I know from a previous conversation with Jessica that the campaign is going to be a series of short videos spliced together. It'll start with this scene, followed by a shot of the two of them coming together, most likely in a heated kiss, and end—of course—with them riding off into the sunset.

"Places, people," Pilar yells.

Rhett and Molly take their places, and Jessica tugs me behind the video camera so we can watch the take. Pilar yells *action*, and Molly saunters into the frame. Her hips sway seductively, her heated gaze trained on Rhett, and when she hits the designated spot, she stops.

I hold my breath, watching as Rhett's head slowly rises, his eyes sweeping up her body—only the heat she's projecting isn't reflected at all on his face.

"Stop! Stop, stop, stop." Pilar throws his hands in the air.

"Damn," Jessica hisses. "Not even a spark."

"How do you know?" I whisper. "Maybe he just needs a second to adjust."

She shakes her head. "Trust me, I know. I've been around the business long enough. Some people have it and others don't."

"Now what?" I ask, secretly glad Rhett doesn't have a *spark* with someone else.

"We'll make it work. They're both too gorgeous not to feel something." She closes her eyes as soon as the words pass her lips and looks over at me. "I didn't mean it like that. I'm sure—"

I hold up my hand to stop her. "It's okay. I understand, and I trust Rhett completely."

She pinches her lips together and nods before turning to watch Pilar. He's talking with Rhett, and when he steps away and calls *action*, everything starts into motion again.

This process is repeated over and over again until frustrated, Pilar turns to Jessica. "We need to take a break, and you need to talk to him. Her tits are perfect, she's sexy as hell, and there's no reason for him not to feel some iota of attraction."

Jessica turns a pleading look my way. "Could you talk to him, please? Try to get him to come around."

"Sure." *Let me convince my boyfriend to drool over another woman. That's exactly what I want to do today.*

As I approach, Rhett's hands are jammed into his pockets, a scowl marring his face.

"Some women may be scared of that scowl, but it sort of turns me on. I suggest you remove it from your face before I force you to have sex with me in the hayloft."

His jaw slackens, the tight line of his lips curving up into a smile. "You wouldn't have to force, darlin'. I'd be a willing participant."

My cheeks flush. I slide my hands up his flannel shirt, un-buttoning the top few buttons as I go because he looks way too uncomfortable. "Maybe if you're good and do what Pilar asks of you, I'll make it worth your while."

"In the hayloft?"

"Anywhere you want."

"How about any way I want?"

Rhett's words wrap around me, caressing my body like a feather.

He takes a step closer, crowding me against the fence. "There are parts of you I've yet to explore."

Oh, God. I know exactly what *parts* he's talking about. It's uncharted territory, but something I'd be willing to give him.

"My body is your playground," I whisper, nipping at his earlobe.

A low rumble emanates from his chest as he presses his thigh between my legs. My nipples pucker tight, my panties growing increasingly damp, and I'm seconds away from beg-ging him to take me now, onlookers be damned.

"Don't. Move," Pilar commands.

Rhett moans as he presses his face against the side of my neck. I wrap my arms around him, embarrassed that we got caught in an intimate moment.

"You." Pilar points to me. "What size jeans do you wear?"

"Uh…" I point to myself because surely he isn't talking to me. "Me?"

Pilar huffs and rolls his eyes. "Yes, you. Jean size."

"Eight, depending on the brand," I reply before whispering to Rhett. "What does he want my jean size for?"

"Not a clue. I just want this day to be over." He pulls his head out of my neck, and I shiver at the loss of him pressed against me.

Pilar claps his hands, catching everyone's attention. "Change of plans, people. Molly is out; Monroe is in."

"What?" I say.

Molly gasps. "You've got to be kidding me." She plants her hands on her hips and marches toward Pilar.

"I need heat, pure sexual chemistry, and those two have it," he says, waving toward us. "Jessica, please tell me you saw that."

Her red cheeks and grin tell me she saw exactly what was transpiring between Rhett and me. "Oh, I saw it, and I agree."

"No." I push away from Rhett, but he grabs my wrist, pulling me back in. "I'm not a model. I have no clue how this stuff works. Rhett can make it work with Molly. Can't you?" I turn a pleading look his way.

He shakes his head. "I think they're right. I am insanely attracted you, and if that's what they're looking for, you're perfect for this."

"This is crazy." My throat closes, making it difficult to breathe, let alone argue my point.

Rhett runs a soothing hand down my spine, and the giant smile on his face tells me he's more than thrilled with the changes.

Jessica motions toward the woman who measured Rhett. "Get her into wardrobe, please. Something similar to what Molly is wearing."

My eyes widen. "Hell no," I protest. "There's no way I'm showing my stomach like that."

Pilar waves me off. "You're gorgeous."

Before I have a chance to respond or argue any more, I'm hauled off to the makeshift changing room Molly was using moments ago.

"Molly looks pissed," I whisper to Jessica as she peeks her head around the corner. I don't even bother to cover up my chest, mostly because I don't have time to react.

She tosses a shirt at me. "She'll get over it. Plus, she's still getting paid, so…" She shrugs. "And we'll pay you too; so don't worry."

"Oh no." I shake my head. "I don't need to get paid."

Her face goes blank. "I think you're the first model to ever tell me that. I won't hold you to it."

"I'm not a model." *What don't these people understand about that?*

"You are now."

———◦———

Rhett

Monroe walks around the corner in a pair of faded jeans, a red and white plaid shirt similar to the one Molly had on, and her favorite Ariats. Her hair isn't in a braid; it's falling down her shoulder in loose curls, casting a shadow across her face. She looks like she's seconds away from ripping out someone's throat if they so much as lay another finger on her.

"You look beautiful." I wrap my hand around her hip and kiss her. "Not that you don't always look beautiful, because you do."

She smiles. "Nice save."

"I'm not used to seeing you with makeup."

"That's because this stuff is the devil," she sneers. "If you pick at the edges, you could probably peel a layer off my face."

I laugh and pull her in for another kiss. "You know what I love most?" I whisper.

"What's that?"

"Those red lips. When this place clears out, I want them wrapped around my cock."

Her eyes glow as Pilar yells, "Let's take our places. Monroe, do you remember what you're supposed to do?"

"Yeah, yeah." She waves and takes Molly's spot by the fence. I have no idea what happened to Molly, and frankly, I don't give a shit, because I've only got eyes for one woman.

"Action!" Pilar yells.

"Wait."

Pilar sighs. "What's wrong, Monroe?"

"Shouldn't we practice or something so I can make sure I get it right?"

"No, we shouldn't. I want this to look natural and unrehearsed."

"Fine. Okay, I'm ready," Monroe declares.

Pilar yells *action* again, and everyone around us goes quiet as I look down at my boots. I can't see Monroe, but I can feel her—I can feel her eyes on me, her body drawing mine in like a magnet. The strawberry scent I know and love floats through the air, making my mouth water. I don't wait for her to hit a certain fence post before I look up. Instead, I look up when I can't take it anymore, when my body screams with the need to see her and touch her.

I lift my head, my eyes starting at her boots and sweeping up her legs as I take in her luscious hips, which are going to fit perfectly in my hands when I push into her from behind later. Swallowing, I trail my eyes over her breasts. Her nipples are puckered beneath the plaid material, and my cock swells inside my jeans. I fight the urge to adjust my crotch as my eyes lock on hers.

Monroe's lips are parted, her eyes wide and smoldering, begging me to come to her, to claim her. I push off the fence. In three measured steps, I'm in front of her. I reach for her hand and when our fingers touch, she takes a shuddery breath. All

I can think about is stripping her naked and sinking my dick inside her tight, warm pussy, making love to her for hours on end. I'm not sure what I'm waiting for.

My fingers glide up her arms, curl around her neck. Her eyes drop to my mouth, her tongue darting out to wet her lips and—

"Cut! Cut! That's perfect!" Pilar applauds. "Absolutely explosive!"

Monroe blinks several times. She steps into my open arms and hugs me so tight I'm afraid we'll be joined at the hip.

"I was ready to strip," she whispers, laughing against my chest.

"Oh, you're going to strip, Ms. Gallagher, and then I'm going to have my way with you."

"This entire day is like foreplay."

Pilar and the rest of the crew set up for the next take as Monroe and I share heated whispers and promises of what's to come. Then we spend the next several hours shooting the remaining scenes. We film a scene of Monroe and me riding the horses through the field. At one point, I slow down enough for her to catch up, and when I take off running, she tosses her head back and laughs, just as Pilar calls cut.

During the next scene, Monroe climbs on the horse with me, only she isn't behind me, she's sitting in the front of the saddle, facing me. Her arms drape around my neck, and her legs coil around my back. One of my hands rests behind her on the horn, the reins dangling from my fingers, and the other hand presses low against her back, holding her to me.

"I bet I could take you just like this," I say softly, feeling her body tremble against mine.

"I'm not sure Sadie would appreciate that."

"Guess we'll find out." I slant my mouth to hers. Our lips

brush once, twice, and a third time.

"Cut!" Pilar turns a pleased smile to Jessica. "One more part."

At the end of the day, after a dinner break, the last video is the two of us riding off into the sunset. Monroe hugs me from behind as we once again share the saddle. The heat from her pussy burns a hole against my ass, and when Pilar calls *cut* for the last time, I ride over to him and stop.

"Are we done?"

"We're done. You two were absolutely perfect." He holds out a hand to help Monroe down from Sadie, but I stop him.

"Do you need anything else from us?" I ask.

Jessica walks up beside Pilar and tilts her head. "No. We just have to clean up, and we'll be out of your hair."

"Good. If you need anything else, Mom, Dad, or Trevor can help you on your way out."

"Oh, do you have somewhere to—"

I give Sadie a tap, propelling us forward, and Jessica's words fade into the wind.

"Where are we going?" Monroe asks.

The wind whips around us. She tightens her grip to keep from falling off.

"Two words," I shout. "Hay. Loft."

"Faster," she laughs.

CHAPTER
Twenty-Nine

Monroe

"Thank you so much. I owe you one," I tell Tess the next afternoon.

"Don't mention it," she says. "We all deserve some time away."

"How's Simon?"

"I'm mad at him, let's not talk about it."

I cringe and she waves me on. "It's fine. I love the damn bird, but he drives me crazy. Tell me what I need to know before you go."

"Here's the key to the spare work truck," I say, dropping it into her hand. "And you've got a key to Animal Haven." She pats her pocket confirming that it's there. "Oh, and I've got tuna in the closet for Pickles. Don't forget I let him stay out. He's no longer confined to his cage."

"I won't forget."

"You've got my number, right?"

"I've got your number."

"And Rhett's?"

"You sent it to me three times."

"You're comfortable taking care—"

"I'm good, Mo. If I have a question I'll be sure to call."

I scan the office one last time, making sure I didn't miss anything.

Tess rests her hand on my arm. "Leave, Mo. I've got it. The animals are in good hands. Enjoy your night with Rhett."

My night with Rhett.

An entire night with him—in his bed without having to be quiet for fear my dad will hear or Coop will walk in.

I grin, picturing Rhett's face when I tell him we'll get to spend the night together. When I mentioned to Sharon that we were going to drive to Houston and back in the same day, she insisted on staying with Dad so we could have the night to ourselves. No way I was turning that down.

"I will."

I give Tess a quick hug and rush home to make sure Sharon has everything she needs. It's four o'clock before I pull into Coop's driveway. The truck is gone, but I know Rhett is home because he was expecting me to drop by after work.

The front door opens before I make it to the porch. Duke and Diesel bound down the stairs, and I squat down and brace myself as they pummel into me. They tackle me to the ground, peppering me with kisses. When I'm able to break free, I look up to see Rhett standing in the doorway, his hands latched on the top of the door frame, and a swarm of butterflies takes flight in my stomach.

He laughs as I struggle to push the boys off so I can stand up. I brush the grass from my shorts and walk toward him, stopping on the top step of the porch. He lifts a brow, but I refuse to go any farther because I know what'll happen if he gets his hands on me.

"Go pack a bag."

His brow creases. "What?"

"Sharon is staying with my dad tonight. Tess is taking care of Animal Haven. We've got the night to ourselves."

Amusement drains from his face. "You're serious?"

"I wouldn't joke about something like this. I was kind of hoping we could drive to Houston tonight, you could show me around your house, and maybe we could grab dinner at your favorite restaurant."

Stepping over the threshold, Rhett pulls me into his arms. "Or, I could have *you* for dinner," he whispers in my ear.

The promise of sex thickens the air. "That works too."

Rhett rushes inside to pack a bag, but not without giving me a heated kiss and slap on the ass for not telling him sooner.

We decide to take my truck so the dogs can ride with us. Once we're all piled in, I toss the keys to Rhett and sit my ass in the passenger seat. With the windows down, radio up, and Rhett's hand resting on my thigh, we make the short trip to Houston.

I must doze off somewhere along Interstate 45, and by the time Rhett nudges me in the arm to wake me up, we're pulling down a long gravel drive.

"Hey, sleepyhead."

Yawning, I stretch in my seat and crane my neck out the window for a better look. "Why did you let me fall asleep? I was looking forward to some alone time with you."

"Figured I'd let you rest up now because we'll have plenty of alone time, and I'm going to utilize every second of it."

The wicked grin on his face causes a tingling between my legs, and I have to look away. If Rhett ever figures out the full extent of the effect he has on me, I'm screwed.

A log house comes into view. "This is your place?"

"Welcome to Casa de Rhett." He puts the truck in park, gets

out, and walks around to my side. He opens the door and helps me out before releasing the dogs. They must be excited to be home, because they both fly across the yard, Diesel grabbing a red ball he finds on his way to the front porch.

"It's even more spectacular in person."

"You've seen my house?" Rhett takes my hand, leading me up the front walk.

"Coop used to show me pictures. I feel like I was here with you when you were remodeling it. Every step of the way he would tell me what you were working on and how the project was progressing. I was so damn proud of you, Rhett. Still am."

We stop in front of a set of ornate wooden doors.

"For what? Renovating a house?"

"Not just for renovating the house—although I am proud that you were able to do the work. It's more than that. You've done all the things you always wanted to. Look at you…you're a three-time world champion bull rider. You've got more endorsements than most bull riders even dream about, a modeling career, *and* your own home."

I pause, reflecting on how different our lives are. "And what do I have?" I mumble. "A high school diploma, a beat-up Chevy, and a free room at my dad's house."

"Don't." Rhett turns me to face him. "Don't put yourself down. You've done so many amazing things. I ride bulls for a living, but you…you save animals from being killed. You find them homes and take care of them. And you've done so, so much for your dad. You've made his life the best it can possibly be. What you do is meaningful."

"I know. I'm not trying to put myself down, but this…" I wave toward his house. "This puts it all in perspective. I had hopes and dreams and—"

"Have. You *have* hopes and dreams, and they're going to

come true. I promise you, Mo."

I sigh, looking up to keep the tears away. "I don't want to talk about this anymore. What I'd like to do is get a tour of this fabulous house."

Rhett smiles, but it doesn't reach his eyes, and I internally berate myself for speaking my thoughts.

He unlocks the front door and pushes it open. Stepping into the entryway is like stepping into *Better Homes and Gardens* magazine.

There are more floor-to-ceiling windows than I can count. Exposed beams run the length of the ceiling, and distressed wood runs the length of the floor. Everything is covered in rich browns and reds, creating a warmth I didn't know was possible.

I move through the space, running my fingers along the mantel above the fireplace and stopping to look over a series of pictures. There's one of Rhett and all his siblings, a few of him and Coop, and tucked in the back corner is a small photo of Rhett and me.

Dust has collected on the aged frame. I pull it from the mantel, wipe the dust off, and stare at the two people in the picture. It was taken after Rhett's first live bull ride. He only stayed on for three seconds, but he was so excited, and I couldn't have been prouder of him. We're standing by the chute, his arm wrapped around my shoulders, and we're wearing the biggest smiles.

"I miss those days," I say softly.

Rhett steps up behind me, wraps an arm across my chest, and rests his head on my shoulder. "Me too."

"Things were much simpler back then."

"Things are still simple; we've just found ways to complicate them."

"I'm surprised you had this up."

After everything that happened, he still kept a picture of us up in his house. Warmth seeps through my veins, wrapping itself around my heart like a warm blanket.

"It's my favorite picture," he says after a moment. "Do you remember what else happened that day?"

I smile. *How could I forget?* "You took me to the diner to eat and then out to our spot under the old oak tree at the ranch."

"And…"

"You told me you loved me for the first time."

Rhett's arm tightens around me. My eyes drift shut as he kisses the base of my neck, and I will him to say the words now, to tell me he loves me the same today as he did back then. But the moment passes, and when I open my eyes, I put the picture back and turn to him with an overly bright smile.

"I want to see the rest of the house."

Rhett follows me through the living room, letting me explore at my own pace, and when I walk into the kitchen I nearly stumble.

"Holy shit," I laugh. "Your kitchen is huge. Do you even know how to cook?"

Everything is stainless steel and oversized. His refrigerator looks bigger than my closet, and who uses a double oven these days anyway?

"I can make a few things," he says, sheepishly.

I stop at the large island in the middle of the opulent room and run my hand along the slick, black granite counter top, admiring how different it feels than the Formica I'm used to.

"Yeah? Can you make me a fancy breakfast tomorrow?"

"Or, I can make *you* dinner now."

CHAPTER
Thirty

Monroe

Rhett's eyes darken as he steps in front of me. He dips down to claim my mouth. His tongue presses between my lips, devouring my words right along with my thoughts. I slide my hands up his chest and wind them around his neck, allowing him to pull me in close.

I push my fingers through his messy hair, then let go long enough for him to peel my jeans and panties off. Gripping my hips, he hoists me up on the counter. He spreads my legs with his knee and steps between them.

Rhett continues to explore my mouth with his tongue. He flexes his hips, pressing his erection against my core. His jeans scrape against my clit, and I reach between us, frantically pulling at the button of his jeans. My hands and feet claw at his pants, pushing them down his legs. His cock springs free, and a second later it's cradled in my hand.

"Condom," I mumble against his lips.

"Damnit," he moans, tearing his mouth from mine so he can reach in his wallet and grab one.

I snatch it from his hand, tear open the foil packet, and

slide it over him.

"I need you," I breathe. "You can make love to me for the rest of our lives, but right now I need you to fuck me."

"Baby," he pants, driving into me with one solid thrust.

My head tilts back, exposing my neck. My breasts bounce between us, still contained by my shirt and bra, and Holy Mother of God, that is not going to work for me.

I yank my shirt off and tug at the top of my bra, allowing my breasts to pop out. They're lifted high and squished together this way, but Rhett doesn't seem to mind. He captures a nipple in his mouth, sucking it deep and hard—the same way his cock drives into me.

"That feels so good." I bury my fingers in his hair, holding his head against my chest. I swear to God this man could give me an orgasm just by sucking my tits.

I draw him closer, locking my ankles behind his back. Rhett releases my nipple with a wet pop and moves to the next, torturing it the same way.

"Oh, God," I groan, watching where our bodies connect. I've always been on the receiving end of dirty talk—never one to offer it—but something about the sight of his cock sliding in and out has me on edge.

"So fucking big, Rhett. God, you're stretching me, and it feels so goddamn good. Don't stop," I beg. "Please don't stop." He groans against my breast, increasing the pace of his thrusts. I buck against him. "Harder. Oh, God, harder. Yes, right like that."

Releasing my nipple, Rhett wraps his hand around my hair, yanking my head back. My eyes meet his, wild and uninhibited.

"Watch me while I take you. I want to see you lose control. I want to hear you scream my name, Mo. You're gonna give me your entire body, do you hear me?"

"Yes," I moan, getting lost in his words, in the moment… in him.

"You're so close, I can feel it. Your pussy gripping my cock, sucking me back in every time I pull out."

Rhett pulls back, pressing my knees as far to the side as my body will allow, opening me up, stretching me.

"You're so perfect, Mo. Your body was made for mine." The sounds of our skin slapping together, along with our heated pants, fill the room. I slam my mouth against his as my orgasm crashes through me.

My legs tighten, jolts of electricity shooting throughout my body. Rhett dips a hand between us and rubs my clit.

"Oh, God, Rhett," I yell, wrenching my mouth from his. I thrash beneath him. "I can't—I can't take it." My body is strung so tight, I feel like he's going to rip me in half, and then I explode, my clit throbbing beneath the pad of his finger.

He slams into me with a deep groan, his eyes locked on mine, and his hips jerk as he spills himself into me. I only wish we could've done that without anything between us.

Rhett buries his face in my neck, his breath on my skin. "You're not leaving until we do that in every room."

"You do that again, and I might not leave at all."

He nips at my neck and pushes into me, setting off a ripple of waves. "Don't say things you don't mean."

I'm tempted to tell him I mean every word, but I don't want to push him, and I don't want to keep putting myself out there if he's not ready, so I keep my thoughts to myself.

Instead I say, "So, you have a really beautiful kitchen—very smooth counter."

He laughs, pulling his head from the crook of my neck. "Would you like to see the rest of the house?"

"Very much."

Rhett helps me off of the counter, and I get dressed while he pulls the condom off and tosses it in the trash. He puts his pants on and reaches for my hand.

We stop first in the master bedroom and bath on the main floor, which boasts a walk-in shower with three shower heads—all of which will be pointed directly at me at some point before we head back. There's an open staircase that leads to two guest bedrooms and a full bath upstairs, which is a scaled down version of Rhett's. Best of all, there are touches of him everywhere I look: pictures and trophies scattered throughout the house to remind me of all his accomplishments and the wonderful life he's made for himself.

"It's perfect, Rhett. Truly perfect."

"Now for the best part."

"You mean the shower with three heads isn't the best part?"

He shakes his head. "Not by a long shot. Follow me."

With my hand clasped in his, we walk back through the house and out the back door. There is farmland as far as the eye can see.

"Wow…are you farming this?"

"No." He leads me toward a large, red barn that sits off to the side. "I rent it out to a local farmer. Hop on," he says, motioning toward a Gator. I climb onto the vehicle.

Rhett pulls out of the barn and drives along the edge of the property.

"How many acres?"

"One hundred." He looks at me and smiles. "I always thought I might put up a new barn and bring some cattle out here. Maybe a few horses and chickens."

"If you're wanting a ranch, you could just take over your father's. I'm sure he'd be happy to hand over some of the responsibility."

"I know he would—and who knows, maybe someday I will—but Allen Family Ranch doesn't have this…"

Rhett pulls the Gator beneath a large tree and parks it. We climb out and step up to a wooden fence. My jaw drops open at the sight in front of me.

"Oh my God, Rhett," I laugh, my smile too big to contain. "This is breathtaking."

His hands land on the fence on either side of me. "This is why I bought the property," he says, following my gaze as I look out at a perfect view of the Houston skyline.

Technically, we're standing on a bluff looking down, so it's more of an aerial view, and I don't think I've ever seen something so beautiful and impressive.

"It's pretty nice now, but you should see it at night," he adds.

"Can we come out here tonight?"

Rhett pulls his phone out and checks the time. "We don't have much longer until sunset, and we've got nowhere to be. We can just stay out here."

"I'd love that."

Pushing away from the fence, I walk over to an open patch of thick, green grass. I kick off my shoes and sit down. Rhett follows, but opts to leave his boots on. Leaning back on my hands, I look over at him.

"Tell me something about you I don't already know."

"Hmmmm," he says, mimicking my position. "There isn't much."

"Come on, there has to be something."

"Lincoln and I took a cooking class."

I gasp. "You did not!"

"We did." He nods. "Neither one of us had a girl, and we were sick of mac-n-cheese, Spaghetti-Os, and takeout."

"Whose idea was it to take the class?"

"Linc's. He used to date a girl who was a chef. We signed up through her."

"Well, did you learn to cook? Is that why you put in a state-of-the-art kitchen?"

"I did learn to cook—a few things at least. And no, I put in a state-of-the-art kitchen because I was hoping one day I'd marry a woman who would put it to good use."

"Is that so?" I ask, laughing.

He smiles and nods. "Yup."

"And what about Linc? Did he learn how to cook?"

"Let's just say some people shouldn't be allowed in a kitchen or around a stove."

"That bad, huh?"

"We made more trips to the emergency room during the course of that class than I have through all of my bull rides—and trust me, there have been many trips caused by the bull."

I bite my bottom lip. "You've had quite a few injuries over the years."

"How do you know?"

"I follow your career, remember?"

"That's right. My sexy stalker."

I swat at his shoulder but miss. "I wasn't stalking."

He winks. "Whatever you have to tell yourself."

We're keeping things light, but I have to ask… "Nothing too serious though, right? I sometimes felt like Coop sugarcoated when he gave me updates."

"Nah. Nothing too serious."

Rhett looks away, and that's how I know he's lying.

"Tell me."

He takes a deep breath. "Three concussions. Fractured pelvis. Dislocated shoulder. Rotator cuff strain." He lifts the offending arm. "A few broken ribs here and there, and a broken wrist."

I open my mouth to ask him more, but he cuts me off.

"Now it's your turn. Tell me something I don't know."

"Nice deflection."

"Thank you. Answer the question."

I scrunch my brow, trying to come up with something fun I've done in the last six years. "I think you pretty much know everything."

"Nah. There has to be a wild, crazy story in there somewhere."

I shake my head. "After dad's stroke, I buried myself in work. Aside from the occasional beer with Claire and Tess, I haven't done much—watched movies with Dad, bartended, worked at Animal Haven." I frown, thinking about all the things I *didn't* do. "I'm boring."

"You're not boring."

"Really?" I lift a brow.

"There has to be a bad date story in there somewhere, or a drunken night with Claire."

I shake my head again. "I'm telling you, there's nothing. I haven't done a damn thing for the last six years—unless you want me to tell you about the time a horse stepped on my toe and I had to have my toenail removed."

Rhett scrunches his nose.

"Didn't think so. I got bit by a stray dog and had to get a tetanus shot. Oh, and one time a skunk got into Mr. Lytle's house, and I helped chase it out, but not before getting sprayed. I went through ten cans of tomato juice that night."

Rhett smiles. "See, you have funny stories."

"About animals."

Sighing, I flop back on the grass and look up at the sky. The sun is starting to set, casting red and orange across the clouds.

"I missed out on so much. I can't tell you how many times I

turned down my friends because I was too tired to hang out, or didn't have enough money to buy myself a beer. Looking back, I wish I would've gone anyway, made those memories." I think about that for a moment and then correct myself. "Actually, it wouldn't have mattered; I still had to stay home to take care of my dad."

"I'm sorry, Mo."

"Don't be. My life hasn't been bad; it just hasn't been very exciting."

Rhett sighs, shifting his gaze to the sky for a moment and then back to me. "You know," he says, running his fingers up the side of my arm. "It's never too late to add some excitement to your life."

When his fingers hit the collar of my shirt and dip beneath, grazing the swell of my breast, my breath catches. "I'm listening."

Shifting in the grass, Rhett props himself on an elbow and leans over me. He delivers a heated kiss and moves to my ear. "I could show you how much fun three showerheads can be. Did I mention they're adjustable and one of them has a pulsating option?"

My throat constricts. "Are they removable?"

"Damn right they are."

Pushing up, I slip my shoes on and look down at a smiling Rhett. "Then what are we waiting for?"

CHAPTER
Thirty-One

Rhett

"I hate hospitals," I tell Mo the next morning.

"Shhh." She shoots me a warning look as we enter the sterile waiting area. "This isn't a hospital; it's a doctor's office, and there are people around."

I look everywhere, doing a three-sixty, and don't see a damn person. "Where? Where are the people?"

"You're grouchy today," she says, motioning for me to sign in at the front desk.

I scribble my name on a piece of paper at the same time the receptionist slides the glass window open.

"I'm going to need your insurance card and a photo ID," she says, using a black marker to cross out the name I just signed.

Well, that was pointless.

I pull the cards she's requested from my wallet and hand them to her.

"You can have seat. I'll get these back to you when we call you in."

I nod as the window closes again. "I'm grouchy because I hate doctors," I say, following Mo.

She walks to the back of the waiting room and grabs a magazine from the shelf. When she goes to sit down, she winces.

"You okay?"

"No, I'm not okay," she whispers, fighting back a smile. "I'm sore."

It takes a second for her words to sink in, but when they do, I grin. Last night was by far the best night Mo and I have had since getting back together. I say that every time, but it's always true.

"I guess tonight I'll have to take your ass instead."

Mo's eyes grow wide as she looks around to make sure no one heard. Lucky for her we're the only ones in the room, other than the walled-off receptionist.

Before Mo has a chance to scold me, a door off to the left opens, and a woman in black scrubs steps out. With a folder in her hand, she looks at Mo and me. "Rhett Allen?"

We follow her through a set of wooden doors, down a hall, and then into another room. She takes my blood pressure, asks a few questions about how I've been feeling—to which I reply *great*—and then disappears from the room.

"I hate these offices," I announce once she's gone. "They're so cold. Look at the walls; you'd think they could infuse some color or something."

"You've seen plenty of them; you should know."

"Really, Mo?"

She frowns, but once again, she gets interrupted. I'm grateful because I'm not sure I want to hear what she has to say. Plus, she couldn't say anything that hasn't already been jammed into my head a million times over.

This is a dangerous career.

What if you get seriously injured?

The next blow to your head could kill you.

"It's great to see you again, Mr. Allen," Dr. Wong says, offering me his hand.

"So, what's the verdict?" I ask as we shake.

He drops my chart on the counter and sits down in a roller chair. With his hands clasped in front of himself, he smiles. "Your physical therapist sent me all of your records, and he seems to think you've made quite a bit of progress."

"Does that mean I don't need surgery?"

Monroe reaches for my hand.

Dr. Wong nods and stands up. "You're correct. You won't need surgery," he says, manipulating my arm into several different positions.

I sigh in relief, and Mo smiles. My shoulder has felt great for the last couple weeks, but the thought of surgery has lingered in the back of my head.

"Does that mean I can go back to work?"

"Yes, I'm clearing you from your shoulder injury to return to work."

He says the words, but his eyes are guarded, and I know there's a *but* coming.

"But I want you to know the risks," he continues. "I've looked over your history, and this isn't your first shoulder injury. On top of that, your rotator cuff is still fragile, so while I will release you, I highly encourage you to start thinking about retirement." He returns to his seat.

"Retirement? Are you kidding me?"

Mo squeezes my hand, but I shake her off.

"I'm nowhere close to retirement. I've got years ahead of me in this career."

Dr. Wong holds up his hands. "I'm not telling you you have to quit. I'm simply suggesting that you start thinking about your future. Another injury like this one, and you'll be out for surgery with months of rehab, and your shoulder still might not get back to a hundred percent. Look," he says, scooting to the edge of his seat. "You're young, and you have your entire life ahead of you. There are lots of things you can't do with a bum shoulder."

"If his shoulder is still fragile, why are you clearing him to return?"

You've got to be kidding me. I shoot a nasty look at Mo, but she keeps her eyes locked on Dr. Wong.

"Because it's healed, Ms…"

"Gallagher."

He smiles. "As much as I would like to, I can't keep Mr. Allen on the disabled list just because I fear a potential re-injury. Bull riding is a dangerous sport, but he knows the hazards, and it has to be his choice. It's my job to make sure he goes in with eyes wide open."

Monroe nods, and thank God she doesn't say another word.

"So that's it?" I ask. "We're done?"

"Almost. I spoke to Dr. Pine about the concussion—"

"I don't need clearance from the concussion to ride," I say, interrupting him.

"I know you don't."

"Wait." Monroe turns to me. "What do you mean you don't need to be cleared after a concussion?" She looks back at the doctor.

"I'm afraid he's right, Ms. Gallagher. The PBR doesn't require medical clearance after a concussion. He's free to ride as soon as he feels up to it."

"But that's ridiculous."

"I'm fine, Mo." I grit the words out, ignoring the nauseating look she gives me.

"Yes, you're fine now. Forget about the shoulder injury; I'm more worried about your head."

Son of a bitch. What was I thinking bringing her with me today?

"That's actually what I wanted to talk to you about next, Mr. Allen," Dr. Wong says. "Dr. Pine wants to see you while you're in the building today."

"I'm not sure if we're going to have time, and I didn't make an appointment."

He nods. "My nurse went ahead and scheduled you one after I talked to Dr. Pine the other day. He just wants to see how you're feeling. It won't take long, and if you're ready, you can go over there now."

"We're ready," Mo answers for me.

"Great." Dr. Wong reaches for my chart and pulls out a piece of paper. "Here's your medical clearance."

"Thanks, Doc." I fold the paper and stuff it in my back pocket.

He reaches for the door and stops. "For what it's worth, you're an extremely talented bull rider. I just want you to walk away from the industry someday with enough of your health left to become an even better husband and father." He glances at Mo, giving her a smile and nod, and steps out the door.

"Mo."

She stands up, pulling her purse strap high on her shoulder. "I refuse to apologize for asking questions that pertain to your health."

"I wasn't going to ask you to apologize."

"Good. Because I won't," she says, walking out.

The silence is deafening as we walk to the opposite side of the medical complex to Dr. Pine's office. Within twenty minutes I'm back in a stark white room, sitting on a bed with that noisy-as-fuck paper.

"Mr. Allen," Dr. Pine says as he walks in. He's a tall man with a gut that tells me he enjoys his dessert as much as I do. Other than a few gray hairs along his temples, he looks the same. "It's been a while."

"That's a good thing, Doc." I shake his hand. "Means I've been healthy."

"Until recently," he adds, turning toward Mo. "And you are?"

"Monroe Gallagher," she answers, slipping her hand in his.

"It's a pleasure to meet you." When he releases Mo's hand, he picks up my chart and flips through. "I assume Dr. Wong told you we spoke on the phone the other day."

"He mentioned it."

Dr. Pine looks up from the chart. "Don't worry, Rhett, all good things. We've both enjoyed following your career."

"I hear a *but* in there somewhere."

He smiles at Monroe while pointing at me. "Is he always this cynical?"

She returns his smile but doesn't answer.

"I just wanted to talk to you about your head."

"My head is good, Doc."

"No blurred vision, floaters, or black spots?"

"Nothing."

"Dizziness or headaches?"

I shake my head, and he continues.

"Numbness or tingling in the extremities?"

"Nothing."

"What about muscle weakness, difficulty chewing or swallowing, memory loss, or trouble concentrating?"

I know what he's getting at, and he's not going to get a positive answer from me. "I'm good. I'd tell you if something was wrong."

"Would you?" Monroe asks, lifting a brow.

Dr. Pine laughs. "I like this one," he says. "She'll keep you on your toes. In all fairness, Ms. Gallagher, Rhett is generally a good patient. He comes to me when he's concerned about something."

She looks at me apologetically, and I smile. As frustrating as it is, I know she's just looking out for me.

"Is that why you wanted to see me today, to make sure I'm still okay?"

"I got a report from the hospital after your recent stay. I was on vacation, which is why you saw Dr. Simpson. That concussion did a number on you, and I wanted a chance to follow up and make sure you weren't suffering any secondary complications."

"I'm good."

"What do you mean it did a number on him?" Monroe asks.

Dr. Pine looks at me. "I'm assuming that since you brought her in here, I'm able to discuss your injuries with her?"

"Yeah, you can talk to her." I drop my head into my hand, running my fingers along my forehead, preparing myself for what's to come.

"Well, Ms. Gallagher, I'm not sure if you're aware, but this wasn't Rhett's first concussion."

"I'm aware."

"He was unconscious for three days, although we believe that was partially due to swelling in the brain after a blow to the head by the bull. The time before this, he was unconscious for four days. These aren't the typical concussions someone playing a contact sport might receive. These are more serious, with the potential to cause severe damage."

I peek through my fingers to see Mo grinding her teeth together. Coop probably *was* sugarcoating things for her. I'll have to remember to thank him.

"He didn't tell me that," she says, not bothering to look at me.

Dr. Pine frowns. "I figured."

"What does this mean? He had scans, right? They did all of that in the hospital. And everything had to come back okay or they wouldn't have discharged him."

"You're right. They did scans, everything came back fine, the swelling subsided, and it was identified as a grade 3 concussion. But it's still considered a traumatic brain injury."

Mo's eyes grow wide. "That sounds serious."

"Any time there's a traumatic brain injury, we take it very seriously. This type of injury can cause bruising or damage to the blood vessels and nerves, as well as amnesia and memory loss."

Lips parted in disbelief, Mo turns to look at me. She holds my gaze for what feels like a solid minute before turning back to Dr. Pine.

"Ms. Gallagher, I know this must seem startling to you, but it isn't new to Rhett. We've had several long talks about the dangers of bull riding, and he's well aware of the implications it could have on his future."

"That doesn't make me feel better," she says.

He pats my knee. "Me neither, which is why I brought him in today. One last-ditch effort to get him to reconsider returning to the arena."

I hate that they're talking about me as if I'm not sitting right here. It's easy for them to pass judgment on my decisions, but I wonder how either of them would feel if I barred them from doing what they loved most. The rodeo is in my DNA. It's what I've always dreamed of doing, and despite the 'risks and implications', as Dr. Pine likes to call it, I can't walk away. Not yet, at least.

"Save your breath." I hop off the table, positioning myself near the window. "I'm not giving it up."

"I've always been a straight shooter with you, Rhett, and I'm not going to change that now. You're risking your life by getting back on a bull. Another blow to the head could cause permanent brain damage or paralysis, and I don't think you understand how serious that is."

"I don't think you understand what my profession means to me," I growl. "You could get killed in a car accident every time you drive to work, but you still do it."

"That's different."

"It isn't!" I yell, even as I regret my outrage. Jamming my hands into my hair, I pace the room. "I get it, okay? I get that each ride could be my last. Every one of us steps into that arena knowing we might not walk out. It's a chance we take. My chances are higher; I understand that too, and I'll walk away when I'm ready. But I'm not there yet, so I'd appreciate it if you two would get off my back."

Mo was with me when I got on a bull for the first time. She's seen me get bucked off more times than I can count. She's seen me get kicked and trampled, and she's always encouraged me to get back on. I asked her to come with me today because she was always my biggest supporter, and I thought she'd continue to be that today.

I guess I was wrong.

Yanking the door open, I storm out of the office, refusing to listen to another warning from Dr. Pine or receive another questioning look from Mo.

Fuck that.

CHAPTER
Thirty-Two

Monroe

"I'm sorry about that," I say, staring at the door Rhett just walked out of.

Dr. Pine's eyes are kind. "Don't apologize."

"I should get going." Standing up, I grab my purse off the floor and reach for the door knob.

"Can I give you a piece of advice before you leave?"

"I'd appreciate any advice."

He smiles. "There are a lot of bull riders in this town; several of them are patients of mine. I've had countless talks with them and their wives, and I've been able to draw one consistent conclusion: bull riding is in their blood. It's something you and I will never understand. Who in their right mind would get on a two-thousand-pound bull?"

We both laugh, and he continues.

"But—and this is a big but that many wives have learned the hard way—if you want to continue to be part of his life, you're going to have to accept that for what it is. Support him, love him, and one of these days when the time is right, he'll walk. But it can't be my decision, and it can't be yours."

I hate to admit it, but I know he's right. The sport has been part of Rhett for as long as I've known him. His passion for it is one of the reasons I fell in love with him.

"Thank you, Doctor." I nod and slip out the door.

Rhett isn't in the waiting room or the hallway. I hope he's in the parking lot, and sure enough, that's where I find him.

Leaning against my truck, elbows resting over the bed, he faces away from me. The need to reach out to him, hold him, and comfort him grows stronger by the second, but there are a few things we need to discuss first.

"If you're going to grill me about quitting, I'd rather not hear it," he announces.

I rest my hand on his back, hating that he flinches at my touch. "We're going to talk about this, but not right now. Right now I'm starving, and you promised to feed me."

Rhett straightens his back and turns to face me. His jaw is set in a firm line, and I reach up and smooth my fingers down the side of his face. The tension eases some; I'll have to work on the rest.

"I'd rather talk about it now and get it over with."

I kiss his lips. "And I'm dying for some food. Isn't your friend Lincoln supposed to have dinner with us before we head home?"

"Yeah."

"Good. I can't wait to meet him, and I'd rather not be cranky when that happens. If we talk about everything now, that's likely to happen."

"I'm not changing my mind on this, Mo. I'm not quitting."

"I know you're not." My hand falls to my side.

Rhett's phone rings. He pulls it out of his pocket and answers with a surly, "Hello?" He listens for a moment. "Yeah, we're heading there now… See you in a few."

"That was Linc," he says, stuffing his phone in his pocket. "He's at The Broken Boot waiting on us."

Rhett opens my door, shutting it after I'm buckled in, and he climbs into the driver's seat.

The Broken Boot isn't far, and within fifteen minutes we're walking through a set of heavy front doors. The smell of smoke is the first thing I notice; the second is the number of cowboy hats.

"That's a lot of cowboys."

"Eyes on me," Rhett says, taking my hand.

We're held up three times as we wind through tables and pass the bar. Rhett stops to shake some hands and talk shop. He introduces me to several men whose names I'll never remember—some are old, some are young, but it's clear they all share a common love.

Bull riding.

The rodeo is these guys' life. It's hanging on the wall, printed on their shirts—it's playing on the TV.

"You must be Monroe."

The smooth southern voice startles me, and I turn. I've never met Lincoln, but I recognize him from the picture on Rhett's mantel.

"And you must be Lincoln Bennett."

I release Rhett's hand, which he barely seems to notice because he's sucked into conversation with an older gentleman. Lincoln curls his fingers around mine, and rather than shake my hand, he kisses my knuckles.

"Rhett could be a minute. I've got a table for us back here," he says, leading me to a booth at the back of the place. I tap Rhett's shoulder on my way past, pointing toward Lincoln, and he nods.

"I'll be right there," he says.

Linc and I slide in on opposite sides. He reaches for his beer and takes a drink.

"Rhett has told me so much about you."

"He has?" That's surprising, considering he hated me until not that long ago.

"I didn't say it was all good."

My smile fades. "Oh." I guess he told Linc everything.

"I didn't say it was all bad, either." He grins.

This time, I roll my eyes. "Make up your mind, cowboy."

"I like you. Figured I would after everything you did. Pretty hard to hate someone who threw herself under the bus to let my boy live his dream."

I'm not sure how I feel about Rhett spilling all of our secrets to his friend. Then again, I've spilled them all to Claire, so I guess that makes me a hypocrite.

"Chill out, princess. Wipe the scowl off your face. Rhett was in a bad place when I met him—fresh off a breakup with you. I was the one pulling him away from the bottle every night. It wasn't easy, but he eventually dusted himself off and moved on. He knew I wasn't going to like you very much after everything I'd witnessed, so he told me the rest of the story. Good thing he did, too, or I'd be trying to talk him out of this." He points his beer in my direction.

Folding my hands together, I lean on the table. "Rhett's the best thing to ever happen to me. I'm not letting him go again."

"I'm gonna hold you to that. Rhett's a damn good guy— best guy I know. He'd do anything for anyone, and he deserves someone who's going to have his back."

"Looks like that someone is you."

"I'll share that role with you. Turns out I've been sharing it with you all along."

The waitress stops by our table. She's a cute little thing.

Black hair, big tits, and a tight shirt. She smiles. "How are ya, Linc?"

"Good. How's the little one?"

"Rotten." She laughs, chomping on her gum. "You having your usual?"

"Yup. But this time add a side of sweet cut corn."

"You got it. And what about Rhett? His usual?"

I shift uncomfortably in my seat. I don't know Rhett's usual.

"Yeah, that'll be fine. He could be over there for a while," Linc says, glancing across the room.

"And what about you, sweetheart?" Her bright smile fades a bit when she turns to me.

"I'll have a burger and fries, and a Diet Coke."

"You got it." She jots my order down.

"What's on your dessert menu?"

She points to a chalkboard above the bar. "Cheesecake is the special. It's really good."

"I'll have that. Bring it out before my meal, please."

"Really?" She lifts a brow and looks at Linc, who just shrugs.

"Dessert before dinner?" he asks.

"Don't judge me."

He holds up his hands. "I'm not judging. Just curious, that's all."

"My grandma always said if you're paying for food, you might as well eat the best thing first. Guess it stuck with me."

"Your grandma sounds like a smart woman. I'll have a piece too, before my food," he adds.

The waitress gives me a *who are you?* look and walks off.

"So this is where you and Rhett hang out?" I ask, looking around. It's big, much bigger than Dirty Dicks, but not as clean. The floors show signs of a life well lived, and the tables have seen better days. But it's warm and has a sort of homey feel. I can see why the boys like it here.

"It is. The arena we train at is only a couple blocks south, so this is where most of the guys come."

"Are these most of the guys?" I look around at all the men.

"Pretty much."

"And them?" I nod to a group of women crowded around a large table in the back. There have to be least twenty of them in all different shapes and sizes.

"Most of them are wives and girlfriends. The buckle bunnies won't roll in for another hour or so."

"Here you go." Our waitress sets two slices of cheesecake on the table, along with three forks. "Your food will be out shortly."

Linc and I waste no time digging in, and when the silky cake hits my tongue, I moan.

"You make that noise again and we won't be here long," Rhett whispers, sliding into the booth next to me.

I smile around the bite in my mouth, and he leans in close.

"I'm sorry I got so tense this afternoon. I know you're just looking out for me."

"Apology accepted," I say, kissing him gently.

He looks at Linc, who's shoveling cheesecake into his mouth.

"Oh, dude. Not you too."

Linc shrugs and takes another bite. "I think your woman is on to something."

"I'm your woman," I say, nudging Rhett in the side.

He drapes an arm around my shoulders, pulling me close. "Damn right you are."

"You getting on the bull?" Linc asks.

I look at Rhett, unsure who his buddy is talking to. I point to myself. "Me?"

"Yeah." Linc laughs. "Cheryl is pretty easy. She won't hurt

you too bad."

"Who is Cheryl?"

"The mechanical bull," Linc answers, pointing to the opposite side of the bar.

Sure enough, there's a large doorway, leading into another room.

"If you're getting on, I suggest you do it before you eat your dinner."

"She's not getting on," Rhett says, stealing a bite of my cake.

I had no intention of getting on Cheryl, but the way Rhett brushed it off makes me want to.

"You don't think I can handle it?"

Rhett's eyebrows lift. "I didn't say that."

"You were thinking it."

"Uh-oh," Linc mumbles.

"That's not what I was thinking."

"You dismissed the idea awful quickly."

I smile as Rhett studies me, daring him to tell me I can't do it.

"Fine." Dropping his fork on the plate, he leans back in his seat. "Do it."

"I will." I take another bite of cheesecake and set Rhett's fork on the opposite side of the table, where he can't reach it.

"Hey, I want another bite."

"Sorry, I don't share my cake with people who don't believe in my riding abilities."

"Oh, I believe in your riding abilities, sweetheart," he says, his voice dropping low.

My cheeks heat, and Linc shows Rhett a knowing smile.

"Move." I scoot toward Rhett, shoving him out of the booth.

Linc tosses his napkin on the table. "This is going to be great."

"Mo, come on," Rhett chides. "You don't have to do this. I don't want you to get hurt, sweetheart."

I whirl on him. "Well, now maybe you know how I feel. Only when you get on a bull, your life is in danger. Mine, not so much."

His hand locks on my elbow as I try to walk away. "Okay, point made—although it's entirely different. You shouldn't risk getting hurt. You have your dad to take care of. He needs you to come home in one piece."

"And I need you to come home in one piece. It isn't just you anymore, Rhett. I'm your who, remember? We're a we now, and one of these days you're going to have to accept that. I feel like you're waiting for me to walk away or do something to mess this up, but that's not going to happen. I'm in this for the long haul, whether you get back on a bull or not."

"Wait a minute, I'm lost. She's your who?" Linc says.

"I'll explain later," Rhett mumbles.

I turn around and walk toward the back room. Sure as shit, there's Cheryl, a big, black mechanical bull sitting in the middle of the room. She's surround by ropes, and the floor beneath her is covered in mats. Several tables sit off to the side, a few of them occupied.

I march up to the man with the Broken Boot shirt on. "I want to ride Cheryl."

"You do, huh?"

Rhett and Linc step up behind me, and Rhett reaches around me to shake the guy's hand.

"Hey, Jimmy."

"Hey, Rhett. How are ya? How's the shoulder?"

"It's good. I'll be heading back to work soon. Just have to wrap up a few loose ends."

I'm guessing those loose ends are me.

"This your girl?" Jimmy asks.

"Yeah." Rhett smiles fondly at me.

"You okay with her getting on Cheryl?"

"Not at all, but I don't have much of a say."

"Do we ever? Damn stubborn women do whatever they want," Jimmy says, nodding toward Cheryl.

"I could say the same about men." I look up at Rhett, a hand on my jutted hip.

Jimmy lets out a laugh. "I like you, sugar. Follow me."

CHAPTER
Thirty-Three

Rhett

"A re you sure this is a good idea?" Linc whispers.

I shake my head. "Hell no. It's a terrible idea."

Linc and I stand off to the side, listening as Jimmy runs over the rules of riding Cheryl. Once he's done, Mo climbs onto Cheryl's back, settles in, and grips the handle. She tosses an arm in the air and nods at Jimmy.

"Oh shit," says Linc. "She's really gonna do it. Not gonna lie, dude, I thought she'd chicken out."

Shit. I'm not sure I can watch this. I rub my hand over my eyes and take a step forward. "You and me both."

Jimmy flips a switch, and Cheryl starts a slow rock. Mo's smile is contagious, and I find myself grinning along with her.

"Fast, Jimmy," she yells.

"Mo." I give her a hard look, but she doesn't see it because she won't look at me. "Monroe," I yell, trying to get her attention.

Jimmy looks unsure of what to do, but when Mo hollers at him again, he kicks it up another notch.

Cheryl's rock speeds up, and this time there's a twist in her movements that has Mo squealing in delight.

"I'm doing it!" Eyes bright, smile even brighter, she finally looks at Linc and me, and I'll be damned if the expression on her face doesn't make me go all mushy inside.

"You're doing great," Linc yells, earning a thumbs up from Mo. "Try going a little faster."

I slap him in the chest. "Are you out of your mind?"

"She's doing good, and the next level isn't much faster."

"I don't give a shit."

"This is great," Linc laughs. "I've never seen you like this over a woman before."

"Because she's not just any woman."

"No, I didn't think so," he murmurs, watching Mo as she spins in slow circles.

"Crank it up, Jimmy!" she yells.

Jesus Christ. "Mo, that's fast enough, baby. You're going to get hurt."

That little shit flips me off.

"Come on, let her have some fun," Linc whines.

"You just wait. Your time is coming, and when it does we'll get the girl you love up on Cheryl and see how you feel about it."

"The girl you love, huh?"

My heart skips a beat inside my chest, and I look at Linc. I've been keeping the words close to my heart, waiting to tell her until... Well, I don't really know what I'm waiting for anymore, but I apparently I don't have a problem telling Linc.

"I've loved that girl since she shoved me in the dirt at recess in kindergarten."

"She know that?"

I look at Mo. She's still the same girl who knocked me down all those years ago, and I'm a lucky son of a bitch because she looks at me the same way she always has—with stars in her eyes. And if that doesn't make a man feel ten feet tall, I don't know what will.

"I've showed her every way I know how."

"Actions do speak louder than words, but she's a chick, man." Linc shakes his head, his eyes on Mo. "Chicks need words. You've got to spell that shit out for her."

"I'm working on it."

"Come on, Jimmy, is that all she's got?" Mo yells.

Jimmy gives me a pleading look.

"Okay, Monroe. You've made your point," I say, stepping up to the rope. "You can get down now."

"No. This is fun. Crank it up, Jimmy!"

The small crowd at the back of room lets out a loud whoop, egging Mo on.

"Jimmy." I lace my voice with warning, but he doesn't listen.

Cheryl starts moving faster, adding a little whip to her twists. Mo giggles, moving her hips along with the bull. She slides to the side, and I suck in a breath, letting it out once she rights herself.

Jerking to the left, Cheryl tosses Mo again, only a little harder. Her eyes widen, the smile falling from her face, and *fuck me*, this is too much. She can't handle something like this.

I turn to Jimmy to tell him to turn it off just as Cheryl bucks, throwing her ass end up and flinging Mo into the air.

My heart lodges in my throat as Mo flies over Cheryl's head, landing hard against the mat. Linc and I hurl ourselves over the rope as Jimmy kills the bull.

I slide to my knees at Mo's side, pulling her into my arms. "Mo, baby, are you okay? Are you hurt?"

She brushes her hair out of her face and beams at me. "That was amazing. A little scary…" She climbs to her feet. "But amazing. The adrenaline rush was crazy."

Linc raises his hand for a high five, and Mo delivers.

"You want to go another round?" he asks, earning a punch in the shoulder from me.

"Would you shut up?"

Mo steps away, ignoring me on her way out of the room.

"Not today," she calls back to Linc. "I think once is enough for now."

"Not ever," I correct, following after her.

The bar has filled while we've been gone, and our food now waits at our table. We slide back into the booth, and Mo finishes off her cheesecake before devouring her burger while Linc and I play catch up.

"Doctor gave you the all clear?"

I nod, taking the last bite of my burger. I toss my napkin on my plate and set it at the edge of the table. "He did. I'm going to have to work my ass off, but a few good rides and I should be able reclaim my spot at the top."

"You'll get there in no time, brother," Linc assures me. "So, you gonna be in Charleston with us next weekend? We're leaving on Wednesday."

"Charleston?" Mo swallows her last fry and looks up.

"That's the next ride. You got a problem with that, princess?" Linc goads.

Always the shit-stirrer.

"Call me that again and you'll get my Ariat shoved up your ass."

He grins.

She scowls.

I intervene. "I haven't been on a bull in weeks."

Linc scoffs. "Yeah, *weeks*, not months. It's like riding a bike. You'll get right back on and do fine. We can get you into the arena tomorrow, and you'll have five days to get comfortable again before we leave."

Mo's hand finds my arm. "Tomorrow?"

I cover her hand with mine and look at Linc. "I'll let you know."

"Your call, brother." He slides from the booth and tosses money on the table—enough to cover all the food and leave a decent tip. "I'm outta here. Nice to meet you, Monroe. And it was good to see you, man. Can't wait to have you back."

I scoot out of the booth and give him a one-armed hug. "We'll talk soon."

I turn to Mo. "You ready?" She takes my hand, letting me help her out of the booth.

We make it halfway to the door before I get stopped.

CHAPTER
Thirty-Four

Monroe

"Oh my God, you're Rhett Allen."

Before my eyes, Rhett transforms into a version of himself I've yet to experience. He releases my hand, positions himself in front of the stunning blonde, and gives her the same smile he has when he's trying to get me naked.

"I thought that was you, but I wasn't sure. I'm a huge fan. My daddy has been following your career for several years."

She bats her big doe eyes, and I fight the urge to rip out her extensions.

"Thank you," Rhett says. "I appreciate the support."

She pulls a pen from her purse, along with a piece of paper. "Would you mind signing this for me?"

"Anything for you."

She blushes, fluttering her eyelashes as he scrawls his name.

Just when I think we're clear, Barbie's friend steps up.

"Can I have your autograph too?"

"Sure." Rhett smiles at the redhead while Barbie steps to the side. He scribbles his name across the paper and hands it back.

"Can we get a picture with you?" she asks, smiling coyly.

It's a look he's probably gotten from women hundreds of thousands of times, but it's a look I instantly hate. *I'm right here, bitch!*

"Absolutely," Rhett says.

Red pulls her phone out of her purse and hands it to Barbie. Rhett drapes an arm around her shoulder and flashes his mega-white smile, then repeats the process with the other woman. When Barbie steps away, she hands Rhett a napkin. I can't see what it says, but I wasn't born yesterday. He looks at the napkin and stuffs it into his pocket.

Oh no he didn't just put her goddamn phone number in his pocket!

"I'll meet you at the truck," I tell him.

Rhett's eyes widen as I shoulder past the women and the rest of the crowd. Once I'm out the front door, I take a deep breath and head straight for my truck.

Rhett is hot on my heels.

"You can't get bent out of shape every time a fan stops me."

"Are you serious?" I say, whirling around. "You think that's why I'm bent out of shape?"

"Isn't it?"

"No!" I pause. "Okay, yes. A little. How often does that happen?"

"I get stopped all the time. I'm not famous by any means, but people who follow the rodeo know who I am. And a lot of my fans are female."

"I don't mean how often do you get stopped. I meant how often do women slip you their number. Because that's another hard limit for me."

"You and your damn hard limits." He purses his lips. "It happens every once in a while."

"I'm gonna need more than that. Once a week? Once a month?"

"A couple times on the weekends after a show, and once or twice a week if I come into The Broken Boot."

"Oh." I give an exaggerated nod. "So we're talking several times a week."

"Something like that."

"And how often do you keep the number?"

He scowls. "Never. I don't keep their numbers."

"Really? Because you stuffed Barbie's number in your pocket."

Rhett's lips twitch. "Barbie? That's cute, Mo," he says, slipping his hand in his pocket as if to show me there's nothing there. Except he pulls out the napkin and stares down at it.

His eyes snap to mine. I challenge him with a look.

"I wasn't going to keep her number." He wads up the napkin and tosses it in the back of my truck. "What was I supposed to do? Tell her I didn't want it?"

"Yes! That's exactly what you should've done. You shouldn't have put it in your pocket with your girlfriend standing next to you."

His eyes soften and he reaches for me. I let him pull me into his arms.

"I'm sorry. I wasn't thinking. I usually just stick the number in my pocket and throw it away later. I had no intention of calling her; you should know that."

"I do know that." I sigh, frustrated at myself for overreacting. "I'm sorry. I shouldn't have gotten mad. You're used to it, but I'm not."

"They're just fans, Mo."

"Not gonna lie, it might take me a little while to get used to other women drooling over my boyfriend."

"As long as you remember your boyfriend is drooling over you. It's just like that photo shoot, right? This is part of my job, but nobody has chemistry like us." Rhett kisses me, opens the door to my truck, and ushers me in. "Let's go get the dogs, gather our stuff, and head out. We can get you back in time to check on the animals."

"I'd like that. I miss them."

"I know you do."

———°———

Monroe

"You got everything?"

"I think so." I sweep my eyes over Rhett's bedroom and bathroom to make sure I didn't leave anything.

With my bag and purse in my hands and Duke and Diesel at my heels, I load my things into the truck. Rhett's phone rings. He digs it out of his pocket and looks at the screen.

"I've gotta take this."

"We're in no hurry," I say, bending down to grab the ball Duke dropped at my feet. "Take your time."

Rhett answers his phone and walks back into the house.

I toss the ball for Duke until he wears out and plops down in the grass. The minutes tick by, and finally curiosity gets the best of me. I go in search of Rhett.

As soon as I shut the front door, I hear his voice coming down the hall. The words I've dreaded hearing stop me in my tracks.

"Yes, you can count on me to be there, and I'll accept the bonus ride… I'm sure… No, I don't need to talk it over with anyone. Nikki no longer works for me… All right, that's perfect… Thank you, sir. I'll see you soon."

With his phone in his hand, Rhett rounds the corner and stops at the sight of me. "How much of that did you hear?"

"Enough to know you're riding this weekend, and you accepted another bonus ride. I also heard you say you didn't need to talk it over with anyone." My voices rises with each word, heat infusing my cheeks. "But what about me?"

Rhett straightens his back, his jaw set in a firm line, his eyes trained on something over my shoulder. "Come on, Mo. You knew this was going to happen. I've made it clear that I'm going back to work, and the sooner the better."

"Would you at least look at me?"

His eyes find mine.

"I understand that this is your job, but I don't like *this*—I've never liked this. When we were younger, I always stepped back and let you take the lead. Bull riding was something you loved, and who was I to stop you? I hope things will be different now, and if I'm going to be part of your life, I'd like to have some input."

"But this is *my* life, and if all you're going to do is fight me, that's not being part of it."

"I'm not trying to fight you—that isn't what this is about. But seeing what my dad has gone through has put things in perspective. I see life for what it is—short, unpredictable, and precious."

"I understand that. Why do you think I'm trying to live it doing what I love?"

"Like you said earlier, I'm just looking out for you, Rhett. I don't want to see you get hurt—or worse, killed. I know you don't want to hear it, but I think you should at least think through what Dr. Wong and Dr. Pine said today."

"I heard them, Mo. But don't you see? It's no different than you doing whatever you had to do to take care of your dad. He was your life. *This* is my life."

"What about us, Rhett? Am I not a part of your life? Does my opinion not matter?"

"You're turning my words around. You are part of my life, and yes, your opinion means everything to me, but I was a bull rider when you started dating me the first time. I was a bull rider when you got back with me, and nothing has changed, Mo. This is who I am."

"And I accept that. I love that you have something you love, but did you not listen to a word your doctors said? You're not making informed decisions; you're reacting. Your shoulder is fragile. The wrong move could result in a complete tear and then what? Surgery and months of rehab, and if you're lucky you'll get back on the bull. And that's if you don't get another head injury first."

"Jesus Christ, Monroe."

I hate that he uses my full name. It feels cold and final.

"I'm not trying to get you to give up. I'm just trying to preserve your future—a future I plan to be a part of, and I want you whole. I want you to carry me over the threshold someday and toss our kids in the air. Most of all, Rhett, I want you alive. If you're not here and breathing, you might as well put me on the bull too, because I won't survive being apart from you again."

"If you don't want me to give up, what is it you want me to do?"

"I want you to make sure you're ready to go back. I don't want you to rush yourself or push yourself and injure your shoulder more. I don't want you to take bonus risks you don't have to. And maybe you could look into a helmet—I've seen some of the newer guys wearing them."

"I'm not wearing a damn helmet."

"Even if it could save your life?"

"Goddammit, Mo. You think I haven't considered what the doctors said? It's all I think about. I'm aware of the risks, and I'm choosing to get back on the bull because it's what I love to do. My doctor cleared me because my shoulder is as good as it's going to get. It may never get back to full capacity, and that's something I'll have to live with, but it has to be my decision, Mo. I know where you stand. I know where my parents stand and where my doctors stand, and when the time comes for me to make a change, I'll involve you in that decision. But that time isn't now, and I need you to trust me." He sighs, shaking his head. "I need you to support me."

"I do support you." I take a step forward. "But you're making it hard. How am I supposed to watch you go back to work when it might be too soon?"

"The doctors cleared me."

"For your shoulder…"

Rhett tosses his arms out to the side. "I don't know what you want from me, Monroe. This is my life. You either want to be part of it or you don't."

"Of course I want to be part of it—I *am* part of it—but I don't want to watch you kill yourself or ruin your chances to continue the career you love."

The air grows thick with tension. Our feet are rooted to the floor, neither one of us willing to make the first move. I hate that we can't seem to find solid ground. I also hate the way he's looking at me.

"I need to drive my truck back to Heaven," he says, still not moving. "I have to be back here tomorrow. So I'll follow you. It'll give each of us some time to think about what we want."

"Shit, Rhett. Didn't you say we don't walk away mad?"

He shakes his head. "I'm not mad, Mo."

I hate the idea of us being apart from each other right now, but maybe he's right. We've been together nonstop almost since he came home. Maybe we need some time to step back and evaluate things. Except I don't need to re-evaluate or think.

"I don't need to think. I already know what I want. I want you."

"I need you to be sure, Mo. Because I can't live with you breathing down my neck about what I do for a living. And you can't live your life angry at me for doing it."

He finally closes the distance between us. "Maybe you should take some time to consider what you want for yourself, too. If your dad moves in with Sharon, you'll have an opportunity to chase your own dreams, Mo, and I want that for you. I want to be part of your dream, whatever it is." His lips, warm and soft, kiss my cheek. "I'll follow you to Heaven."

We gather our things, and he holds the front door open for me, locking it after I walk out. I climb into my truck. He whistles for the dogs, who jump in with him, and we all pull out and head toward the highway.

I meant what I said—I don't want Rhett to give up what he loves. I might prefer that he not get back on the bull or chance it on bonus rides with his history of injuries, but I would never ask him to walk away before he's ready.

The irony of the situation isn't lost on me, though, because I walked away from what I loved. I walked away from Rhett and my chance to be a vet. And he didn't have a say in any of that. Yet here I am, asking for a voice in his future.

We've been back together just a short time, and already he consumes me. He's all I think about, all I dream about, but he's right—what about me? What do I want? I have to exist outside of Rhett and my father. I just hope that whatever I choose to do—even if it turns out not to be convenient or moves us farther away from each other—Rhett will support me.

But I already know he will.

I glance in my rearview mirror.

He's right behind me, the strong, supportive presence I've always known him to be, and now it's my turn to step up.

This time I'll be who *he*'s told me he needs me to be, not anyone else.

CHAPTER
Thirty-Five

Rhett

The ride back to Heaven is too quiet. The dogs are asleep in the backseat, and Mo is a few hundred feet in front of me—though it feels like she's a thousand miles away. This is the part of the job I hate—the part I've always dreaded. I've seen my friends go through it with their ladies. Some relationships have made it through; others weren't so lucky.

It killed me to tell Mo I was going back now whether she likes it or not, but I have to. Not going back isn't an option. And the longer I wait, the harder it will be to get back on a bull again. Despite what Mo and the doctors think, I have listened. Every warning is branded into my head, but I can't walk away after an injury—I can't let a bull decide the fate of my career. Getting back in the arena is something I have to do for myself, to prove I can overcome this, that I can still have this career. I'll regret it for the rest of my life if I stop now.

Now Lucifer, he's a different story. Accepting that bonus ride was purely selfish. They doubled the offer—making it something they knew I wouldn't turn down—but this time it's about more than the money. It's a chance at a rematch, a chance to prove I can conquer that bull. And I will conquer him. This time I won't walk away injured. I'll walk away with a hundred thousand dollars in my pocket.

That's enough to buy Mo the ring she deserves and have plenty left over for a honeymoon—that is, if she chooses to stay with me. And I really need to her to choose me. I need her to choose us.

But before she can do that, I think she has to choose herself. Her life hasn't been easy, and for the first time in a long time, she has the opportunity to make choices about a future she thought she'd lost. She just has to be brave enough to do it. And I will support her and make sure she follows her heart wherever it leads, even if that's away from me.

That thought twists my stomach.

My eyes flick from the road to Mo's truck up ahead.

What will I do if she chooses to go back to school? What if she moves away and we're right back where we were six years ago, trying to make a long-distance relationship work? Can I handle that?

The answer is quite simply *no*. I just got Mo back, and I'm not ready to let her go again. I don't want to live a life between two homes—always passing each other in the wind, hoping for a night together before we have several more apart. With my job, that's exactly how it could end up.

But my thoughts about my future have been changing.

The logistics of how we could make this work roll around my head for the rest of the drive. Mo passes the exit for her house, instead taking a left toward Animal Haven, but I keep going straight. A couple of minutes, later I'm pulling down my parents' lane. I put the truck in park and shoot Mo a quick text because I'm sure she's wondering where I went.

I have to run a few errands. I'll meet you at Animal Haven

in a little while.

Dad is sitting on the front porch when I pull up. I roll the windows down for the dogs, rather than letting them out. We won't be here long. I just need to get some advice from the person I trust more than anyone.

"Thought I might be seeing you soon. What did the doctors say?"

I shrug and bound up his front steps. "Same ol' shit, different day."

His eyes watch me. "Lucifer did some damage, huh?"

"Little bit."

"When are you heading back?"

Propping my hip against the porch rail, I look at my dad. "You don't want to try to talk me out of going?"

"Nope." He tilts his head. "You do want to go back, don't you?"

"Yeah." I pause. "I mean, I think so. Hell, I don't know."

A slow smile spreads across his face. "What did you really come out here for, son?"

I worry my bottom lip between my teeth and decide to go for it. "How did you know you were ready to retire?"

"I didn't retire," he says, waving toward the ranch. "I might not mount the bull, but I trained you and your cousin. I still live the life."

He's going to make me spell it out. "How did you know you were ready to give up that part of the life?"

"I was never scared of getting hurt. I was a lot like you; I always heard the doctors' advice and kept doing my thing because it's what I loved. And then one day I realized I loved your mom more than I'd ever loved the bull."

"I love Mo more than I love the bull."

"Then what's the problem?"

I look out toward the ranch for a moment. "She scares me more than any bull ever has. Lucifer can break every bone in my body, but those bones will heal. I might not ride again, but I'll heal. Mo broke my heart, and I've never quite been the same. She says she's all in, swears she won't leave me again, but how can I be sure? What if I walk away from bull riding to be with her and she changes her mind?"

"Has she asked you to walk away?"

"No, but she was with me at the doctor's appointment. She heard everything they had to say, and she questioned my return to the PBR. If I'm going to change my life for her, I need to know she'll support me through all my decisions, even if that means I return to bull riding."

Dad pushes himself out of the rocking chair. He steps in front of me and lays a hand on my arm. "Then you need to make her show her hand first."

"What do you mean?"

"Give her the chance to prove herself, and once you have your answer, you'll be prepared to lay it all on the line or move on with your life."

Make her show her hand first. I nod. "I think I know how to do that."

Hope unfurls in my gut, along with a sliver of fear. This could go well or very, very badly. But it has to be done.

"Thanks, Dad." I wrap him in my arms, clapping his back.

"What are you going to do?" he asks as I jump off the porch.

I open the door to my truck and turn around. "My first ride will be in Charleston next weekend. I'm leaving on Wednesday. You coming?"

"I wouldn't miss it."

"You'll find out then."

He nods as I hop in.

I tear down the lane and turn toward Coop's, where I'll put my plan in motion. At Coop's place, I print off the documents I need, pack the rest of my shit in my truck, and make the short drive to Animal Haven.

Duke and Diesel don't even lift their heads when I put the truck in park, and this time I don't bother shutting off the ignition. I grab the extra badge from the glove compartment, along with the papers I printed at Coop's. I've only used the badge a handful of times—always for one of my siblings—but now I'm going to use it the way it's intended.

Mo walks out of Animal Haven. She looks exhausted and a little bit sad and definitely like she's ready to talk, but that's not happening today.

In three strides I close the distance between us. She startles when I slam my mouth against hers. It's a frenzied and sloppy kiss—our teeth knock together—and I sure as hell hope it isn't our last.

When I pull away, she touches her bottom lip and smiles.

"Can we talk now?" she asks.

"Soon, baby, but not today. There's something I need you to do for me first." She frowns, but I continue. "Not too long ago you needed my forgiveness. I gave that to you because I believe in us and what we have the potential to become. Now I need you to do the same for me."

I hold the badge out.

She eyes it curiously as she takes it from my hand. "What's this?"

"My first ride is Friday night at seven at the Civic Center in Charleston, West Virginia. Take this badge to the guest relations counter, and they'll show you where to go."

She frowns and shakes her head. "I can't afford a plane ticket, Rhett."

"No excuses, Mo." I hold out the papers. "I paid for a plane ticket. Everything you need is here."

Taking the papers from my hands, she looks down at them. "What if I can't find anyone to cover for me or take care of my dad?"

"Figure it out," I say.

Her eyes widen.

"Go home," I continue, my voice softer. "Talk to your dad, think about what you want to do with your life and whether you see me in your future. If you see an *us*, then get your ass on that plane and be in your seat when I mount the bull. That's what I need from you right now."

"And if I can't get there?"

God, please don't let that happen. "Then I'll trust you had a damn good reason."

Mo blinks, but she doesn't move. She doesn't try to stop me from climbing back into my truck, and she makes no attempt to chase after me.

I pick up my phone and scroll through my contact list. Linc answers on the first ring.

"I'll be back in town in two hours. You up for a late night?"

"I'll meet you there."

CHAPTER
Thirty-Six

Monroe

I stand outside of Animal Haven for a long time after Rhett's taillights fade away. I know what he's doing—he's giving me the space to choose. He wants me to decide for myself. If he'd let me talk, he'd know I've already chosen him. But evidently that's not enough. He wants actions, not just words.

I understand that, and I want to give him what he wants. I just have to take care of something else first.

I finally turn to lock up Animal Haven and climb back into my truck. I should take care of my own life before I insert myself into someone else's.

I type out a quick text to Tess and Claire.

Can you meet me at Dirty Dicks in an hour?

Claire replies back almost instantly.

Did you think I would say no? ☺

Tess's reply is simple.

Yes.

The drive home is too quick, barely allowing me a chance to think about what I'm going to say, but that's okay because my future is all I thought about on the drive home from Houston.

When I step into my house, I know what I want; I just have to have the courage to ask for it.

"Hey, Daddy." I bend down to kiss my dad on the cheek.

From the corner of my eye, I can see Sharon gathering her things.

"Would you mind staying a while longer?" I ask her. "There are a few things I want to talk to Dad about, and I'd like for you to be here."

Sharon looks between me and Dad for a moment and then puts her purse back on the hook behind the door. She comes to sit on the tattered La-Z-Boy. Dad's wheelchair is pulled up next to her, and I sit opposite them on the couch.

"I've been thinking a lot about what we talked about, Dad, and I think you should do it," I begin.

"D-do what?" he asks.

"I think you should move in with Sharon."

He smiles.

So does Sharon.

Tears fill my eyes. I can't believe I'm doing this. Six years of taking care of my father every day, and things are finally going to change. I can barely comprehend what that means. As excited as I am for my future, I'm also sad.

"I want you to be happy, Daddy, and if Sharon makes you happy, I don't want to hold you back and keep you from living your life."

"Mo." Dad moves his wheelchair closer to me and reaches out with his good hand. I wrap my fingers around his and smile. "You are th-the best daughter a m-m-man could ever ask for. You have n-never held me b-b-back. It's me who h-has held you b-back."

Pushing up from the couch, I wrap my arms around him. "I'm going to miss you."

He buries his face in my hair, and when I pull back, his eyes are filled with tears. "Y-you'll still see m-me plenty. This is a g-good thing, M-mo."

"I know." I nod, smiling tremulously at him. "I know it's a good thing, but it's a big change, and change is scary."

"Life is s-scary, but you have t-to live it. You can't l-let your life p-pass you by, Mo, or one d-day you'll look back and h-have a mountain of r-r-regrets."

"I know."

Sharon reaches for Dad's hand, and I can't help but smile. I want that. I want to grow old with Rhett and be his rock. I want him to be the person I turn to when I have a problem or need to smile. I want him with me every single day, and I'm ready to take the steps I need to to get that.

"I want to go back to school," I declare.

Dad's smile wobbles. "I was h-hoping you w-would say that."

"But not to be a veterinarian," I add. "I want to take some business classes, work toward a degree. If it's okay with you, I'd like to keep Animal Haven and grow the business." That might be a pipe dream. I'm not sure I'll ever be able to afford to expand, but that's what this conversation is about—dreams—and this time I'm not letting mine get away.

"Animal H-haven is yours, Mo. It h-has been f-for the last s-six years."

I shake my head. "I'm not sure what the value is on a business like Animal Haven, but I want to do this the right way. I don't expect you to just give it to me."

"I w-want to. Let me d-do this, M-mo."

Sharon kisses my dad on the cheek and turns to me. "Let him do this, Monroe. He's talked about signing it over to you for a long time now. He's just been waiting for you to want it. He didn't want to push it on you."

Smiling, I laugh. "Okay, Dad. Thank you. And I promise I'll do great things with it."

"I know y-you w-will." His smile is bright. He watches me for a second and then asks, "What a-about the house?"

"Well…" I look around at my childhood home. "I don't know. What would you like to do with it?"

"Y-you live here until y-you get through s-school and get s-settled, and then we'll s-sell it. Unless you w-want it?"

"You want to sell it?" I don't know why his answer surprises me. This house holds a lot of good memories, but even more bad.

"It's j-just a house, M-mo. It's been m-more like a prison to b-both of us over th-the years, and I'd l-like for that t-to change. But if y-you want it, y-you can k-keep it."

"No." I shake my head. "I think your plan is good. Once I get on my feet and can afford a place of my own, we'll sell it."

Sharon pats Dad's hand and stands up. "You two are making so many big decisions tonight. I feel like this deserves a celebration, and I've got a fresh plate of brownies."

"My favorite."

Sharon smiles back at me. "I know." She winks and slips out of the room.

"I'm happy for you, Daddy. I'm glad you were able to find someone who makes you smile the way she does."

"Th-thank you. She's s-special."

"I know she is. You deserve someone special."

"I've been trying to tell him that for years," Sharon says, laughing.

She hands me a napkin with a giant brownie on it. Pulling a tray from the corner of the room, she clips it on Dad's wheelchair and sets his brownie there.

I eat my brownie silently, watching Dad feed himself. Sharon doesn't fuss over him or hover, but when a chunk of brownie lands on the side of his lip, she wipes it off and smiles warmly. That's when I know for sure I've made the right decision.

One of many right decisions to come.

She'll care for him with a gentle, loving hand, and I can't ask for more than that.

"If you two are good here, I've got a few more errands to run."

Dad looks up as though he just remembered I was in the room, and Sharon answers. "Sure, sweetie. We're good. Take your time."

I wad my napkin up and toss it in the trash before returning to give Dad and Sharon each a kiss. On my way to the door, Dad stops me.

"What a-about Rhett?" he asks.

My heart skips a beat as I turn around. "What about him?"

"What does h-he think about y-you going b-back to school?"

"I haven't had a chance to tell him yet," I say. Then I walk out the door, shutting it softly behind me.

On my drive to Dirty Dicks, I make a mental note of all the things I need to do. Not only will I have to get Dad's things packed, I'll have to contact the medical equipment company and transfer everything to Sharon's. I'll also need to call the local community college and make an appointment with an academic advisor to find out where to start.

So many things to do, and I welcome the chaos with open arms.

When I pull up to Dirty Dicks, I see Tess's car in the lot, as well as Claire's. I climb out of the truck and walk in, waving to some of my regular customers along the way.

Claire and Tess are sitting in a booth along the back wall. They smile when I walk up.

"I ordered you a beer," Claire says, handing me the brown bottle.

"Thank you." I slide in the booth next to Tess, who's looking at me funny. "What? Why are you looking at me like that?"

"Oh, I don't know, maybe because I don't think you've ever initiated a girl's night out."

"She's right," Claire says. "What's going on?"

"Nothing." I smile. "Maybe I just wanted to hang out with my friends."

They look at each other and then at me. "Sorry," Claire says. "Try again."

"Fine." I roll my eyes. "My dad is moving in with your mom. He's giving me Animal Haven, and I'm going back to college."

Tess throws her arm in the air, signaling the waitress. "We're going to need more alcohol for this."

Claire's eyes are wide. "What do you mean your dad and my mom are moving in together? Are they…you know…sleeping together?"

"See, I told you we'd need more alcohol," Tess pipes in.

"No." I shake my head. "They aren't sleeping together."

Sean drops off another round of beers. Claire grabs one, takes a giant swig, and wipes her mouth with the back of her hand.

"Okay," she sighs. "Start from the beginning, and don't leave a damn thing out."

"It's a long story."

"We've got all night."

CHAPTER
Thirty-Seven

Rhett

I haven't heard another word from Mo—not that night after I left her at Animal Haven or any other night leading up to my ride. It's been almost a week, and I'm going out of my mind, wondering what she's thinking and how she's doing. Several times I've picked up the phone, wanting to hear her voice, but I can't get myself to make the call. I miss her, more than I ever did when I left for Houston six years ago. How I went that many years without talking to her or seeing her beautiful face, I'll never know. The dull ache in my chest is a constant reminder of how integrated into my life she's become.

But I keep reminding myself: I told her exactly what I needed from her, so it's up to her to come through.

By the time Friday night rolls around, it feels like an entire year has passed. My crew and I have worked around the clock, perfecting my movements and getting me comfortable on the bull again.

"You ready?" Dad claps my shoulder.

"Born ready." I give him the same cocky grin I always do,

and with Dad on one side and Linc on the other, we wind our way through the back pens.

"You scored an 89.87 on that last ride." I punch Linc in the arm. "I'm proud of you, fucker."

He grins but doesn't say a word. He's struggled the last few years, and he doesn't like to talk about it. I make a mental note to celebrate his success tonight when we go out after the event.

If we go out after the event.

I had plans to celebrate with Mo, bringing her out with the guys, but if she doesn't show up, I might be nursing a beer by myself in the hotel room.

Linc has offered several times to check and see if Mo is here, but I've refused. If she didn't, I don't want to know until the very last minute. That way I can channel all of the anger and pain into the ride. And if she did...well, that'll just give me the reason I need to go out and do my best.

I survey the full stadium, purposefully looking away from where the riders' guests sit. Like all the times before, I climb up the fence, swing my leg over, and position myself on the bull. Ruckus thrashes to the side, unhappy that I'm on his back. We wait for him to settle, and then I wrap my hand in the rope, take a deep breath, and look up. It only takes a second for my eyes to find Mo. She's exactly where she should be—perched on the edge of her seat, her eyes wide, hands clasped beneath her chin—and my heart soars.

Seeing her in the stands, sitting with the rest of the wives and girlfriends, is all I need to get my adrenaline pumping. Whatever she's decided about her future, I know it includes me. She stepped out of her comfort zone to be here tonight, and that tells me more than words ever could. Suddenly I'm like a caveman banging on his chest, desperate for his girl to see him succeed.

Her face lights up with a breathtaking smile, and I give the nod.

The gate opens, and Ruckus flings himself into the arena, twisting every which way, bucking and jostling my body from side to side, but I hold on.

It's the longest eight seconds of my entire life, this first ride back, but finally the buzzer sounds. I release my hold, wait for the right moment, and jump off.

Ruckus flings himself around the stadium, kicking up dust, but my eyes aren't on him, they're on Mo. She's jumping up and down, clapping, her hair a wild mess around her head, and I'm absolutely mesmerized.

"Rhett!"

I blink, jerking my head to the right just in time to jump over the fence before Ruckus rams his horn up my ass.

"Shit," Linc laughs. "You got a death wish or what?"

"Or what."

"What were you looking out at there?" Dad asks.

"Mo." I grin.

Linc doesn't.

Neither does Dad.

"You need to keep your head in the game, son. You can't get distracted out there or you'll get hurt."

"I know that." I'm laughing even though it's not funny. I can't help it. I've never been this happy. When I walk out of this arena tonight, I'll be walking away with Mo—with the woman I want to spend the rest of my life with.

My next ride is similar to the first, only this time I'm on Bruiser, and he isn't nearly as accommodating as Ruckus. His kick is higher, the twist faster, and I only make it seven seconds before I'm flung into the air.

I land on the unforgiving ground with a loud thud that feels like it echoes through the stadium. The force is enough to knock the wind right out of me, and it takes a second to catch my breath. Bruiser is corralled, and when I'm certain I can stand up without passing out, I get to my feet. My head spins, tilting the world to the left. I stumble, but Linc and Dad are there to catch me. Scanning the crowd, I find Mo. She's standing up, one hand covering her heart, the other tucked tight against her stomach as though she's keeping herself from being sick.

There's not much I can do to ease her fear, so I tip my hat in her direction to show her I'm okay. I hope she understands. I can't go to her or comfort her, and that kills me. I glance back at her several times as Linc and Dad lead me out of the arena. When I make it safely through the gate, she falls back into her seat.

I have a little time between rides, but I have to spend it getting checked out by the house doctor—which also pisses me off because I miss Linc's final ride. When I get the all clear, it's time to make my way back the chutes.

The third ride is much more like the first than the second. Demon kicks and spins, doing his best to throw me off, but I manage to hold on until the buzzer. When my feet are safely on the ground, I look for Mo, expecting her to be cheering along with the rest of the crowd. Except she isn't. She's sitting down while everyone around her hoots and hollers on their feet. Our eyes connect for a brief second before I'm dragged away.

"Awesome ride, brother. You are killing it tonight," Linc says, guiding me through the back pens. When we hit the locker room, Dad stops.

"What's wrong?" I ask.

"You good for a few minutes?" he asks, looking between me and Linc. "I'm gonna step out and call your mother, see how she's doing."

That's odd. Dad doesn't usually check in with her until the event is over, but whatever. "I'm good," I assure him.

He nods and walks off. Linc and I go into the locker room and grab a drink while we watch a replay of my rides tonight.

"Can you pull up my last ride with Lucifer?" I ask.

"Sure can."

Linc punches a few buttons, and I watch again as I'm thrown from the bull. This time, when I see myself lying on the ground, all I can think about is Mo hurdling over the bar and crying in Coop's arms.

I close my eyes. "Turn it off."

"I can't believe you agreed to this," Linc says. "You're crazy, you know that? No man in his right mind would willingly get on Lucifer—especially *again.*"

I look up at him. "I have to."

"You don't." Linc shakes his head.

"If you're trying to prove something, forget about it," he continues. "It isn't worth your life. Did you see what happened to Rodriguez out there earlier tonight?"

"No, and don't tell me. I'd rather not know."

"It's not too late to back out," he offers.

"I'm not backing out."

"Is this about the money? Because you don't need the money."

I'll always need the money, but that's not what this is about. "I need to do this for me."

Linc takes a deep breath and looks around. When his eyes return to me, they're full of spit and fire. "Then you better stay on that bull for the entire eight seconds. So help me God, if you don't walk out of that arena, you'll wish you'd never accepted this ride. For the first time since I met you, you've got something more than the bull and buckle to go home to, something to live and breathe for, and she's a whole hell of a lot more important than conquering some bull."

"I know."

I realize that the bonus ride is a needless risk now that Mo is back in my life, but I have to do it anyway, for myself. Her showing up tonight is all I needed to confirm that she's in this just as deep as I am, and I'm ready to walk away if that's what we decide is best. But it's a decision we'll make together. I'm ready to hang up my rope and hat and help her chase her dream and our future, whatever that may be.

"I'm going to be fine," I assure him.

"I sure as hell hope so. Come on, we've got to go get you ready."

Five more guys ride, and then the bonus event is announced. The crowd goes wild, people rising into a standing ovation while I get myself into position on Lucifer. Slinging my leg over his back, I let it slide down his side. His eyes dart back, locking on mine, and it's as if the damn bull remembers me. Thrashing to the left, he slams us against the gate. My crew lifts me up before he can crush my leg. He continues to thrash around for several seconds before finally settling down, and that's when I realize my dad is still gone.

"Where's my dad?" I holler to Linc.

He glances around and shrugs. "He'll be here. Get yourself situated."

It takes a little longer than normal to get my hand positioned in the rope. Adrenaline rushes through my veins, causing my arms and legs to tingle. I shake my free hand out, wiggling my fingers as though I'm warming up, and that's when I realize it isn't excitement that has me riled up. It's fear.

In that moment, my whole life stops.

What if something happens? What if I get thrown off, kicked in the head, and have permanent brain damage? What if I never get to see Mo's beautiful smile again, or hear her laugh?

What if I never get the chance to tell her I love her?

I can't breathe.

I can't speak.

All I can do is frantically search for Mo in the stands, because I need to see her. I need to know she's still here.

"What's wrong?"

I hear Dad's voice behind me. I want to ask him where he went and what took him so long, but I can't focus on anything but Mo.

"Where's Mo? She isn't in her seat."

"Don't worry about Mo," he says. "She's fine. You need to concentrate, because you're about to ride this bull, and you have to focus on what you're doing."

I hear him. His words float around me, but they don't register because all I can feel and think about is the incredible sense of dread weighing down my stomach.

"Come on, Rhett," Linc hollers. "Snap out of it. They've already announced the ride. They're waiting on you."

I blink, searching the crowd one last time, and when I come up empty, I turn to Linc. "When I get off this bull, you better have a path clear for me to get straight out of this goddamn place, because I'm going after my girl." I've got to find out why she left.

"Not sure you'll have to go far, but okay."

Tightening my grip on the rope, I lift my hand and nod.

Lucifer flies out of the gate with a frenzy only he's capable of. The muscles of his back shift beneath my thighs as he bucks and thrashes around, tossing me from side to side. The roar of the crowd is deafening as I squeeze my thighs together, hell bent on staying on his back.

It feels like a lifetime, but the buzzer eventually sounds. The crowd goes wild, and in a not-so-graceful dismount, I fall to the ground. Lucifer jumps, charging for a rodeo clown as I scramble to my feet.

CHAPTER
Thirty-Eight

Rhett

As promised, Linc clears a path, and I rush through the gate, weaving through the back pens and ignoring the announcers and fans calling out for me. My head spins with all the places Mo could be, and I just want to find her and hold her and tell her how much I love her. I also need to apologize for getting back on Lucifer.

I'll do whatever it takes, because now I know for sure that all I want in this life is Mo's happiness.

I turn a corner and run right into her.

"Mo." Relief rushes through me, and I yank her into my arms. "God, baby, I thought you left. I looked up in the stands, and you weren't there."

"I'm sorry." She shakes her head, and I notice the tear stains on her cheeks. "I tried to watch, but I just couldn't. I think your dad realized that, because he came and got me."

"Wait. What? My dad came and got you?"

She nods. "I need you to listen to me, Rhett. I know this is what you do…what you love, but it was so much harder to sit there in the stands than I thought it would be." Her words come out in a rush, along with a few fresh tears.

I wipe them away. "I know, baby."

"No." Her head shakes. "You don't. It's different than when we were younger. When we were sixteen, we were invincible, with the entire world at our feet. I don't see things like that anymore."

"What do you see?"

"I see a future. I know we're not there yet, but I see babies and a tire swing in the front yard. I see family dinners and a golden retriever and teaching my daughter how to ride a horse. But when they announced the special event, all of that went away. All I could see were the ways that future could be ripped away from us. I had visions of you getting thrown off again, kicked in the head, trampled on, and I realized I can't do this."

Her voice splinters, along with my heart. She tries to pull away, but I don't let her.

"I can't sit here and watch you put your life and our future on the line." Brushing the tears from her face, she blinks up at me, her big, beautiful eyes full of so much love and pain.

All the blood drains from my face. A wave of dizziness washes over me, and I reach for her arm. "What are you saying, Mo?"

"I can't ask you to walk away before you're ready, but you can't ask me to watch."

Oh, God. She's leaving me.

"No!" I shout, my grip on her tightening. "You can't leave me. You don't have to ask me to walk away. I'll just do it. I'll walk away and never look back. I'd do anything for you—you can't break up with me again."

"Break up with you?" Confusion clouds her eyes.

My words continue to come out in a rush, my brain not exactly processing her question. "My life doesn't work without you, so if bull riding is a hard limit, I'll stop. I'd do that because I love you."

Mo sweeps a hand up my cheek, curving her fingers around the back of my head. "What did you just say?"

"I love you. I've never stopped loving you, and I'm sorry I didn't say it sooner, I just—"

Slamming her lips against mine, Mo shuts me up. And when she steps back, she's smiling like she won the lottery.

"You love me?"

"More than I've ever loved another human being." I press my lips to her forehead, lingering there while I catch my breath.

Mo grabs my hands and brings them to her heart. "The first time you gave me your heart, I broke it, but I swear it won't happen again. And I know that means my life is going to change, but I want that, I'm ready for it. Dad and I talked a lot this week, and there are some things I want to run by you when we get home."

Home. "Does that mean you're sticking with me? Because I don't think I could handle life without you. When I climbed on Lucifer and didn't see you, all I could think was what would happen if I got hurt and never got the chance to see you again, or tell you I love you, and that scared the shit out of me. I'd rather get trampled by a thousand bulls than feel the pain of not having you with me."

She smiles. "You're stuck with me, cowboy."

The weight on my shoulders lifts, finally making it easier to breathe. "But you said you couldn't watch me put our future on the line."

"I can't," she says. "Every time you climbed on one of those bulls, I thought I was going to have a heart attack. I left the stands because I couldn't physically watch anymore. I support you, and I will be here for as many shows as I can, but I can't be in the stands. I'll wait in the wings. The less I see, the better. Your dad said your mom was the same way. It's one of the reasons she doesn't come to your events."

"I didn't know that."

"That's okay with you, right? If I'm here but not in the stands?"

"That's more than okay." I kiss her once, and then again. "But that doesn't change what I said. Your support means everything, but I want our future, too. I want us to move forward together, make choices about my career together. I promise not to shut down when you offer your opinion, and when we get home, we're going to talk about my retirement."

"Rhett." Her eyes widen. "I don't want you to give up your dream. I would never ask you to do that."

"I know you're not, and I'm not giving up my dream. I'm adding to it. I finally have reason to heed the doctors' warnings. Everything I do moving forward I'll do for you—for us."

"Oh, Rhett." She tangles her fingers in my hair. "It's not going to be easy, and we have a lot of things to work out, but I'm going to start living my life again, make the choices that are right for me—for us."

Warmth flows through my veins as a smile stretches my face. "You're worth so much more than the buckle or the bull or the adrenaline rush. I can live without those things, but not without you. You're it for me, Mo."

"Rhett." She chokes back a sob. "I love you so much."

"I love you too, baby. I promise I'm listening. We're in this together, all the way."

"Together." She presses her lips to my heart.

I take a step back because I'm covered in dirt and sweat, and I probably smell like a damn bull. "Careful, baby. I'm dirty."

"You're sexy." With her arms around my neck, she hops up to wrap her legs around my waist. I catch her, cradling her ass in the palms of my hands. "And now you're going to take me home, and we're going to make dirty, sexy love."

"I like the way you think."

CHAPTER
Thirty-Nine

Rhett

Mo's face is smashed against the passenger side window. Her hair is a wild mess, and I'm pretty sure she's drooling, but I've never been more in love with her than I am right now. In fact, I think I fall more in love with her with each passing moment, although I don't know how that's possible.

"Babe, wake up." I brush the hair out of her eyes. She stirs in the seat, blinking as she sits up.

"Are we home?" she asks, yawning.

We had a late night last night. After the event, Linc, Dad, and I took Mo for a much-needed drink, and then I took her back to my hotel room, where I kept her up until the early-morning sun filtered through the windows. We made love more times than I can count, and about the time we drifted off to sleep, the alarm went off, and we had to get up to make our flight back to Houston.

Thanks to an upgrade to cozy first class, Mo and I were able to catch a few hours of sleep. She says she doesn't have to be back in Heaven until early tomorrow morning, which means

I've got her all to myself for another night, and I'm going to take full advantage of it.

Mo sighs as we come to a stop in front of the house. "I love this place."

She slides from the truck, and I come around to meet her. Hand in hand, we walk up the stairs to the front porch. I open the door and turn to scoop Mo into my arms.

She squeals, wrapping her arms around my neck. "What are you doing?"

"I'm carrying you over the threshold."

"But we're not married."

"Don't care, Mo." I kiss her lips and step into the house. "This is our house now."

I lower her to the ground, and her eyes shine up at me. "Our house, huh?"

I nod. "If that's okay with you. I know we have a lot to talk about, but I love it here, and I was thinking we could keep it."

"I love it here too. Of course you should keep it, especially since it's so close to your training facility."

"About that…" I reach for her hand and lead her to the couch. She sits down next to me, and I pull her legs across my lap. "I think the doctors are right. With my history of injuries, it's getting too dangerous for me to continue."

Mo takes a deep breath, pulls her feet from my lap, and straddles my legs. With a knee pressed to the couch on either side of my hips, she rests her hands on my chest. I hold her waist and wait for her to talk.

"Don't do this because of me. I'm here for you, Rhett, and I'm not going anywhere. I want you to retire because *you're* ready for it."

"That's the thing. I am. Last night was wonderful, and it felt final. I put Lucifer in his place, and I've achieved all I could ever want. Before you, I didn't have much to come home to. I think deep down I didn't worry about getting hurt, because it was just me. But that's different now. I don't want to risk my future with you for eight seconds on the bull."

"What will you do?"

"I've thought about training other riders, but mostly I think I'd like to take over Allen Family Ranch."

"Really?"

I nod. "I've always loved working there, and Dad is getting ready to start cutting back. Trevor's heart is in firefighting—he doesn't want the ranch to be his career—so this is perfect timing."

"What about your sponsors?"

"I'm not sure. I'll have to look into that. If anything, I might have to finish out the season, but it's almost over."

"That wouldn't be so bad. If you start working at the ranch, does that mean you'll move back to Heaven?"

"Yeah. I'll buy a house, or build one, but like I said, I'd like to keep this place, too."

Mo's face lights up like a Christmas tree. "I have the perfect place for you to build."

"Us. For *us* to build."

Her eyes shine with happiness, and my heart soars.

"Tell me about this perfect place," I urge.

"You remember that spot at Animal Haven where my dad always wanted to build?"

"Yeah. By the pond. It's gorgeous out there."

"*We* can build there."

I can't believe we're talking about this—making plans for a future, talking about building a house. It's all a little surreal.

"And what about your dad?"

"I sat down with him and Sharon after you left last Friday.

He's going to move in with her just as soon as I get everything situated."

"Wow. That's a big step. You're okay with this?"

"More than okay. There's more." She grins. "He's giving me Animal Haven. Once I get a few things with my life figured out and get on my feet, we can build out there. It might take a couple of years, but we'll get there."

We'll get there sooner than that. I have enough money saved up to build her dream home. But I also know Mo, and she won't go for that right out of the gate. I'll have to work her up to the idea.

"What do you have to figure out?" I ask.

"I want to go back to school."

I can feel a smile splitting my face. "I'm so proud of you, baby. You're going to make a great veterinarian."

"No." She shakes her head. "I want to take some business classes, something that will help me with what I love now. What I love now is running Animal Haven. I'd like to figure out how to hire some help so I'm not killing myself, and I want to grow it into so much more—take on more animals and offer obedience training. I've even looked into a program where I would team up with inmates to train dogs who can then be adopted."

"I've heard of those programs."

"It'll take time and patience, but I'm willing to put in the effort."

I nod. "And I'll be there to help you. We'll grow it together."

"You'd want to help me with Animal Haven?"

"Have you listened to a word I've said over the last twenty-four hours?"

She laughs when I nibble her neck. "We're in this together. It's me and you moving forward. We build this life together."

"I like the sound of that."

"Yeah?"

She laughs. "Yeah."

"I love you, Monroe Gallagher. I always have. Can I show you something?"

———◦———

Monroe

Rhett lifts me from his lap, grabs my hand, and leads me toward the barn. We hop on the four-wheeler.

I wrap my arms around his waist and drop my chin to his shoulder. "Where are you taking me?"

"It's a surprise."

I squeal, tightening my grip when we take off, and when we pull up to the same lookout spot he brought me to before, I climb off.

"Sorry to disappoint you cowboy, but this isn't really a surprise—although I do love it out here."

"I love it too, and there's something else I want to show you. Something better," he whispers.

"How can there possibly be anything better than this view?"

"See that tree over there?" he asks, pointing off to the left.

I turn my head, and he takes the opportunity to press a kiss along the side of my neck.

"That one?" I ask, pointing to a tree about thirty feet away. I didn't notice it last time we were out here.

"That's the one. It's a Red Sunset maple. It's only about twenty feet tall now, but it'll grow to be fifty. In the fall, it turns a stunning shade of red. I planted it out here as soon as I bought the property."

"Just because?"

Taking my hand again, Rhett moves toward the tree. We're

a couple of yards away when I see a heart engraved near the base. Pressure builds behind my eyes, but I refuse to look back at Rhett.

With a hand covering my mouth, I step away from him and kneel in front of the tree, running my fingers over our initials. They're carved into the base of this tree, just like the ones on our old oak tree at his parents' ranch.

"Rhett," I breathe, finally looking up at him.

His hands are in his pockets, a thoughtful look in his eye when he smiles back at me.

"I bought this place after my first win with the PBR. Didn't tell a soul—not Dad or Coop, not even you."

"You were so young."

"Age doesn't matter. I might've been young and dumb, but I knew what I wanted. I planted this tree the day of the closing because I wanted to have a place to bring you…a place like our spot at the ranch."

I blink down at our initials, trying to picture him out here carving the tree with nothing but me in mind. If he'd known I was going to break his heart, he might've done things differently.

"After you…" He pauses, his eyes darting to the side.

"Lied," I finish for him. "It's okay; you can say it."

He smiles and reaches for my hand, pulling me to my feet. "After that, I hated this place. I hated this tree and everything it represented, because I'd bought this place for us. I tried over and over to convince myself I could still live here, sow my wild oats, and eventually raise a family with someone else. But that never felt right. I tried to bring women here—"

"Rhett." I hold up a hand and take a step back. "I'd really rather not hear this."

He snags my wrist, drawing me back in. "But I need to say

it. Just hear me out, okay?"

I nod.

"I tried to bring women here to prove to myself that I could move on, that you weren't still a part of me, but I never made it farther than the driveway. Every single time, I came up with an excuse to leave or go back to their place, and do you know why, Mo?"

Swallowing past the lump in my throat, I shake my head.

"Because every time I looked at the house, I saw you. So I tried to sell it. Couldn't do that either, because every time I put it on the market, I got physically sick. Selling it was like admitting whatever we had was gone. I believe now that my heart knew we weren't over. That's why I couldn't sell the house. That's why the only women to set foot inside have been my mom and Adley.

You and I, we were always meant to get to this place," he says, cupping my face in his hands. "It just took us a little longer. We had a few obstacles to overcome, but we made it. I don't regret the empty nights when I drowned myself in the bottle, or the anger I felt toward you, because all of that—all of those feelings—led me here." His soft lips land on mine. "And here is the place I've always dreamed of."

"Rhett." My throat clogs, making it difficult to speak. I grip the soft flannel of his shirt in my fist, holding him to me as tears stream down my face. "I'm so sorry I did that to you."

"No. Don't do that to yourself. We've been through all that. I didn't tell you this to upset you. I told you because for the last six years, you've gone about your life thinking I'd moved on, and that kills me. I need you to know you were always here." He lifts my hand, placing it over his heart.

He drops his forehead to mine, kisses my nose, and then kisses away my tears.

"Thank you." I give him a tremulous smile. "I love you so much."

"Say it again," he whispers.

"I love you."

"One more time."

"I love you," I say with every fiber of my being. "I'm always going to love you—I always have loved you."

"I love you, too, baby."

ACKNOWLEDGEMENTS

First and foremost, I have to thank my husband, Tom. The endless amount of support and encouragement you give me while writing is truly amazing. Thank you for making sure the house stayed clean, the laundry got done, and the kids were fed. Thank you for taking over nighttime duty so that I could stay up late and write. Your love and support is what gets me through the day and I'm so incredibly thankful for you.

Mom and dad. Thank you for always supporting me and encouraging me to follow my dreams. And thank you for watching my kids when I'm desperate to hit a deadlines. I love you both more than you'll ever know.

Keshia Langston, Kristen Proby and Rebecca Shea… 'Thank you' seems so insignificant. You've encouraged me, supported me, and laughed with me. Your kind words and friendship has been the highlight of many of my days. Thank you for always being there, no matter the question or concern. Each of you mean so much to me and I love you <3.

Jessica Royer Ocken, my amazing editor. Thank you for being patient with me, and for taking my often scrambled prose and transforming it into something beautiful. Your opinion means the world to me, and I am so grateful that you edited this book. You're stuck with me forever.

A big huge thank you to Kari March for creating such a beautiful cover. You know my vision better than I do.

Stacey Ryan Blake, aka the best damn formatter in the world, thank you for making the inside of my books look beautiful. And, thank you for putting up with all of my last minutes changes. You're amazing and you're never getting rid of me ;)

Alison Evans-Maxwell, thank you so much for proofing this book. Your hard work is appreciated more than you'll ever know.

To the staff with Give Me Books… THANK YOU for taking me on and cheering for my books. I appreciate all of the hard work and dedication that you put into each and every project. Your love of the book world shows and I'm proud to be part of it.

Last and certainly not least, thank you to every single one of my readers and all of the bloggers. Thank you for taking the time to read my books and share them. I hope you swooned over Rhett as much as I did. Your support means so much to me and without you and I wouldn't be doing what I love.

ABOUT THE AUTHOR

Photo by Perrywinkle Photography

K.L. Grayson resides in a small town outside of St. Louis, MO. She is entertained daily by her extraordinary husband, who will forever inspire every good quality she writes in a man. Her entire life rests in the palms of six dirty little hands, and when the day is over and those pint-sized cherubs have been washed and tucked into bed, you can find her typing away furiously on her computer. She has a love for alpha-males, brownies, reading, tattoos, sunglasses, and happy endings…and not particularly in that order.

OTHER BOOKS BY
K.L. GRAYSON

A Touch of Fate Series
Where We Belong
Pretty Pink Ribbons
On Solid Ground – a Harley and Tyson Novella
Live Without Regret

Other Titles
A Lover's Lament
The Truth About Lennon
Black

Made in the USA
Middletown, DE
26 July 2019